ALSO BY ELIE WIESEL

# A MAD DESIRE
# TO DANCE

# A MAD DESIRE TO DANCE

A NOVEL

## ELIE WIESEL

*Translated from the French by Catherine Temerson*

SCHOCKEN BOOKS, NEW YORK

Translation copyright © 2009 by Catherine Temerson

All rights reserved. Published in the United States by Schocken Books,
a division of Random House, Inc., New York, and in Canada by
Random House of Canada Limited, Toronto. Originally published in France
as *Un désir fou de danser* by Éditions du Seuil, Paris, in 2006.
Copyright © 2006 by Éditions du Seuil. This translation originally
published in hardcover in the United States by Alfred A. Knopf,
a division of Random House, Inc., New York, in 2009.

Schocken Books and colophon are registered trademarks
of Random House, Inc.

Library of Congress Cataloging-in-Publication Data
Wiesel, Elie, [date]
[Désir fou de danser. English]
A mad desire to dance / Elie Wiesel ; translated from
the French byCatherine Temerson.
p. cm.
ISBN: 978-0-8052-1212-9
I. Temerson, Catherine. II. Title.
PQ2683.I32D4713 2009b    843'.914—dc22    2009051065

www.schocken.com

Printed in the United States of America
First Paperback Edition
2 4 6 8 9 7 5 3 1

*For Elijah*

*and Shira*

*from their grandfather*

*Arbaa nikhnessu lepardes:* Four Wise Men entered the orchard of secret knowledge. The son of Azzai looked at the orchard and lost his life. The son of Zoma looked at the orchard and lost his reason. Elisha, Abouya's son, looked at the orchard and lost his faith. Only Rabbi Akiba entered in peace and left in peace.

—The Talmud, Khagiga Treatise

Why, young friend, do you say that happiness doesn't exist? That love is only an illusion? If true, why say it? And why say it, since it is true?

Long ago, you loved a gracious and beautiful woman who lived on the other side of the oceans and mountains. And you suffered from it.

Well, in that distant Orient where she hoped to share memorable moments with you, she remains gracious and beautiful. Head lowered and smiling, she is waiting for you. And every time my eyes meet hers, I know that love causes madness and happiness.

—One-eyed Paritus, in his "Message to a Student Who Is Frightened of Becoming Old"

# A MAD DESIRE
# TO DANCE

# 1

She has dark eyes and the smile of a frightened child. I searched for her all my life. Was it she who saved me from the silent death that characterizes resignation to solitude? And from madness in its terminal phase, terminal as we refer to cancer when incurable? Yes, the kind of madness in which one can find refuge, if not salvation?

Madness is what I'll talk to you about—madness burdened with memories and with eyes like everyone else's, though in my story the eyes are like those of a smiling child trembling with fear.

You'll ask: Is a madman who knows he's mad really mad? Or: In a mad world, isn't the madman who is aware of his madness the only sane person? But let's not rush ahead. If you had to describe a madman, how would you portray him? As a marble-faced stranger? Smiling but without joy, his nerves on edge; when he goes into a trance, his limbs move about and all his thoughts collide; time and again, he has electrical discharges, not in his brain but in his soul. Do you like this portrait? Let's continue. How can we talk about madness except by using the specific language of those who carry it within themselves? What if I told you that within each of us, whether in good health or bad, there is a hidden zone, a secret region that opens out onto madness? One misstep, one unfortunate blow of fate, is enough to make us slip or flounder with no hope of ever rising up again.

Careless mistakes, an impaired memory or errors of judgment, can provoke a series of falls. It then becomes impossible to make ourselves understood by those we call—rather foolishly—kindred souls. If you will not grant me this, I will have a serious problem, but you must not feel sorry for me. Tears sometimes leave furrows, but never very deep ones—in any case, not deep enough.

There, this is what you have to know for a start.

That said, since I'm eager to tell you everything, you should know that I'll be telling you this story without any concern for chronology. You'll be made to discover many different periods of time and many different places in a haphazard fashion. What can I say? The madman's time is not always the same as the so-called normal man's.

For instance, let's begin this narrative five years ago, in the office of Thérèse Goldschmidt, a healer of souls, well paid—I'll tell you how well later—thanks to her vast knowledge. She expects to prod me into knowing the dark, innermost recesses of my ego, in order to help me live with myself without my dybbuk, but that's an assumption to which I plan to return.

Later on I'll talk to you about Thérèse; I'll talk about her at length. Inevitable Thérèse, there is no way around her. She's the one who made me talk. It's her profession. She spends her life probing the unconscious—that strongbox and trash bin of knowledge and experience, those subterranean archives that can and must be deciphered—and asking childish or harebrained questions. And in my case, these questions summoned not answers but stories.

Why do people make fun of madmen? Because they upset people? Didn't Molière mock the hypochondriac? Doesn't the man who *believes* he is ill need treatment?

Am I way off the beam? I don't think I'm completely irrational. Is being mad being disabled? Can one speak of a gangrened mind, of thought beaten to death, of a mutilated, damned soul? Can one be mad in happiness as in misfortune? Can someone take vows of madness as one takes religious vows, or devotes one's life to poetry? Can a person slip breathlessly into madness with a slow, muffled tread, as if to avoid disturbing some secret demon feigning absence or asceticism? At times I'm afraid of shutting my eyes, for I see an unreal world with its dead. I open them again and fear has not left me. Madness may just be a sensation resonant with futility: as in Franz K.'s castle, we are waiting on the landing, in front of a closed door, for something that has already happened and will paradoxically happen too late. Am I insane? Thérèse was going to tell me. Does that word bother you? You would rather not use it anymore? I have others to offer you: disturbed, unbalanced, crazy, unhinged, nuts, loony, daft, demented, maladjusted, retarded, half-witted. Am I a paranoiac, a schizophrenic, a hysteric, or a neurotic? Do I just have an ordinary inferiority or guilt complex that a simple antidepressant could cure? That's possible. Am I guilty of having freely abused my freedom? Or of having simply lived a life that wasn't mine by succumbing to the torture of both excessively vague despair and excessively transparent hope—thus, of having survived thanks to my madness, in its various phases and darkest depths? But who is to say whether guilt and madness are compatible or incompatible? And who decides that I'm not entitled to both madness *and* despair? That madmen are beyond redemption, thus hopelessly condemned, except in the privileged area of art? Van Gogh, before dying, whispered: "Sadness will last forever." Sadness. No. Madness lasts much longer. Tolstoy said that thinking about the future is the beginning of madness, but Maimonides said the world would be saved by madmen. Which of the two will succeed in guiding me to a different reality?

I thought: Thérèse will help me; she'll save me. She has a degree. This is her work, her goal, her mission. To rescue by listening, through words. Open doors. Rummage around in the darkness. That's not easy in my case. She admitted as much. Can madness, like memory, be forced open? Difficult, I'm told. Madness is both beneficial and subversive: it takes a path that constantly changes directions; stumbles as it rises; tells lies while shouting "believe me"; forges ahead while stepping back; aims to please and displease simultaneously; seeks the company of others as a way of sublimating solitude. It searches out the origins of Creation in order to sink into eschatology. Didn't Kleist, the great mad poet, describe existence as a bridge going from nowhere to nowhere? And, he added, it is hard to live between two nowheres . . .

I remember saying all this to the doctor. I talk to her, talk on, sometimes freely, sometimes at her command, of my mute delusions and fits of rage, managing to tame their violence momentarily. I tell her of my disappointments, my repressed ambitions and lived fantasies, the glow of my proud suns as well as their sudden blinding descents; I reveal some things to her in order to hide other truer and more intimate things, those that fill my thirsting soul with meaning as well as truth—and I quote Augustine, who said about the Maccabees that men learn how to die for truth! I call up old memories that will be born tomorrow or might never even come to light. But I make no mention of my conscience, within which everything breathes misfortune and illness. I can wait, she says, to reassure me. Sooner or later, we'll get there. Later for whom? For the aging man that I am, who, like a beggar invited to the feast of the gods, implores the future for the alms of a few years?

He remembers, yes, the patient remembers. As a child, he feared being abducted by thieves. And one night, in a waking dream no doubt, the abduction did take place. Strangers broke into his bedroom; a tall, mustached man and a heavy-breasted woman lifted him up. He wanted to cry out for help, but no sound came from his throat. A second later, he found himself under thick blankets, in a wagon pulled by two frenzied horses. And the heavy-breasted woman said to him: "It is not you we are taking away, but years off your life; we'll sell them at the market."

Another dream, given the therapist loves dreams: I'm traveling by plane. The captain announces that due to mechanical problems, he has to make a sea landing. Cries of anguish inside the aircraft. A child bursts into tears. His mother can't pacify him. Stroke of luck: the aircraft lands on an island. A jubilant crowd welcomes us with strange dances. Speeches are made that no one understands. A woman tries to lead me away; her blood-stained eyes blot out her face; I resist. I say to myself: she's a witch or she's mad, stark raving mad; mad as a hatter; they're all mad. I'm right. Law doesn't rule here; madness does. It has seized power. I look for the aircraft; it has disappeared, sunk into the sea. The pilot? Gone as well, along with the passengers, possibly tortured, punished, sacrificed. And all of them strangers. I didn't exchange a single word with them. And what if it was a conspiracy? And they had set this trap for me? The woman says: "We're in the theater, we're putting on a play about madness. It's a world overrun by madness. Everyone has a part. And so do you. You can choose: you can be the executioner or the condemned man." Overcome with panic, breathing with difficulty, I cry out: "I refuse, do you hear? I refuse." The woman insists. She calls for help. A bare-chested maniac grabs me by the hair. He yells: "You're in our country, so obey! If you don't, you'll wake up beheaded!" I reply: "No, it's my dream and you're all in it; I have the right to drive you out."

And the dreamer woke up in a sweat.

Why these nightmares, Doctor? Dreams, that famous product of and guide to the unconscious, that's your area of predilection; here you find your bearings as you do in your bedroom. Please explain: Why, when I shut my eyes, do I always have the feeling of being in hostile territory?

Another dream: I'm a child again and I hear a voice that says: "You see that road; it will lead you to God. Run, my boy, run. God is waiting for you at the far end!" So I run until I'm out of breath; I run to get there as fast as I can. But when I get to the end of the road, the voice says: "You're mistaken, child; God is waiting for you at the other end." Gathering up all the strength I have left, I retrace my steps—but the voice has fallen silent. And the child cries out: "Where are you, Lord?" No answer. "And what about the voice I heard, where is it?" No answer. Then I remember a book I never part with. I start to leaf through it. And on page 13 I read: "God is also the road that leads you forward and backward." Commentary: "If you really wish to love Him, you must sacrifice reason, human knowledge of things and beings."

Did I really go astray in my words as in my life? At my age, this is very possible, indeed normal. At any rate, even if she thinks it, Thérèse doesn't criticize me. Besides, I can get away with anything; I'm not ill for nothing.

My "healer" often frightens me, as I frighten myself: I'm afraid of saying too much or concealing everything—in short, of emptying myself of what I am, a kind of madman whose soul has been amputated, in search of his excessively rich and burdensome past, so he won't see it extinguished before his death. But that madman's past no longer exists; thieves have taken it to a doomed city, wiped out by the blood-soaked rays of a violent, crimson twilight. There every woman is a goddess, a young, red-headed goddess with slender, soft hands, who prevents joys from being eradicated by hatred, the sound of a kiss from becoming a roar from hell, and the melodious voices of happy children from turning into howls. But this woman, this goddess, has a face like no other, a face with the eyes of a child, a smiling child who is afraid of me.

Sitting on my stool, I can sometimes spend hours staring into the void in the hope of filling it with the sand borne by the tears of widows and orphans, or the laughter of beggars inviting happiness only to flee from it as soon as it comes; I then have the feeling that I know everything but understand nothing, or else that I know nothing but understand things that others fail to comprehend.

Moreover, everything happens to me yet everything passes; I retain nothing. Stubbornly resistant to childish happiness and shame, a victim and author of hallucinations both morbid and funny, eager for shortcuts, I want to think of myself as impervious to how long things last. Visions and images burst under my eyelids only to be instantly dispelled, burning hot. Memory moves forward or backward in fits and starts. I am stricken with nausea and a splitting headache. Constant dizziness, unremitting and oppressive. I speak when I am silent; I am silent when I howl. Past and future merge. In a flash the familiar world capsizes; as for me, where do I fit in? With me everything occurs in spasms: spasms of anger, of decisions, of desires that last only an instant. Oh, if I could only become a cloud set on fire by the sun, a torrent that knocks down powerful armies in its path. If I could only unravel the web of dreams and phantasms that haunt me, disentangle time and duration in the consciousness of philosophers, the amused knowledge of psychologists, the lived experience of saints attracted by violence; might I be an epiphenomenon? A veiled reference from dead gods? Am I running toward the summit, or have I moved away from it with giant steps while keeping still? I am asked my name and I give a silly answer, that it's a beautiful day when the sky is dark. Or I say I hear the heartrending laughter of the heavens through the shower of stars. And I say . . . the devil, I don't know what I say anymore.

Often—though I don't know since when or for how long—I have the feeling of living cut off from the world; no sound reaches me from the outside. The sighing of lovers, the moaning of sick people, the neighing of horses, the howling of wolves, the stealthily approaching heavy clouds: I see and hear nothing. I feel nothing. It is as if time is suspended, awaiting a sign to start up again. I am alone, irrevocably alone, because I am confined. But the next day, or the next minute, in my brain, there's a crush of people gasping for breath, looking wild and cruel, running all over, heading for precipices. Or there's the railway station, where frantic travelers insult one another in front of closed ticket offices and locked doors because they've missed their train, as though this is their last chance to escape an invisible enemy.

After these attacks, I tell myself that I'll go crazy, that I already am. Then I am beset by a greater lucidity. I convince myself that it is I whom every torturer is hunting down, I whom every jailer curses.

If I was still living at my uncle's, I would wonder if I was possessed. Am I a target? And of whose dybbuk?

*I am writing to you, my dear mother and father, because I know that sooner or later we will meet again. After a long, very long separation, we will be reunited. At least, I hope so. For this separation has lasted, lasted far too long, indeed for a whole lifetime, my life from before.*

*Everyone changes, but not you. You remain frozen in eternity, so young, so cheerful, in search of a future outlined on my features.*

*I am writing to you so you will know everything about me: who I am and what I'll become. Will you recognize me? Do you know what I've been through, what I've acquired and lost, since your gaze rested upon me with tenderness and confidence for the last time? That gaze has now become mine. Together we'll look for answers to the questions that define man and his destiny.*

*Do I still exist in your memory as you exist in mine?*

*I live in fear. The fear of disappointing you.*

*I won't tell you about anything heroic or glorious. Only about things that appear simple and fill a threatened existence.*

*Like you, I didn't experience the Nazi concentration camps. I found out about the Warsaw Ghetto uprising in 1943 and the liberation of Paris in 1944 from books. We suffered together through the deaths of my older sister and my little brother; we kept them shrouded in discreet silence but not in oblivion. The fear of line-ups, the lump in one's throat, resignation, terror, blows, death inside the barbed-wire fences—images, words found in the narratives of survivors. Thus, every now and then I smell the acrid, sickly sweet, repellent odor of burned flesh. And I feel nauseous. But when I think of the people's jubilation on victory day, or three years later, for Israel's declaration of independence, I feel like dancing in the street.*

*All these events came to me from afar, from outside. They glided over my consciousness like warm water, or like sand.*

*However, this isn't what I would like to tell you about. With a bit of luck, everything I could tell you about took place mostly inside me. I imagine you have immense powers over me, but can you read what is not said aloud? Can you guess what the heart manages to conceal from the brain? Do you know what it's like to feel madness in oneself as one feels blood flowing in one's veins? A living kaleidoscope of colors and shapes, faces and destinies: Is it my being splitting in two? I feel I am simultaneously a child and an old man; do they hate each other? Not at all! Here they are embracing. At the edge of a river, I see myself on the opposite bank. One minute I am living among biblical characters, but a second later I am in the midst of a crowd applauding the takeoff of a spaceship bringing travelers to the moon of their dreams.*

*Wherever you are, you may be smiling and saying to each*

*other with pride: Oh, what an imagination, eh? Only that's not what it's about. It's about something much more serious.*

*I am writing to you because I love you very much. And also in order to prepare myself and prepare you for our inevitable reunion. Will it be a bolted door or an opening?*

You know whom I owe a lot to? To a dead patron. And on another level, to an old, erudite tramp—unless he was a young fallen god who thought he was an elderly invalid. One autumn evening, he offered to teach me the truth.

I was still living with my uncle. I was strolling in Brooklyn, among its bearded Hasidim with their suspicious, feverish eyes, expecting to be stopped by a fanatic who would urge me to repent, when a sickly-looking stranger asked me to help him walk; he was having trouble with his crutches. An image came to mind: What if he was the Messiah, who, according to the Talmud, waits to be called from among the wounded and the ailing in front of the gates to Rome? How could I refuse to help him? In a weak voice, he asked me: "Would you like me to teach you the truth?"

After taking a few steps, I replied: "Of course. I've been trying to track it down for ages."

"Well, believe it or not, I've found it."

"Bravo," I said, feigning admiration. "Explain it to me."

"Truth is a mask that hides under other masks."

"You're disappointing me," I answered.

"The truth is there is no truth."

A young Hasid came up to us and asked us if we'd already recited our evening prayers.

My companion of the day became angry. "You're disturbing us," he said. "Don't you see that we're praying?"

Looking vexed, the intruder murmured: "You'll end up in hell, you'll burn in its flames, and then you'll remember me."

The beggar didn't condescend to answer; he just sniggered.

"And what about God in all this?" I asked him.

He stopped and stared at me with pity. "You poor fool," he said with a sneer. "Haven't you understood yet that—"

"Don't say another word," I begged him.

Suddenly, I was overcome with panic. I felt my interlocutor was going to make me plunge into blasphemy.

". . . don't you understand that God isn't God, for man is no longer human? That in an insane world, dominated by violence and hatred, in the service of Evil and Death, God Himself is like you and me? He too needs to be liberated, needs to be helped so He won't lose hope?"

"But then—" I cried out.

"Then what?"

"Then what's the point of our quest for God? What should we do about our craving for God, our faith in an all-powerful and merciful God?"

The beggar looked at me, nodding in commiseration.

"One day, poor fellow, you'll understand."

Yes, one day, I say to myself, one day I'll be at the end of my wits, and I'll understand.

What will I understand? That there are times when madness is preferable to what seems rational? That one can settle into it with no fear of disappointments and betrayals?

And could this day have already come?

I don't mention my dybbuk to Thérèse, who is supposed to cure me, but I tell her about Rina, with whom I shared a hurried encounter—correction: to whom I got close, I think, for the duration of a smile. An enthusiast of everything occult, this strange woman despised life, and life certainly repaid her in kind. Had she ever been in love? Impossible to know. Though thirty or forty, she dressed like an old grandmother. As I talk about her, I don't know why, I think of my first and last true love. Could you be too young for me? Your maturity belies your age. I love you for your smile, even if it's the smile of a frightened child. Frightened of growing up? Yes, frightened of growing up in a world that, in spite of protesting grandiloquently, doesn't like children, but uses them instead as targets for its disappointment, its lack of self-confidence, and for its revenge.

"Tell me about Rina," the doctor insists.

"I think of her without joy."

"Why?"

"She was a fortune-teller, or rather, a misfortune-teller."

"Yet mysticism doesn't leave you indifferent."

Indifferent? Nothing leaves me indifferent. I tell her about my attraction to Buddhism. In India, in some ashrams, not listed in guidebooks, they teach wisdom and serenity, in others, madness. Yes, you go there to become mad. There you can see a woman walking around naked and laughing, another singing, a third moaning, but in fact it is always the same woman.

Unbearable images for a simple visitor: an adolescent grown old in a minute, an old man sucked up into the heavens. That is the veil that envelops the existence and world of men.

"An illusion then?"

"A beautiful illusion that hides a reality that isn't an illusion."

This brings back the memory of my meeting with Rina. "Who are you?" a woman inquired one day, in a gentle, slow voice, a woman who believed in love's inability to change life.

It was after my first trip to the Holy Land. We were in a bus going down Fifth Avenue. A gloomy autumn day. Depressing. I had walked for hours to dispel my low spirits. I said to myself that my life was somewhere else, on the other side. I saw myself again as a child. My parents had no suspicions: the thieves had left a little boy in my place who looked just like me. And who, totally delirious, contemplated the world and didn't find it pleasant.

I got off at a stop near Central Park. I sat down on a bench.

A second later, a young woman with short, brown, curly hair, wrapped in a black coat, sat down next to me. I realized it was the woman who had questioned me on the bus. Had she followed me? She looked at me in a strange way, as though I wasn't there, as though I wasn't me; she was at the same time terribly present and terribly distant, neither seeing nor feeling the snow falling on her tousled hair. And I wondered: Could she be the heavy-breasted thief? No, she is better dressed. She remained silent. Because she still thought I was distant? Yet I needed to hear her voice. Understand me, Doctor: I looked at her; her eyes became bluer than the blue of the firmament, and their pupils darker than the wrath of jealous gods. Suddenly she stood up. With a gesture, she invited me to do the same. We walked down the street to a coffee shop, where it was warm.

"You didn't answer my question: Who are you?" she asked.

"I'm someone who is looking for a child."

"What about me? Who am I?" she asked me.

"How would I know?"

"My name is Rina."

"What do you do?"

"People who know me think I'm a witch."

"Oh, I see. So you're fond of demons."

"No. Not demons. Only their master," she said.

"I see."

"Satan."

"In our sources, he's called Ashmedai."

"You're Jewish."

"Yes. Jewish," I said.

"So you know that Ashmedai has a wife."

"Her name is Lilith."

"I know. It's me."

I was rendered speechless, thinking: She's boasting! In the texts, Lilith is very beautiful. Rina seemed to read my mind. "You don't believe me," she said.

"You're right, I don't."

"You might have to pay dearly for that."

"Pay dearly? How?" I asked.

"My husband's punishment."

"For example?"

"We can make you incapable of loving."

She had just entered my life, a minute ago she hadn't existed, but not knowing why, I told her I hated her, had hated her since I was born, and perhaps long before.

"You're mad," she answered. "Stark raving mad, mad as a hatter." She hesitated, then went on: "And perhaps mad enough to love."

She stopped again, as if to invite me to understand on my own that in the cold, cynical world where we live, you have to be mad to love.

A cold, colorless, neutral voice. Ready to become impassioned? A face of stone, but of living, human stone; yes, she had dark, baleful eyes, an astonishingly steady gaze, and a smile verging on laughter. For a moment I felt like touching her face, yes, touching it to punish myself by making each one of her features a little less human. She held out her hand to me, and I was afraid of grasping it.

"So, would you be mad enough to love me, me the wife of the other king of the universe?"

So as not to fall into her trap, I let my thoughts wander back to my parents: Where are we? Where am I? In the jungle of Paris or of Manhattan? In the valley of the gods, where the gardens are in bloom and springtime is eternal?

*Answer me, for the love of God and the hatred of beings like Lilith and Ashmedai. Say something, Father. Answer me, Mother. If only to shatter the silence howling in my blazing head, in my heart gone mad.*

When the dead don't want to speak, no one in the world can force them to. Confined, locked up, as in a hostile enemy fortress.

And, like them, I remained silent just to listen to a song they alone could pick up and decipher: the song of the stones complaining of being stones.

As a result, I felt a renewed strength come over me. Nothing frightened me. I leaned toward her to gaze at her and assess her endowments. Was there a better way of reacting? Finally, something in her face moved. A word tried to come out of her throat and stopped short. Then another word. And more words. I could see them; I saw them swarming about restlessly like flies.

"I know you have questions; I'm listening to you," she said. "They interest me as much as you."

"I would rather listen to yours," I replied.

She didn't answer right away. "Might you be afraid of suffering, of dying perhaps?"

"Not anymore."

"I'll proceed. Let's imagine that I fall in love with you. What would you say?"

"I would say you're crazy."

"And if I was," she said, "would that change anything? Would you be in love with me, say, if you knew everything I know and everything I know how to do? Would you love me insanely?"

"You're crazy, I tell you." And I added that in my studies I learned a great many things about the world of demons. Their powers, their likings, their perversities. But no source mentions their insanity. I'll have to fill that void.

"You know nothing about us," she hissed between her teeth. "You don't know who we are and what our desires are. You reject my love not because I am who I am, but because you are who you are: a man doomed never to love. Too bad for you and for me. If you had wanted to, you could have rescued me by loving me. Yes indeed, dear Mr. Purity, do you know that I live in the mud, the mud of the world? And with the curse upon me, the curse of his creatures?"

I started to ramble, yes, I was rambling, but I couldn't do anything else. Tell her about my life, lived foolishly, mutilated, claimed by evil gods? The extent of my illness, the reasons for my real or imaginary guilt?

"I curse you!" Lilith cried out. "May you remain without love all your life!"

Did she know I was mad, therefore crippled? Had she forgotten this? Could she have gone mad too? What was she seeking in me: the pure and innocent love I was reserving, in my subconscious, for the woman of my dreams whom I don't want to talk about yet? But does pure love exist? For years, each time I meet a stranger, I wonder about this. Until when will I have to wonder about it? In fact, all those who know me, or think they know me from my words and silences, wonder about the same thing: about solitude erected as a screen, a wall, and also as a mirror.

Is madness contagious? All those who come close to me are stricken by this curse—why?

Okay, I'm exaggerating a bit, perhaps a lot. Not all are affected, and those who aren't really cursed. And what of it? If they're free to choose reason and happiness, I'm free to want neither one. My obsession: one minute before sinking into madness entirely, to shout the truth to men's faces, even if it makes them go mad.

Like the dybbuk, I take refuge in my madness as in a warm bed on a winter night.

Yes, that's it. It's a dybbuk pursuing me, haunting me. Taking my place. Usurping my identity and giving me his fate. No more doubt: it's a dybbuk disguised as Doriel. So, I am really another? And would the other be me? This explains my constant distress, the changes, the sudden metamorphoses, with no rites of passage, the despondency bordering on mindlessness, the vagueness of heart that characterizes my illness. In other words: Could I be living another person's life, the life of a stranger, in fact? And who is the other person's dybbuk?

"What's a dybbuk?" asks Thérèse, truly interested.

"Badly formulated question, Doctor. You should say, who?"

"I'm sorry, but I don't understand."

"You should say: Who is a dybbuk?"

"Very well. Who?"

I tell her about S. Anski's play, a great play, in which two Talmudic students are bound by an oath: if, one day, one of them has a boy and the other a girl, their children will marry. But one becomes rich and the other remains poor. You can imagine the rest. Leah didn't marry Hanan. He dies of grief. And his soul steals its way into his betrothed's soul.

"But then your dybbuk should be a woman."

"Not always, Doctor. A dybbuk can be a stranger, an identity thief, who says 'me' through my mouth, in my place. A wandering, exiled soul, lost in the immense emptiness that makes up the universe of men and the memory of God. For reasons known and unknown, the dybbuk hides from the sight of angels and demons. He feels safe only in the soul of another being. I am his hiding place. His life becomes mine; it is made of excess, anguish, and ill-defined remorse. I fear that my dybbuk may be mad, and I struggle to understand the germ of his madness. Is it, in his case, the rejection of a religion that he considers not demanding enough or, on the contrary, worth no greater demands? Is it just thought rebelling against itself? The dybbuk's thought never stays still; it runs until it is out of breath, and I run after it, to hold it back. The dybbuk's heart knows neither love nor hatred but is jealous of those who feel either. Perhaps he repudiates tradition in the name of all traditions, rejecting a heritage accepted unthinkingly, so as to feel freer."

The therapist stops nodding and manifests an incredulous air. "But which of you two is ill? Who am I supposed to take care of?" she asks.

"Me. Him. More specifically: me who is him."

I explain it to her in a few hasty words: when he invades a person, the dybbuk is omnipresent, cunning, but not always diabolical, because he is suffering. However, he too is motivated by a need that is within the province of the sacred. Doesn't his soul, though damned, aspire to the tranquility promised by transcendence? Nimble, unpredictable, determined and unscrupulous, he pulls me along like a prisoner burdened with chains; his salvation depends on mine, but at the same time mine is conditioned by his.

"And what about me?" asks the therapist without looking at me. "Where do I fit in?"

The dybbuk bursts out laughing, and so do I.

In every form of madness there smolders the desire to escape so as to find oneself again and renew oneself, to experience rebirth through death, howling in order to keep quiet.

I have so many things to keep silent about, so many things to talk about, but where are the words? The words are hiding, they elude me, they hate me; therein lies my madness, Doctor. It's the words. The words I need in order to cling to life, to find my fervor again and pray—yes: in order to live. Where are they? Why have they vanished? Out of fear of being isolated? There are sounds and words that can't bear being alone; each one summons the next and becomes linked to it, and no force can separate them without reducing them to powerlessness. Is that the secret of poetry and music?

And of madness?

I made too much use of words, their suppleness and their density, as a way of captivating the first passerby encountered in the street or at the fair, and I am overcome by a desire to repudiate them. Then, especially in the morning, I feel an irresistible need to just sink my teeth into life, and to hell with the fear of others and the shame of living among them. After all, the point is to like what one possesses and what one is, in order to better get rid of them. The devil take future pleasures in heaven; the earth is here so we can savor its fruits, and the body to demand an impossible happiness. A vain hope? Cries directed at a deaf world? And if I'm taken for a madman, too bad. Remember Zarathustra, Doctor, expressing himself through the mouth of that other great madman, who committed suicide after a long silence: "It is night. Now, up higher, rises the voice of gushing fountains; and my soul too becomes a gushing fountain." Do you think his silence drowned him in his own delusions?

I shut my eyes. Somewhere, in my village in Poland. A small cloud, a dark smile, the snow that keeps falling on the face as if to erase the lost orphan's smile. Don't ask me what the connection is, not you of all people, Doctor, especially not you. It's you who is constantly annoying me with your habit of reminding me that association of ideas is essential to therapy. It's you who requests, demands, and commands me, in the name of all the saints of holy therapy, to let my thoughts wander, run wild, plucking an image here, extracting a sigh there. Bah, Doctor, I for one don't believe in that catastrophe-theory stuff according to which the truth about the world and man is hiding out of fear or shame—

"Fear? Shame? Why?"

"I have no idea, Doctor. You want me to say whatever comes to my mind, absolutely everything, including what's unclear, or has no meaning, so that's what I'm doing, understand? I'll let you guide me, but I'm also entitled to ask you if what comes out of my brain helps us progress; is that true or not? You say nothing? All right, then I'll keep quiet too."

"What if we went back to fear and shame?"

"I also said the word *truth*. Remember? Do you know the Gaon of Vilna? He used to say that the goal of redemption is the redemption of truth. No, I see you don't know him. But Plato you know, right? Plato is dear to me, but not as much as truth."

"Let's drop the Gaon. Let's forget about fear and shame. Let's talk about truth."

"I see you don't understand a thing. All of this is connected. People like you surely think that truth causes shame, causes fear. But what if someone told you that's not it at all? That truth is fear as well as shame?"

She continues to provoke me with her monotonous voice, and for my part, I think she's afraid of the little cloud smiling down on the orphan. She wants to make me talk about the place of women in my life, and I don't feel like it. To tell her that they've always intimidated me? That I don't know what behavior to adopt with them? I prefer to stay on my cloud. The cloud is an orphan too, and it weeps. Its tears turn into flakes of snow and blood. I catch them in my mouth and out comes a howl; I'm afraid of strangling myself. It's that I imagine the strangler, his twisted face, his monstrously large hands, unwieldy and unclean; I imagine and visualize his conqueror's grimaces. As though he is announcing to whomever wants to hear it: I'm destiny, I'm above time and the heavens, I'm the force that crushes you. Have I actually seen him, or just seen him in a film or maybe in an illustrated book? A Jewish child in hiding, flushed out by shifty eyes, surrounded by murderers with gleaming daggers. He is alone, the future little orphan, so alone, my little brother. Who betrayed him? I know that I should run to him, take his hand, do anything to protect him, show him my solidarity and affection. He's frightened and I'm frightened; he's frightened and I'm ashamed. And that's the truth. To touch lightly on the truth without desecrating it, to wish for it without attaining it—if only I could. And what if I told you it may be time to unfasten the bonds tying man to his destiny and to expose the sham: Rina doesn't exist, the madman of this narrative doesn't confide in his therapist; he is simultaneously his own question and his own answer, and the rejection of both. Thérèse Goldschmidt exists only in my illness, and in me too.

"So, what is madness, Doctor, if not a dybbuk, in my case? A new form of asceticism? A divine punishment?"

She doesn't know.

*But you, to whom I am writing, you're supposed to know everything, to foresee everything. So tell me what I will someday learn from you: What is human madness exactly? Falling into a trance? Denouncing reason until one is short of breath? Listening to the silence explode in one's brain and not being able to gather its bits and pieces?*

Am I really me? And the other one, who is he when he says *I*? Is he still me?

*You see? I tell you everything; at least I take pains to. It's important to me to know that you'll accept me in spite of all the obstacles. Your consent will make sense only if it is offered as a supreme act of lucidity.*

*Do you wish to follow me?*

# 2

An image: A village somewhere in Poland. It is Sunday. The church must be full. The sound of its bells fill the countryside, as for a funeral. A room in a house at the edge of the woods. A bed, an old couch, two chairs. Books on a shelf, newspapers on the floor. A frustrated, unhappy little boy. Frightened, his senses on the alert. His father tells him to pay attention, to watch for the moment when, with a bit of luck, they'll have the right to go out into the street. And never to show he's frightened. Too many enemies, too many dangers threaten them outside. The sky is blue, cloudless. And under the fruit trees everything is so calm. The child wants to go out. Warm himself in the sun, play. Pluck an apple, some plums. No, says his father. Not today. Why not today? Because. When will he be able to go out? Tomorrow. "But tomorrow you'll say, Not today again." "No, tomorrow I'll say, Let's wait." The little boy is me. I'm six years old, I'm too young, I don't know how to respond. So I say, "If Mother were here . . ." I cut myself short: What if Mother were here? Would she be nicer with me?

"But she wasn't there," remarks the doctor. "Did you resent her for that?"

No. But the little boy feels like crying.

———

Is it because of the incomplete memories and the many twists and turns I hide in, aging and tired, ever since I've been left all alone? The doctor is talking and I answer, but I'm thinking about something else; my mind is elsewhere. Will she help me? Will I hurt her? So many interlocutors I've met during my peregrinations sooner or later have lost hope or reason, and at the very least, part of their being. You'd think I was casting my shadows on those who talk to me and putting a curse on those who behold me. A retired physician and bewildered widower, a swindler released from jail without having disclaimed his crime, an unemployed actress, a former industrialist who cheated at chess—they have all been affected. There were young ones among them and not-so-young ones, foreigners and natives, intellectuals and ignoramuses, poets and technicians: they all experienced the same fate, each in his own way.

Could I be the last one?

Everything explodes within me: images, looks, noises and memories, chimerical angels and diabolical monsters. How can I find something to appease me? The man who pursues me has climbed up so many mountains and followed so many trails—how can I name him? Where does he come from? Who sent him?

One morning, a passerby heard my enemy howling like a beast at slaughter. When notified, the police had to break down the door to his apartment. They found him on his bed, his head covered with blood. Questioned as to the identity of his aggressor, he could only keep repeating the same sentences: "She had the smile of an innocent child. A shame. I would rather have said the smile of a frightened child." But who is the enemy? Not me?

"I don't understand," says the therapist.

"But it's simple: the child I see in my mind's eye always has a frightened smile."

"But you mentioned a woman. Who is she? A sorceress? A

lover? A stranger? Was she with a man? How could they get into your house since the door and the windows were shut?"

Like a blind man groping to find his way, or at least looking for something to lean on, the interlocutor preferred to think about his dream rather than the assailant; he could only mumble the same words: "She had a smile, the smile of an innocent child, but not frightened, not at all frightened."

I remember the police inspector: a grandfather with a mustache and a wise and kindly smile; he nodded several times to let me know he understood me. Who did he think I was? An orphan abandoned in the middle of the fair? The idiot of Chelm, the legendary village whose inhabitants had a reputation for touching naïveté according to some, stupidity according to others?

"I remember," said the wounded man. "We met on a cloud."

"Is it she who put you in this state? Don't worry, we'll find her. She'll go to jail."

"To jail? I'll go join her."

"What was she like? We need a description."

"Long hair, dark eyes. And the moving smile of a child who is waiting but isn't frightened. She didn't like my name."

"Is that so? Your name. And what is your name?"

*I remember:*

*After having reflected for a long time, Mother took on a solemn expression: "Who are you?" she asked.*

*"My name is Doriel."*

*I no longer know why, but I was having trouble breathing.*

*You didn't like it. That's not a name, you said. I like it. It doesn't belong to anyone. It's an announcement, an ancient message, a new agenda. And yes, it's a name, my very own name, a name I sometimes hate or love for no good reason, but it's mine. Do you hear me? Do all of you hear me? I'll have to keep it, even if I have to drag it around like a burden, a sack filled with shadows.*

In my head, a scaffolding of noises and images, sniggering or blank faces, men running in all directions and soldiers advancing toward a bottomless cemetery. Then the building collapses and, from this thundering noise, my brain bursts. I look for something to lean on, and it proliferates into 144 points. I want to understand, and I become more deeply confused than ever.

What could be more natural, I take refuge where no one can follow me. First in my dreams, but the walls weren't solid, so I opted for madness.

From the many beginnings of my conscious existence or dream life, I never stopped astonishing my family circle. When still in the crib, I used to play with my mother by pinching her cheeks or bosom. I heard her boasting to visitors: "Just look at my big rascal. If he weren't so little, I'd say he's crazy about me." My hair used to change colors suddenly. Brown in the morning, blond in the afternoon. Black in my dreams. I sometimes gulped my meal down in a flash, though I had taken four hours the previous day. "Oh, yes," said an old Gypsy with wrinkled skin and a hoarse, unpleasant voice. "He's crazy, this little one. Crazy about life that death chases away, or conversely."

In the evening, abandoned by my father, who used to quietly sleep in a corner of the barn, I visualized myself in a stranger's arms, or perched on his shoulder, while he ran toward the woods where priests, half naked, were celebrating ancient victories and defeats in a diabolical tribal ritual, by dancing around a blazing fire.

Yes, I visualized myself among them, silent and frightened, anticipating the moment when I would be carried to the altar to expiate some forgotten sins. I feared pain more than death, but deep down, something else happened: I was saved by a woman whose dark hair fell over her ample bosom. Was it the woman who had abducted me long ago and was now repenting? She put herself between the dancers and me; she whispered comforting and tender words in my ear—not to be afraid because she was there, to tell her when I was thirsty, for she would give me something to drink. I asked her who had sent her, my mother or my father. Then she looked deeply into my eyes with her dark gaze and shook her head. "Don't ask questions, my child, no questions, not yet. Learn to wait, it's an art—you'll understand that when you grow up." In a flash, I see myself projected into the future: a young prince, almost an adolescent, I am lost among the dancers. Here again, it is a little boy they are preparing to sacrifice. I scrutinize him as hard as I can; then suddenly I turn my head away so as not to see his head anymore. Is it my little brother, Jacob? Is it me? I wake up with a start, frightened. But I'm not certain that my awakening isn't itself part of the dream.

As for the woman, what color were her eyes when she smiled? Could I have forgotten the most important thing?

"Whom did she look like?" asks the therapist, curious, as always.

"I don't know, I don't know anymore. In the dream everything is distorted."

"Did she look like Rina?"

"What do you know about Rina?"

"Nothing. Except the time before last, at one point you mentioned her name."

"In connection with what? You must have misheard."

"But the woman in the dream: Did she look like your mother?"

"Leave my mother alone."

"You don't think about her anymore, is that it?"

"Leave her alone, I tell you."

"Okay. Let's talk about the woman you loved."

"Which one?"

"Any one of them."

"I didn't love her."

"Not even for a brief moment?"

"A brief moment of intoxication and delirium doesn't count."

"Given what concerns us, everything counts."

"I say no."

"I'm talking about—"

"About whom? The woman I loved? She doesn't count. She doesn't count anymore. She never counted. I didn't even touch her."

"But you wanted to."

"Yes, maybe. Wanted to touch her, that's all. But that lasted only a split second. Nothing to do with desire."

"But a split second—"

"Don't be so exacting. I've done lots of things in my life without really doing them. One fine morning, my features distorted, I woke up a troubadour; I visualized myself singing in the streets, palms outstretched, imploring passersby to listen to me and acknowledge my existence. Did I do it? Of course not. The same is true for Maya."

I can't remember who put me in touch with her. A mutual friend who wanted to help me or play a trick on me? An enemy who hoped to see me sink into disgrace? A heavenly or earthly court, anxious perhaps to protect me from the dybbuk who was leading me to violate taboos by blaming others and myself? Certainly not. I met Maya by the strangest of coincidences. On my way to Israel in the 1950s, I stopped in Marseilles, where I wanted to meditate at my parents' grave. And I found myself in this place where, according to a Brooklyn acquaintance, Jewish refugees from central Europe met for business or simply to pass the time. Why in heaven did I have to enter a room where a lecture was taking place, a lecture to which I hadn't been invited? I didn't know the lecturer; I knew nothing about his subject.

Was it a colloquium of intellectuals or a political meeting? I didn't understand their language. Actually, I had seen well-dressed people go into a building with an elegant façade that looked like a theater or museum. Prompted by an uncustomary curiosity, I followed them in. Just to see. The room was jam-packed. The ambience rather sophisticated. Some people were sighing, from emotion probably, or possibly impatience; others were chatting to while away boredom. Suddenly, everyone stood up; the orator had just arrived. He mounted the small platform and began talking, and everyone nodded as he spoke. Since I couldn't understand a thing, not least what I was doing there, I was soon eager to leave, but being too shy to attract attention, I looked around me. I wanted to see if my neighbors also found the lecture obscure, which would not have been surprising since the lecturer's French was riddled with words and names in Yiddish and Hebrew, and his way of expressing himself was long-winded, terribly so, and his voice sugary in a way that I found boring.

A young dark-haired woman was sitting in front of me, perfectly still. Something about her intrigued me. I had the strange feeling that she wasn't alone, and yet no one was accompanying her. Solitary like me? And what if she was the unknown woman of my dreams, one of my first unfulfilled loves, whom I often thought about with remorse and shame, for I owed her so much? Just thinking about it, I felt the blood rush to my brain. Was it a memory or dream already stifled and consumed in a fog suddenly and even more quickly dispelled? Oh, Lord, let it be her. If only I could see her from the front. What if I touched her shoulder to make her turn toward me? Would I dare?

I dared. She turned around and looked at me with an expression more amused than angry. She wasn't the stranger from the bus. But she too smiled at me. A second later she stood up and went out. I followed her into the street. A light drizzle washed the streets and houses. The woman took my arm in silence. We went into a café and sat down at a table near the entrance to the terrace. She ordered tea for two. Her voice, deep and sensual, aroused me.

"Talk, I'm listening."

I told her that I didn't understand French. Fortunately, she spoke Yiddish. She wanted to know why I had followed her; I replied that I didn't know myself.

Why was I spending time in this city?

I told her.

"Is it your first visit here?" she asked.

"Yes."

"Your first visit since the war?"

"Yes."

"In other words, you don't know the city."

"No."

"How will you find the way to the cemetery?"

"I'm counting on you," I answered in a serious tone of voice.

It was true. I didn't know her, but I was counting on her. Perhaps because I liked her melodious Yiddish.

"You have a strange way of staring at people," she said.

"No."

"What do you mean, no?"

"I look at eyes that look at me. And what about me, how do *you* look at me?"

"I wonder if you're part of my past or my future."

"I don't know the first, but you're in luck: the second interests me."

We chatted for a long time. Good fortune smiled on me that day. She seemed older than me and worked in a Jewish organization. I convinced myself that she was going to help me.

"I have an offer to make to you," I said. "Be my guide. Stay with me until my departure in two days. Take me to the cemetery. Show me the city. The Jewish neighborhood, if there still is one. I'll pay you well. Don't say no. Not yet. It's too soon. You'll tell me the next time."

"You're a funny guy. When will the next time be? And where? In what city? In what lifetime?"

Should I tell her that I was staying at the Hotel Splendide?

"I have no idea. Let's leave it up to fate."

Suddenly a feeling of panic came over me. I went on quickly: "But what if we don't see each other again?"

"It would still be a lovely romance."

That's when I realized she had the smile of an innocent, peaceful child, and dark shadows under her eyes.

Like my mother?

Suddenly, I was embarrassed to realize I no longer remembered the color of her eyes.

But everything that I never dared to say or even think about my mother, I can now say about Maya.

Maya's eyes were dark, at least so I believed. Never in my life have I seen eyes like hers. Whoever saw them plunged into them as into a beckoning river promising dreams and adventure.

I never forgot those eyes and I never will. I'm emphasizing this because, even if I'm wrong, I think it's important for the story; they were cheerful, of a remarkable, uneven blue-black color, at once disquieting and soothing. Dark blue like a spring night over the ocean, or the sky over the desert. One minute, they seemed fiery to the point of pain; then, unperturbed, without transition, they opened up, under their delicate eyelids, like an offering. And you felt like searching them endlessly, caressing them with your gaze, attributing to them a secret meaning, kissing them. What poets and novelists say about eyes and their power is both true and untrue. Mirror of the soul? Window into the unconscious? Yes, without a doubt. But Maya's were more, far more than that: they stirred your stomach and shook your guts. She had only to look at me and say the word and I was prepared to take her to the ends of the earth. She had only to take my hand and I would have let death carry me off to the final ecstasy where no compromise is possible.

It is because of her that blue remains my favorite color.

"You look at me and I look at you," she said, smiling slightly at the corners of her lips. "That's enough to imagine the impossible and even to live it, isn't it?"

"Enough for whom?"

"For couples in the making," she said, her eyes lighting up, gleaming mischievously. "Am I wrong, Mr. . . . who?"

"Doriel. My name is Doriel."

"What a strange name. I don't like it."

She took me to the cemetery and, being discreet, left me alone. I visited ancient graves before visiting my parents'. I recited the Psalms with my prayer: Do you recognize your son? Watch over him when he goes astray.

That's the story of Maya. That meeting binds me to other encounters, of another kind; that's the way things are in life. Every human being is unique, but his or her stories aren't. From a quasi-mystical point of view, it could almost be said that the stories are all alike. And yet I didn't know that many years later I would meet other Mayas, with other names, smiling like sensible children grazed by fear, but never close enough to be able to talk of a fulfilled love.

Blushing like a schoolboy on his first date, my heart racing like a wild beast chasing its prey, I see myself again with Maya by the sea in Marseilles. We had just left the cemetery in silence. I felt close to her. Nothing had faded. This is how the past survives in the present. Speechless, I saw myself in the little Polish village whose surrounding mountains I loved. Now, I loved the sea. Hypnotized, I gazed at the waves that recounted their eternal stories to me lost and swallowed up deep in their unfathomable mysteries. Suddenly her voice struck me. More affectionate than before. She was smiling at me. She looked like a worried child, but she was smiling. What was she hinting at? What did she see in me? Her own youth, perhaps? Her loss of faith? The opportunity to convey to me her experience of shared desire? As a result, I began to forget all the strange women that, because of the fear of God and my arousal on seeing them in the streets of Manhattan and Brooklyn, I had unsuccessfully tried to blot out of my consciousness. None had her charm or imagination. Or her freedom. She spoke to me uninhibitedly, as though we were alone in the world. For Maya, everything seemed simple, at close range. The word was innocent, gesture much less so; everything in her exuded naturalness.

"Is it your dead parents? Are you grieving for them?" she asked me, still in Yiddish. "I lost mine too. We must not let them weigh us down," she added. "Despair can have a kind of beauty, provided it remains in the sphere of memory. Your memories paralyze you; mine do not."

She wanted to celebrate life but instilled in me an anguish that dragged me down. How had she guessed my appalling frame of mind? How did she know that I was unhappy? She took my hand and held it for a long while, and in my heart, darkness gave way to a spark of enthusiasm and joyfulness. But while her body said yes, mine replied no. Is it my fault? Must I feel guilty for that too? Guilty for not having extended and fecundated this tie that, in plain sight of the sea and sky, might have united us in a moment of happiness, though fleeting and therefore deceptive? And what if I stayed in Marseilles, canceled my trip to Israel, and took her with me to the United States? All these thoughts swirled around in my head.

Many things happened afterward. Was it too early or too late? They all led to the time of separation. But no matter. In a diseased brain, time follows a special rhythm. In the past, at my uncle's, life seemed more orderly. In the past? When was that? What was it? A pause, an invitation? A warning from destiny? Let's put in a crossroads. In the past is far away.

"When it comes to destiny, everything is a challenge," Maya said. "But who comes out the winner? That is the question."

Our second meeting took place a few years later in a seaside café in Tel Aviv, a city that is constantly growing in successive maelstroms of fury and joy. Was it chance? Was it destiny? The Jewish tradition—for, you see, Doctor, I remember it—doesn't believe in fate. And yet. Everything in every creature's life is part of a grand design. Even the rolling stone or swaying tree. Everything is preordained. I might not have come here today. I might have come to see you at an earlier time, or later. And you'd have known nothing about my life. The same is true of Maya. No doubt this will seem to you childish and absurd, but an inner voice had whispered to me that I would see her again in Israel. In Jerusalem? On a kibbutz? But why did I want to meet her again? Out of curiosity? Simply to prove to myself that I was capable of loving? Or to pursue our sad romance, in any case doomed to failure? But Maya had other plans. I wasn't that important in her life. And was she in mine? Where and for whom had she concocted dreams for months?

I saw her arrive, holding a young officer's arm. She was glowing with pride. Having eyes only for her companion, she didn't see me. With a heavy heart, I wondered whether I should attract her attention.

I left the place, tiptoeing away through a hidden door. Like a thief.

*I have so many things to keep silent about, so many episodes, and I search and search for my words. They hide, evade me. Why don't you try to capture them for me? You have given me so much, for one thing, life; now give me the words I need in order to love, to understand, and to open myself up to serenity.*

Late November, 1973. Sitting in a café near the center of Jerusalem, I'm waiting for an old friend of my uncle's, a Haredi, as pious as he. I listen distractedly to the discussion between two journalists at a nearby table. They're talking about the debacle at the beginning of the Yom Kippur War. The shameful deficiency of Israeli military intelligence. Never had the existence of the Jewish state been in such danger. And never had there been as much talk about divine intervention and miracles. Especially in the first few days: helped by the Soviets in the south, the Egyptian forces had crossed the Suez Canal and advanced into the desert, while in the north the Syrian army was winning unprecedented victories. Here, there, and everywhere, disabled tanks and airplanes were being replaced too slowly and too inadequately. In some circles, people mentioned in an undertone the possibility of the Third Temple, symbol of the new Jewish state, being destroyed. Young soldiers, thanks to their courage, stopped the invasion. The price was high: three thousand dead in combat and more than ten thousand wounded. And Europe remained indifferent to the anguish and suffering of the Jews. When the United States finally agreed to deliver arms to Israel, none of the European countries gave the military planes permission to refuel in their airports. You'd almost think France, Germany, and the other countries had accepted the possibility of a Jewish tragedy on a historical scale. Though anti-Zionist, my uncle's friend hadn't concealed his grief and fears from me. Fortunately, Tsahal, the Israeli army, had crossed the Suez Canal as well, taking the rear of the Egyptian army by surprise and threatening Cairo.

I sipped my lemonade thinking not about my studies, so frequently interrupted, but about my uncle and aunt. They lived in New York and must have been fretting: I was nearly thirty-eight, but if something were to happen to me right then, they would sink into a possibly irreversible depression. For in a country at war, the tragedy is not just death but uncertainty. That's why their anguish kept haunting me during my long nights wandering around the world.

"And our future, what's become of it?" a voice in back of me suddenly asked in Yiddish.

I gave a start and exclaimed: "Maya! Where have you been? What are you doing here? Are you on a special assignment?"

"I came to surprise you."

"You knew I was in the country?"

"I had no idea."

"Well then?"

"Well, nothing."

"You're the goddess of surprises."

"All the better."

"For whom?"

"For couples unexpectedly in the making."

Couples. Again, almost the same thoughts she had expressed the first time, in Marseilles. She alluded to it once more; then, taking on a professorial tone, she explained: if surprises didn't exist, life would be nothing more than a bad novel about mediocrity. She still had her beautiful low voice, suggesting unsuspected profundity. But it wasn't her voice that made her attractive; even then, it was her dark, haunted eyes and her childlike smile, not frightened but amused. Could this be a disease, Doctor, which psychiatrists will have to deal with, the disease of "blue eyes" and of "a childlike smile"?

"You look at me and I feel like smiling at you," Maya said in her melodious Yiddish. "And talking to you about us, and maybe about myself too. I look at you and you seem as lost and as unhappy as the last time. Is it because of the squandered years?"

"It's not our fault. If we just met again, it's because it was meant to be."

Did I still love her?

*I asked myself this question a long time ago. Today, as I speak to you, to you who are no longer here, and to you too, Liatt, while*

*I write to you, I would answer: something of this love has re-mained in me. It is not nothing, but no more than that. Today I am writing to you, and not to her.*

Yes, I loved her in my way, not in hers. I loved her because her voice took me back to my childhood and those miraculous moments. And because she had dark blue eyes and dark rings around them. And an open face. And she forgot nothing. She requested—she demanded—that I take up the bet of candidly narrating a novel to her about the future we could have had. I briefly invented a languorous engagement, a wedding celebrated by mystical beggars in a bewitched forest. And then I loved her because it was a pure, naïve, innocent love. I told her that I used to think women liked me and were attracted to me. Now, no women smiled at me. None, except her. Then Maya in turn described the same period since we had first met but dwelled on aspects of a coupledom marked by unfulfilled love and ending in a cruel disease. She described a hospital room, physicians, visitors, flowers on the table, and the river view from the window. She said she married to counter destiny; she thought she would be able to demonstrate she had powers over it. But it always wins in the end. She seemed so young still. And already a widow.

"You look at me and I feel like smiling," she said again in her melodious Yiddish.

And I felt like crying.

This was our third meeting, though there really wasn't a second one.

I remember: She was best at talking and I was best at keeping silent, unlike with you, Doctor. She repeated simple but strange words. As though she were reciting, in Yiddish, poems by Markish, short stories by Peretz, verses on death culled from esoteric ancient works from Tibet, Egypt, and Babylonia. I listened to her with the same anxiety as the first time. Doctor, was I already then the man you see today? Was the dybbuk already haunting me? Maya dreamily recalled our hours of imaginary happiness, whereas my thoughts drifted to the finality of suffering. The Angel of Death, the only one to have escaped madness, now made his presence felt under his anonymous and indifferent masks. Nasty, pernicious, he prowled through the streets populated with Jewish and Arab children and on the sunlit hills of Judea, ready to strike the descendants of Moses and David.

Many years have gone by since then. I had pleasant affairs, and though some were not so lovely, they were never dull. I studied, made a few breakthroughs in the interpretation of texts, traveled across exotic countries, got close to some great masters, played with the children of my friends, spent money left and right, founded shelters and health-care centers for the disinherited, and did my best to help people resigned to regaining a little bit of hope. I took care of the unfortunate orphans whose parents were victims of war.

When I'm sick, which at my age happens more and more frequently, children come to see me. Irene, so young and so sickly, kisses my hand. Little Avrémele, who lost his mother, looks at me with a sad expression; he wants to know where it hurts. I answer I don't know. He's surprised; if I don't know where it hurts, it must mean it doesn't hurt. Logical, isn't it? Then he caresses my forehead and says: There, it doesn't hurt anymore. And my chest: You see, it doesn't hurt anymore. I smile at him and tell him that I love him. Between two hospital stays, I have work that sometimes gives me a feeling of satisfaction. I give adolescents private courses on medieval Jewish history. That's my area; don't ask me why, Doctor. Perhaps because, at my advanced age, I thought it would make my elderly parents happy, my parents who died young, so young. First I grieved over the death of my mother. Then over that of my father. Yet they died together, on the same day; I know when, where, and in what circumstances. I also know that I should have done more for them and better . . . I grieve over the deaths of my sister, Dina, and my brother, Jacob. She, so graceful, so intrepid; he, so frail and vulnerable. Is it because of them that I expect so little out of life?

I told Maya all this, and she interrupted me. "Of life?" she asked. "What life are you talking about? Yours or mine? Or the one suggested to you by your fantasies?"

When two destinies beckon to each other, Doctor, the gods always intervene. Either they applaud or they get angry.

"And you," I said, in order to hurt her back, "what couple are you talking about? Yours or mine?"

"Ours, you poor fool. We could have lived together, spread happiness in a world doomed to suffer and cause suffering. We could have . . ."

She was dreaming.

Should I question her about our "second" meeting? She was with an officer. Who was he? Her future husband? And if I had joined her, would she have left him?

We brought our heads closer. Around us, the world continued on its restless course. For us, time stopped.


At the frontiers of the desert, war was too exhausted to strike again; hundreds of families were grieving over the heroic deaths of their close ones; journalists talked of scandals involving the military and politicians; commentators demanded resignations, but the two of us, in that café, we thought only about our little quarrel.

"Tell me a story," Maya begged, her blue eyes becoming bluer than the sky.

"A story?" I asked, half surprised. "Here? Now?"

"Why not?" she replied with a serious expression. "Is there a special time for stories?"

I could have answered yes, there's a time for revealed stories and a time for those that remain hidden away in the shadows, a time for tears and another for songs, except that tears can turn into songs. "Would a memory do?" I asked.

"Instead of a story?"

"Why not?"

"I prefer stories. Memories are often too sad."

"And stories aren't?"

Maya stopped smiling. She must have been weighing the pros and cons in her mind.

"Very well then," she concluded. "A memory will be okay."

How could I avoid making her sad? I told her about the tradition that existed in our family, transmitted from generation to generation. It concerned my maternal great-great-grandfather. He lived in a small village tucked away in the Carpathians. He kept a tavern and inn, where he lived with his wife and children. In spite of the difficult times in that region for our people, he never complained. Was he happy? Like all Diaspora Jews, yes and no. On the Sabbath, he and his entire family glowed with happiness. Yet he had his share of hardships. Up to his neck in debt, threatened and occasionally beaten by fanatical hooligans, especially during Christian holidays, he was convinced that only the arrival of the Messiah would bring an end to the curses hanging over his household and the greater house of Israel. Thanks to this belief, he overcame sufferings and misfortunes. Then, one winter night, when everything was closed in the sleeping village, someone knocked at his door. A shabbily dressed visitor, probably a peasant or coachman, asked if he could sleep at the inn until daybreak. He was exhausted and penniless. My great-great-grandfather wanted to know who he was and where he was from, but the visitor evaded the questions and said, "What does it matter where I'm from? Actually, I'm from where you're from. And you'll be going where I'm going." With that, he turned away and walked toward the hearth to warm himself up. My great-great grandfather brought him some hot tea, a fur pelisse to wrap himself in, some dried fruits, and an oil lamp. Worried, he didn't go back to bed but kept a watchful eye on the sleeping visitor. It was Rabbi Israel, son of Eliezer and Sarah, the man who would become the Ba'al Shem Tov, the Master of the Good Name.

Maya waited for me to continue, but I kept silent.

"That's all?" she cried out, disappointed.

"No," I said. "That's not all. That's only the prologue."

"Well, then, tell me the rest! There's a sequel, isn't there?"

"Yes, this memory, or story, has a sequel."

"What is it? Don't be cruel!"

"I'm not cruel; you know that."

I asked her not to press the matter: "Be patient. Now you know there's a sequel, and that one day you'll know it. Let that be enough for you. It's dangerous to run too fast. Only madmen take that risk."

Being intelligent, Maya pretended to be sad, but she didn't press the matter.

I know, Doctor, I know what people are saying: "He's gone mad, poor Doriel's gone mad." Oh yes, mad, me. I raise again the question that comes up at all our sessions: What is being mad, Doctor? Between a normal storyteller narrating the story of a madman and a madman describing the death of a normal man, which one would require your treatment, Doctor? If the world tells me I'm mad, whereas I know I'm not, which of us is right? Thus, being mad is what? Starting a story or a sentence and not finishing it? Inventing a life one hasn't lived or loving a woman met in another lifetime? Is it clinging to unsatisfied desires? Having a blazing head and a heart frozen in terror? Living on the fringes of time in a country where everything is orderly just as others go off to live and dance at the ends of the earth? Yes,

I'm chained to my madness, to its fury, caught up in its violence. My brain is mush, Doctor; my mind is in shreds. And what about the soul, Doctor? The possessed, desecrated soul. Does the madman's soul leave with his reason, or does it become mad too? But then what does this madness consist of? Is it attracted by the black flames of a fire like the ones, during a pogrom, that devour the hearts and bodies of the living and the dead, and even of babies still to be born? And this ailing soul, disconsolate or raging, how can it be healed without knowing the true nature of its shackles and wounds?

"Yes, he's mad, Doriel," that's what people mutter, adding, "Poor guy," or "Nice guy," it all depends, for they claim the right to pass judgment, to censure a person who refuses to be like them, a person attached to his life as though it were a sleepy planet or a planet in turmoil, who might ruin them by unmasking them.

What do they know of the dybbuk who thumbs his nose at me, these men and women who have never felt the throes of hunger and fear? Since when does a full stomach fancy himself a spiritual adviser, or the client of the best tailor set himself up as an expert in social ethics?

All these people chatter morning and night, while working and resting; they'll say anything about anything, without wondering whether their words reflect a desire to enrich the world with a new truth or an ancient promise. I'm sure that the parents of my students go so far as to reproach me for the ignorance of their offspring . . . The teachers accuse me of competing with them. And hypochondriacs of stealing their physicians. I remain impassive. I find more interest, life, and independence in words than in those who utter them. Sometimes, always unexpectedly, a word vanishes; it's impossible to recapture it, for it has already become a face. And this face, stunningly beautiful and fascinatingly ugly, at once young and decrepit, coarse and majestic, enjoys attracting and repelling me, and I say to myself, laughing and crying: it is the face of a god struck by the madness of demons, and the madman is me.

I have a question for you, Doctor: Does a madman think he is the only person who is mad or that all men are mad? Am I mad *so* I can be alone or because I *already* am? Sometimes in a fit of a certain indefinable something, I ask myself: Since there's such a connection between solitude and madness, how can one know whether human beings, in their opaqueness and pettiness, didn't succeed in driving mad all of Creation, saturated and disgusted with their stupidity?

Sometimes the madman wants to fling the plain truth into their faces. Remind them of the puerile fantasies of power that they boast of avoiding in order to better grab them. The madman is less cunning but more experienced than they; his memories reach back farther. But what is the point of attracting their attention? They won't even get angry; they'll guffaw and slap their knees: "Oh, he's funny, our poor Doriel, he's rambling, it probably helps him; it entertains him." Well, no; it doesn't entertain him. Sometimes, he just assumes the role of the solitary dreamer who sees the light coming from another age. And suddenly, the light changes into a fire; it's the fire, the fire that a demented woman sees in the train bringing her and her starving children, and their silent grandparents, to the kingdom where all life plunges into death; she sees gigantic flames nipping the sky, and set ablaze, it opens like a tomb where the sparks of souls said to be immortal are snuffed out. Then the mad dreamer begins to sob uncontrollably and says to himself that if he sheds enough tears, who knows, perhaps the tears will extinguish the fire; and God himself in a burst of remorse or gratitude will thank him.

Oh, dreamer, where is the fire that set the night ablaze? You know, Doctor, you know what's happened to it, that feverish and terrifying night that the madman carries deep down and that crushes me relentlessly with the weight of its tormented ghosts?

I'm talking to you, Doctor, even when I know you don't understand me and never will. I am talking to you the way I used to talk to a woman whom I thought was close; she left me like an illusion, and in her flight, she filched more than my earthly clothes. She didn't just steal the joys and hopes that are offered to us during our life span. She dispossessed me of my dreams and desires for an absolute.

You listen to me; that's your function, your duty. In order to mollify me, you pretend to be opening up to my voice. You say: "I keep silent for your own good; so you'll allow your thoughts to range freely in the plowed, known, and unknown landscape of your memory. So as to cure you of your phobias and manias." You're thinking of the guilt complex every son feels with regard to his father, and every person with regard to his elder or his heir, and that's why you wish to make me speak freely about myself, without censuring me, is that it? But submitting oneself to your method is not self-evident. Of course, I sometimes feel guilty, though not responsible, for a lot of blunders, errors, and other wrongdoings, guilty for living a life that isn't normal, and never was, but how would you know this unless I opened up? And what if I die in the middle of my confessions, in the middle of a sentence that was going to reveal a spine-chilling truth? Who will know how to complete the sentence for us?

Admittedly, I told you about Maya. Maya is the past. Which doesn't prevent me from describing her, much more than the sensuality of her lips or the melodious tone of her Yiddish, the beauty of her blue eyes, so intense, so true, hardly softened by the dark shadows under them, and her smile, yes, her smile too. It's very simple: Maya is my bygone youth. I loved being with her. In order to better isolate myself? Of course not. Love implies rejecting isolation. When one loves, one loves everyone. When I think of the woman I love, I love even those walls that separate me from the world and myself. But you're going to interrupt me; I know it, I feel it. No? I'm wrong? Good. In that case, perhaps I should start by telling you how I became mad, when the dybbuk took possession of me. But I repeat, Doctor, answer me, you who have learned to know everything. How can you tell if someone's a lunatic? Where does it start? How can he be recognized? From his abrupt ruptures or their internal logic? From his need for chastity or for debauchery? What must he do or say for us to know that he is undermined by an affliction that can't be defined? If I start to laugh, and make you laugh by telling you tragic stories in an amusing way, stories that should make you weep, would you take me for a madman? And what if I told heartrending tales in order to entertain you, and cause you to burst out laughing; it would be the same, wouldn't it?

Listen, Doctor. We've been seeing each other for months and seem to be complying with the requirements of a ritual that is still partially obscure. Do I know you any better? No. Do you know me any better? No. So what could be the aim of our meetings, except to make us admit that they are irrevocably doomed to failure? If only I could at least fall in love with you while talking to you or opposing my will to yours. You would replace Rina, Maya, Ayala—yes, there was also Ayala. After all, why not? A gesture from you would suffice. But your professionalism would prevent your making this gesture, or am I deluding myself? No, surely not. Your masters, whom you claim to follow, are keeping an eye on us; you'd never dare displease them. This applies to mine too, though for other reasons, ethical rather than professional.

Where are mine?


Sometimes, I think of what happened to my sister, Dina, and my little brother, Jacob, but I don't see them anymore. Why are they suddenly hidden from my view, Doctor? Could this be another sign of my illness: not seeing the invisible anymore? Swallowed up into a dense, frantic, and confused crowd, they've lost their identity. Are they looking for me the way I am looking for them? Are they looking for our parents? Among the old men, walking unsteadily, which one is my father? Among the motionless women, which one held me to her breast? Help me, Doctor: Whose son am I? What have I done, what error have I committed that I can no longer remember my roots? Could that be my illness: choosing oblivion in order to justify my life? Could memory be the tool my dybbuk is using? Could that be why your Freud distrusted it? Yet you've often explained to me that mental suffering can come not from forgetting everything but from desperately trying to remember everything.

I don't forget my parents, Doctor. I've never forgotten them, believe me. Every time I think of them, I feel like crying, but I hold back my tears. I think of them so my tears will flow, but they don't flow. And if they choke me, too bad. Let my tears decide. I am ready to let them carry me to nearby rivers and faraway peaks. Would my life then become a tear?

What of it? Let it make the ocean overflow.

Maya, you wanted me to tell you a story? Listen:

In the Orient, where I went in search of solitude and serenity, I made friends with an ascetic fugitive forced to wander, a penitent like me. At night, under a sky with a thousand stars both near and far, we listened to the rustle of the trees bending in the wind, herald of a life-giving rainfall.

My friend, still young, younger than me, told me about his past, which he himself described as criminal, and I thought of mine, unable to say whether it was completely innocent.

"Listen to me, brother," he said. "Listen to me closely, from beginning to end. Try not to interrupt me, not even to ask for more facts, or clarification. Listen to me and then tell me which of us has more to blame himself for. Wait, I said from beginning to end. Was I wrong? And what if I suddenly wanted to start with the end or with what leads up to the beginning? And also, brother, did I give you the impression that I wanted to tell you just one anecdote, just one thought, just one episode? And what if I had several up my sleeve, even a thousand, why not? Which ones should I present to you first? Wait, I haven't finished questioning you while questioning myself; I said 'a thousand episodes,' hence a thousand anecdotes, a thousand glimmers, a thousand moments. And what if it was always the same destiny intent on being told, but in a constantly changing rhythm and according to a structure forever renewed?"

I remember thinking as I listened: I could appropriate his words and say the same thing, in the same tone of voice. I too am haunted by questioning, I too have "a thousand stories" teeming in my brain; all they want is to come out and live again in the sunlight with the reward of being shared or to dissipate in the mist of anticipated suffering. I could have . . . but I wouldn't do it. If one day I started speaking, my lips would describe my father's melancholic face and my mother's noble smile on the day I left them—or rather, on the day they left me. I saw them, but as a result I felt incapable of uttering the slightest word to describe them. Could that be the reason why I felt so ill at ease and guilty? Was it too late to try? I should have confided in my ascetic friend, but I didn't have the strength. I was drained.

Over there, in the Orient, both miserable, each in his own way, wandering far from our roots and our homes, melancholic but not in despair, close to each other, we derived from our association a feeling of plenitude that only friendship can provide.

"In the beginning," said my friend in a tone tinged with nostalgia, "there was happiness . . ."

It occurred to me that I could say the same: in the beginning, there was probably happiness. I didn't always remember it.

When I wasn't myself, I couldn't find its trace either in my body or my memories. Yet, in every fiber of my being, even if I couldn't really apprehend it, I knew it must have existed at a specific time and place. When I was with my relatives, all my relatives, before the breakup of our family circle. And later, when my parents were reunited. But afterward? Yes, that's man's tragedy: there is always an afterward.

"I remember," said my friend. "A forty-year-old man, his still-radiant wife, an unusually well-behaved little boy. They are sitting at the table, lit by a faint yellow light. Somewhere far away, in another city, or in another neighborhood of the same city perhaps, war is raging. With cannons and knives. Brothers and neighbors, driven by a need for vengeance or conquest, define their ties through blood and violence. Death is what unites them. Then, after a brief meditation, the father sighs and bows his head as if to pray. 'We're poor, but let's not complain of anything anymore. For we're happier than the wealthy. We have bread before us, and cool water. And no hatred in our hearts. That's sufficient. The rest doesn't count. The rest will come in time.' And after a silence, he goes on: 'May God forgive me. I expressed myself badly. I said the rest doesn't count. It counts, it must count, since, not so far away, among people like us, human beings are killing or being killed. For them, the rest won't come anymore. And yet, aren't our happiness and our serenity whole? Shouldn't we feel diminished, guilty, or at least concerned?'

"So then," my ascetic friend added, "deep down, I said to myself: My father isn't guilty but mad; and if he isn't mad, I am."

"Very well," I remarked. "Your father was mad. But who was guilty?"

"Me," said my friend.

"Guilty? You? Of what? You were the little boy, weren't you?"

"Yes, I was. And I was innocent, even more so than my father.

But I became guilty later, when I chose the wrong path. I rebelled against poverty and misery. The idea was romantic, the means less so. Some friends and I robbed a banker. We didn't know that he had a heart condition. He died a few days later."

"But why did you do that? Did you love money?" I asked.

"No, on the contrary: I hated it. In order to hate it, I first had to have some."

Should I have told him about Samek and his gift? What would he have thought of me?

I tried to answer him with a smile, and being a believing Buddhist, he would have understood, but I changed my mind. The deepest and most powerful cry, a Hasidic rabbi used to say, is the one we keep locked up in our breast.

Like remorse. And desire.

## 3

*From where you are, close to everything eternal, you know my past. In fact, you may even know my future. How can I explain to you why I undertook this therapy? What is its true aim? To know more about you and me? Will she bring me closer to you or, on the contrary, raise a permanent wall between us? Is it my illness that prompts you to answer me, or my hypothetical recovery?*

*Whatever happens, since I owe you everything, I'll tell you everything.*

*Yes, everything.*

EXCERPTS FROM DR. THÉRÈSE GOLDSCHMIDT'S NOTES

Doriel Waldman was recommended to me by a non-Jewish colleague, Dr. John Gallagher, who thought that, given my origins, my professional training, and my experience in so-called Jewish therapy, his case would interest me. Actually, my first impulse was to refuse. I don't like categorizing medical science using ethnic or religious criteria. There is no such thing as specifically Jewish therapy. A competent Protestant or agnostic therapist is perfectly capable of treating a Muslim patient, just as a Jewish specialist should be able to handle a Catholic schizophrenic or a depressive atheist. Freud and Jung, at variance on many things, are both concerned with human beings and their illnesses, whatever their roots and affinities. But my eminent colleague insisted: "Receive him and you'll see. I trust your judgment. Do you remember our three patients five years ago? They helped give us a deeper insight into some of man's dark and dangerous drives."

"Do you mean that this patient is like them?"

"No, he's different."

"And you think I'll be able to help him?"

"See him and decide."

Fine, let's not be too rigid.

Gallagher deserved my trust. The three unusual cases we had treated jointly had taught me a lot. Did Gallagher know they presented fascinating though disturbing similarities to the experiences that had haunted the sleep and infrequent joys of my parents? They had lived through the time of horrors. So I agreed to see his protégé while thinking, I don't know why; still, it's strange he didn't keep him.

An appointment was made with my new patient for a month and three days later. A Thursday afternoon. I unintentionally kept him waiting; I had to calm down a young movie actress in the throes of a severe nervous breakdown. I couldn't possibly send her away given the state she was in. Delayed by a quarter of an hour, I took a short time to glance at the file Dr. Gallagher sent. Biographical facts: about sixty, single, in-depth Jewish studies, numerous activities but no fixed employment, active in several associations devoted to aiding the disadvantaged, research trips to Israel, Africa, and Asia. Insomniac, loner. Complains of frequent anxiety attacks and various ills that prevent him from working. Or from being happy. And far worse: they disrupt his very existence. In short, he's unwell.

Sitting at my desk, I hold out my hand and invite him to sit down. Doriel Waldman barely hides his annoyance. As usual, I'm polite, courteous, even kind, but not overly so. I ask him what seems to irritate him. His first words, uttered with a sneer: "I hate waiting."

First impression: he's angry; the whole world wishes him ill, including me, since I didn't receive him immediately. Bah, I didn't waste my time at the university: I also learned how not to respond to provocations; that's part of the profession. I say to him: "It seems you need my services."

He replies with a shrug: "Who told you that? Dr. Gallagher? He refuses to treat me."

"He thinks, no doubt mistakenly, that I'm better qualified than he is."

"Perhaps, but that's not the real reason."

"Oh yes? What's the real reason then?"

"He's an anti-Semite; that's why he refused. He doesn't want to help the Jew that I am."

I can't refrain from laughing. "Dr. Gallagher happens to be a close friend. He was my favorite teacher. In some ways I owe my career to him. He's a decent, honorable person. Anything racist and ugly is repellent to him."

"Well, it's possible to be anti-racist and anti-Semitic."

Very soon, something about him intrigues me. Nervous energy, pathological touchiness, personal ghosts that make him angry. Obviously, he has suffered a lot. Too much perhaps? That's meaningless. To each his yardstick. Each person has his own conception of what is too much and too heavy a burden. Hegel talks about excess knowledge. Can there also be excess memory? A mildly unpleasant remark for one person is as unbearable as a bludgeoning for another. Therefore? While observing my visitor and taking mental notes on this first meeting—or should I say first confrontation?—I wonder, What makes him tick? as they say. In other words, what motivates his behavior? What should his illness be called? What disturbs him in his social relation-ships? What misconceptions does he have that disrupt his perception of reality? What aberrations did he live through? What pains him at night and frightens him in the morning? Is he just suffering from a pathological nostalgia for a lost paradise, filched by strangers?

I explain to him briefly what I have in mind—one or two (well-paid) sessions a week to start, length of treatment unpredictable—and I expect him to tell me I'm too expensive, but he interrupts me: "Forget money issues. It's very kind of you to accept me as a patient, but I'm entitled to my say in the matter too, am I not?"

Surprised, I quickly answer: "You can't pay?"

"Pay? I'll pay whatever you want. And more, if necessary."

"So money isn't a problem for you—"

"Are you making fun of me, or what? I can pay; I've always paid for everything. And don't ask me the source of my revenue. It's none of your business. Besides, that's not what I want to talk to you about. Would you have the kindness to listen to me?"

"Certainly. Go ahead, I'm all ears," I say.

"Since we're going to spend a lot of time together, it's important to me to know who you are."

"That's no concern of yours."

"Sorry to contradict you, but if I understand correctly, it's my mental health, if not my life, that's at stake. Don't I have the right to know in whose hands I'm putting them?"

I try to keep calm and explain to him, very summarily, Freud's conception of psychopathology, trying to adapt it to the circumstances. Association of ideas. Essential mutual trust. Mandatory distance between therapist and patient; eliminating it would jeopardize the cure.

He objects. "I've read a lot about hysteria, neurosis, psychosis, and schizophrenia. I've even studied split-personality syndrome. But Freud is dead, may he rest in peace. It's not him I'll be ambling—or living—with for months or years to come, but you. You'll find out everything about me. I'll have to reveal my innermost secrets to you, if I understand your approach correctly. And meanwhile I'll know nothing about you? Where you're from? Who your parents are? Whether you have brothers, or cousins? Friends, devoted or hypocritical? Whether you're married? Whether you love your husband? Whether you've been unfaithful to him, if only in your thoughts? And whether you're happy when you're alone? So finally: Will you answer my questions, yes or no? If it's no, then I'll leave you, and may that anti-Semitic bastard Gallagher go to the devil!"

I frown and keep silent for a while. What should I reply? That I'm Jewish and the only daughter of survivors who refuse to talk about their past? That I love my profession? That I'm married, faithful, and have no children? That happy people may have problems but no story to tell? I just reply with all the sincerity I think is fitting: "Very well, Mr. Waldman. Your argument isn't without merit. I'll make a deal with you, or if you prefer, a wager: Let's proceed on the basis of exchange. I'll do everything I can to get to know you better, and you'll do the same thing. And we'll see who'll be the first to succeed."

He accepts the deal—and I wonder which one of us will be the first to regret it. And why.

I ask him what he lives on; he answers by shrugging. Can he really afford to pay me? Another gesture, almost of disdain. He talks and behaves as if this is the least of his worries. Is he really that wealthy? Could that be his problem?

So the show is on the road. That's how the treatment began. It wasn't easy. The first fifty-minute session went rather badly. First, he refused to lie down on the couch. Then he didn't want me to sit behind him, notebook in hand. An unpleasant discussion—it nearly ended in a quarrel—took up all the time I had decided to grant him. As he got up, he said, "I'm not sure I want to come back." I replied that he was free to do as he pleased; he could just phone my secretary and cancel the next appointment. He took an envelope out of his pocket and put it on my desk; it contained a check covering an entire month's treatment. One of these days, I thought, if we continue, I'll have to question him—discreetly—about his financial resources.

He didn't phone.

He arrived for the second session in a bad mood, but it ended comically.

"I don't think you can help me" were the words he assailed me with at the door. "I came back because I'm interested in you. I have a feeling you need me more than I need you."

I replied that if I lost my patients, my husband wouldn't like it.

And then, again, he refused to lie down. Never mind. Since he lost the first battle and reappeared, why not let him win this one? He insisted that we sit facing each other. Very well, we placed two chairs accordingly. He didn't look comfortable, nor, I imagine, did I. A heavy, hostile silence set in. I asked him in a dry, cold, neutral tone: "What are we going to talk about?"

"You're the physician. You suggest the topics."

"We could start with the present. What did you do and how did you feel this morning when you woke up? Did you remember your dreams? Were you in a good mood?"

"Let's hear your second suggestion."

"We could talk about your parents."

"What for?"

"So I can get to know you better."

"No."

"Do you ever dream of your mother?"

"Yes."

"When?"

"When I'm awake."

"Never when you're asleep?"

"I sometimes see her in my sleep. Then it's no longer sleep."

"Do you see her otherwise than in a dream?"

"Sometimes."

"How is she dressed?"

"White shirt, light blue skirt."

"What is she doing?"

"She's resting."

"And your father?"

"He's resting."

"And you?"

"I look at them rest."

"Are they kissing?"

"They kiss me."

"And when they're alone?"

"You're annoying me, Doctor. I don't feel like talking about them anymore."

"Why?"

"Because I don't understand what you find interesting about them."

"But I find everything you say interesting."

"Especially my mother, right? She's the one taunting you. You'd like to hear me say I was in love with her. Come on, I know what's up. You're not the only one who's read Uncle Sigmund, as we call him in certain literary circles. Be a bit more original, Doctor. And a bit more daring. Why don't you start by throwing your routine questionnaire in the trash can?"

Then he clammed up. I tried goading him, but in vain. I brought up other subjects: nothing doing. The silence persisted and became unpleasant. Doriel got up five minutes before the end of the session, headed toward the door, and, without turning around, gave me something of a warning: "I told you a lot of things this afternoon. If you didn't hear anything, you have only yourself to blame. It's your fault, not mine. Better yet: if, for all your studies and experience, you still don't know that each person has his own questions and his own distinctive way of elucidating them, you should change professions. At any rate, what I have to tell you now is simple: the session we just had doesn't deserve payment."

He left without saying whether he would return.

I hoped he would.


"So, in order to help me get better, you want to know everything about . . . my disease, my illness. And about my life. Well, I promise I'll make an effort."

"I'm listening."

"I'm frightened. And when I'm not frightened, I'm frightened of not being frightened. Frightened of losing my stability, my reason. Madness, Doctor—let's not be afraid of saying the word—that's what I dread. When my illness appears, it doesn't come from others but from myself. Its seductive capacity as well as its destructive power, its ability to shake everything up, to invade everything, to envelop everything: I fear these. To escape its grasp, I sometimes use the biblical images of punishments and curses: in the morning I call for the night, and at night I wait for the day. It's an enemy that's always on the lookout, a dagger in each hand, ready to stab me. Sometimes I feel like running to the other end of the planet and hiding. But I don't move. I know that there is no refuge in my life against what is called mental illness or madness. Do you understand what I'm saying, Doctor? Do you honestly think you'll be able to show me that this refuge exists and tell me where?"


Doriel is on time. Sullen, taciturn, he doesn't greet me, goes over to the couch and sits down. The next minute, he gets up and settles in his usual chair.

He doesn't look at me. Motionless, he stares at a specific point in space. As though I didn't exist? Rather, as though I alone exist. In order to better get ready to confront me, defy me, contradict me.

The hands on the little wristwatch Martin gave me for our first wedding anniversary move forward, painfully but stubbornly.

"How about telling me about your day yesterday?"

He pretends not to hear. In the closed world he's locked himself up in, perhaps he can't hear. Does a man who is born deaf hear noises in his sleep? Does he think everyone is like him, deaf to the music of words and sounds?

"Doriel," I say, "the fact that you're here means you think I can help you. But if you keep remaining silent, I can't continue."

You'd think I hadn't said anything.

He's trying to annoy me; that's obvious. Destabilize me, make me vulnerable. What's his aim? To prove to me I'm weak when faced with his desire to create a space between us, a space that I, whom he sees as an explorer of the human soul, will never be able to cross? Well, he won't succeed. I can be strong, stronger than he can imagine. I speak to him in a calm, very calm, unruffled tone of voice: "Apparently you like silence, Doriel. That happens. There are men like you. They've given up on speech. In their despair over language, they choose silence. As a goal or a means? They're not the same. As a means, silence can last indefinitely. It can be explained and is translated into a rejection of language as being another form of silence. But as a goal, silence implies speech if it wishes to delve deeper and justify itself."

Doriel says nothing, walled up in his determination to reject any attempt I make to approach him.

By then, imperceptibly, we are more than halfway through the session.

"Is it because I didn't tell you anything about myself that you're silent? Is your silence meant to punish me? Meant to force me to confide in the stranger you still are, for me and for yourself? Are you trying to inflict a lesson in modesty on me? Go on, put me to the test, ask me some questions, just one for a start, on my professional or private life. Ask me anything. In your situation, the challenge will be less offensive and more fertile than your retreat into silence."

I lean toward him. Should I touch his arm or his shoulder? I feel like doing it. After all, I can't just wait for him to pull himself together and snap out of his torpor. But I decide against it. In my profession, physical contact with the patient is forbidden. But what if he remains in this hypnotized and aphasic state for the next fifteen minutes? How will I let him know the session is over? It is coming to an end and we're sitting here, each of us conscious of our powerlessness, condemned to endure the eternal absence of communication between human beings who are each experiencing the moment in a different way, even though they're on the same quest.

I get up. A minute later, he gets up too. He heads toward the door. He opens it and stops, probably hesitating about leaving me without saying a word. He decides to turn around. And suddenly his expression changes. A smile appears on his face for a fleeting second. A sign of victory? As if to say: You see, Doctor, I won. I feel like conveying to him, with gestures, that we're not playing a game.

But he's no longer there.

Anxiety mixed with vexation. Has he left for good?


In the evening, at dinner, trying unsuccessfully to control the tic that makes his eyelids flutter, Martin stares at me with a troubled expression. "Bad day?" he asks. "Is your work giving you trouble? You seem on edge."

My husband knows me well; he can guess—this happens once in a while, but rarely—what I'm trying to hide from him. But why worry him? He has his own share of problems. At the library, wealthy donors keep complicating his life. Never satisfied, they assign him absurd, if not unfeasible, tasks. They each come up with ideas for attracting more people. Some would like to see movie stars photographed reading the latest fashionable writer. Others suggest that students distribute old books door-to-door. Or that they read to the elderly in old people's homes, in the presence of journalists and photographers. In vain, Martin explains that, as a chief executive officer, he does not count publicity his area of expertise, or his dream, and that if they're serious about their harebrained publicity stunts, they should hire a professional. But with what budget? The institution has far more important needs when it comes to finances. In their stubbornness, the donors assail him over and over again.

"So?" Martin asks. "You're not answering. Was your day beyond bad?"

I tell him about my day. My unbearable eighth patient. He wants to be helped but does everything to prevent it. It's like pure sabotage.

"Oh, he'll get over it," Martin says. "Eventually he'll fall in love with you and all his problems will be solved. And mine will begin."

This is Martin's miracle cure. He's convinced that men can be divided into two categories: the men who have already fallen in love with me and the men who will; he thinks I have occult powers. When I object, he replies: "Isn't that method the one you used to solve my problems?" And it is up to me to settle the matter by saying, "You're incorrigible."

But not tonight. Suddenly I wonder, And what if that happened? What if Doriel became infatuated? Impossible? Quite the contrary, rather probable. Transference is a common occurrence in analysis: the patient becomes enamored of the analyst. And what would I do then? With a wave of the hand, I reject this thought as premature, if not frankly indecent. Should I have a word with Dr. Gallagher? Ask his advice? After all, he foisted this burden on me—me, his former student.

"You're right," I say to my husband. "He'll get over it."

Naturally. Next time will be better. If there is a next time.


Decision: Not to go back over what happened. Not to mention the incident. Avoid traps. A kind of silence: taboo.

Besides, I have no reason to worry. Doriel seems in a good mood. Amiable, docile. Ready for anything. As soon as he sits down, he launches in.

"So, shall we start?"

"Fine."

"You know I come from a religious milieu. But I'm not unfamiliar with literature and philosophy. How about you? Do you know Nietzsche? Not the philosopher or poet but the psychologist. Somewhere he says that man is his own dearest enemy: Is this true for you too? Are you afraid that this enemy will break down your resistance and shatter your hopes? Have you ever been frightened, yes, frightened, of finding yourself disarmed before invisible enemies, in a hostile universe where all victory is denied to you ahead of time? Frightened of no longer understanding or accepting what is happening to you, whether good or evil? Have you ever felt suddenly detached from your environment, separated from your fellow men, thrown into an abyss by the very people who loved you and whom you loved? In other words, Doctor: Have you ever been frightened of losing your bearings, your reason?"

I jot down his questions in my notebook. I feel they have a meaning. They contain keys that will be useful to me. I underline *Nietzsche*. His influence? A feeling of being torn. After a fit of insanity in Turin in 1889, he didn't write another line before he died in 1900. If my patient wants to upset me, he's succeeding admirably.

"I'm waiting," Doriel says.

Since I don't answer, as I'm busy jotting everything down, including his last remark, he repeats: "I'm waiting."

"I see. And what are you waiting for?"

"For your answers to my questions. I know, they might be too personal, even intimate, but if you agree to answer them, Doctor, it will help our work together; you'll see. I promise."

"Of course, I'm frightened at times, like everyone," I say. "It's human. Frightened of solitude. Failure. Separation. Frightened of disease. Of shame and humiliation. Frightened of death. Someone who isn't frightened isn't human."

"You didn't mention the only word I care about: *madness*. I'm asking you if you've ever been frightened of going crazy, nuts, being cracked or just plain mad."

He's no fool. Nothing throws him off. If he's hooked on a word, he won't let go.

"What can I say, Doriel? As a student I lived among mental patients or close to them. The courses of your beloved Dr. Gallagher, for instance, were in psychopathology. Once a week, we attended his conversations with patients. And, to satisfy your curiosity, they often instilled fear in me."

"Why? Why fear rather than repulsion, helplessness, or indifference?"

"What I felt was fear. Fear of seeing someone live in a reality that would remain forever out of my reach."

"But not fear of waking up one morning imprisoned in that same reality?" he asked.

"Probably that fear too."

"And what did you do then, and what would you do now to overcome your fear?"

His question disconcerts me. How can I elude it? It impinges upon a secret area of my being. I say to myself: The man is clever. Now, all of a sudden, he's the therapist and I'm the patient. And I have to come up with an answer, if only so I won't lose face.

"I look at patients and I say to myself that they don't know my fear; as to theirs, perhaps they're hiding it by integrating it into their fragmented, if not filched, lives. For them, everything makes sense, whereas the world is in a thousand pieces. They live in an environment of organized, structured madness, frozen in mental acrobatics. I listen to them and I say to myself: They have ready-made answers; for me, they become questions again. In this way, by following my thought processes, unconsciously I get rid of my fear."

Doriel gazes at me intently. His smile, icy from the beginning, fades. There is a solemn, pained look in his eyes. I must make an effort not to be moved.

"Thank you," he says in a low voice, his head slightly bowed. "Thank you for your candor. Your honesty in playing the game inspires trust. Now, I'll do the same. Listen, in the Orient, my ascetic friend had said: 'When you reach your sixties, you'll be in great danger somewhere, far from here; call me and I'll come to your rescue.' Well, the appointment he gave me is now. I called him and he didn't come. What should I do, Doctor? I wrote to him and he didn't answer. Is he still alive? Free or locked up again?"

Unfortunately we have only three minutes left. And the schedule, as Uncle Sigmund said, is immutable, hallowed, sacred.


That evening, during dinner, I can't help bringing up the subject again, which preoccupies me more and more. I tell Martin that there's something important about my patient's behavior that escapes me. True, the afternoon session was rather encouraging, but I sense he resents me; he treats me with animosity, whereas with other people he must be much more docile, generous, and even warm. On the one hand, he's paying me, so he must trust me. On the other, he gets irritated, loses his temper, and is always watching me, judging me, and complaining bitterly. Why this special, strange attitude on his part?

"You're asking me? What can I tell you, since I've never seen the fellow?" says Martin.

"That's just it. Because you're—how can I put it—on the sidelines, you might have a more objective view of the situation."

"Well, you want me to make a guess?"

"Go ahead."

"In my opinion, he's stricter and harsher with you precisely because he's frightened."

"Frightened? Of what? Of whom?"

"Of you. Frightened you might uncover the true nature of his illness, its true roots."

# 4

As he wanders down the streets in no rush to get home, Doriel tries to get a better understanding of his own state of mind. Whom can he confide in? His thoughts go back to the Orient, back to his old friend. There was someone he could confide in. Why does this woman, Thérèse Goldschmidt, arouse such strong but ambiguous feelings in him? Will he really end up having heart-to-heart talks with her? What is it about her that makes him want to contradict everything she says? Subconsciously, does he admire or desire her? She isn't the most beautiful or most brilliant woman he's ever met or seen. Besides, she's married and clearly in love with her librarian husband. Is it so he could have regrets about his bachelor life that, of all the therapists listed in the medical directory, he ended up with a married woman with whom he could fall in love?

From far away, his friend in the Orient, always present, affectionate but tactful, would have answered him without a moment's hesitation. "Brother, you've done a lot of things in your life. Some have made you wiser, others more rebellious. At times you dreamed of rising up to the heavens; at other times you were ready to bury yourself in the darkness. Sometimes you wanted to live in the future and sometimes in the past, sometimes immersed in the misfortune of disappointed flirtation, sometimes in the happiness of a rare true love. What can I say, brother, sometimes you confuse everything. And so you've forgotten the most important thing: For a man who wants to quench his thirst at the spring, aren't intelligence and passion frauds? For fulfillment, whether in ecstasy or a fall, man must cling to the present. Though fleeting, the instant holds its own eternity, just as love and even desire conceive their own absolute. If man aspires to transform being and time, and their interrelationships, he will end up adopting Platonic thought, which ultimately leads him away from his destiny, leaving him in the undefined, misty, cluttered realm of decline, followed by insanity. In this ambiguous universe, full of pitfalls and boasts, strength lies in the act of creating one's own lucidity and mastering one's own truth. The person who loves, who creates or re-creates if only for a split second, has already won a victory over the absurdity of fate."

Doriel imagines his friend in his great wisdom: the friend breaks off, holds his breath, and glances at him with a smile, as though advising him to follow his example. "You will say to me: And what about the future in all this? It exists, brother, of course it exists, but as a threat. Disease is a prison, old age a humiliation, and death a defeat. These are things I know about: I had happy parents, I told you about them; their bliss was the envy of the village. What I didn't tell you was that they died in an epidemic that devastated the region. As for my school friends, most of them were killed in the war. For years, I lived in anger; I kept railing against the injustice of fate and of men. Then, with a great master as my guide, I understood we were given lips not just to cry out but also to sing and kiss. To brave the wrath of the gods by saying: You want to prevent me from experiencing happiness. Well, I'll bite into it with gusto! There: faced with suffering, that's the only valid response. To reject joy under the pretext that it has no right to exist and can only be imperfect would be, for me, surrendering right at the start."

Doriel would tell him that one is defeated well before the start; he would say that being born is more like exile than liberation. No sooner do you arrive with the plan of asserting yourself in an indifferent world than it is already too late.

"Too late for whom? For the infant maybe, but not for his parents. Or his own future children. You're so eager to give a meaning to destiny that you'll end up thinking you're destiny or, worse, not allowing destiny to do its job. That's the mistake! You can be the friend of your fellow man or his enemy, but you can't be his destiny. He carries his destiny within himself."

Wise words, not entirely devoid of sense and humanism. As he thinks about it, Doriel pulls himself together. He remembers that, back in the Orient, he hid something from his friend who was so poor. He did not tell him about his wealth.

# 5

Today, for the first time, Doriel Waldman stretches out on the couch and stays there. Bravo. How can I thank the gods for small victories? Without waiting for my first question, he returns to his fear of illness.

"Usually capricious, it slowly infiltrates the humdrum of everyday life, or it bursts violently, even more readily than in periods of tragedy. A movement of the head or arm, a suppressed or awkward caress, one word too many is all that's needed to make the world around me, or my inner world, cave in and drag me along. Then images and drawings, memories of tears and laughter, become jumbled and interwoven before disintegrating into a neutral blur, a strange, weightless atmosphere cut off from time. True, there are occasional breakthroughs, even glimmers of light in the fog, but one second later, everything starts up again. And in this depressed state, I no longer know who is who, and who I am."

As I'm jotting everything down in my notebook without comment, he goes on: "Yes, Doctor, a fleeting guilty kiss, nothing else before or after, was all it took for the order of things to be forever disrupted. Don't ask me if I'm speaking from experience—perhaps I'm speaking of yours."

He speaks of a kiss. Should I ask him to elaborate? Best not to interrupt him. He's in excellent form; let him continue.

"Therefore, blind in facing the future, dispossessed of all hope, yesterday's unfortunate lover expects nothing from others now and even less from himself. Yet before he believed in the future fervently, with all his heart and soul; now he no longer does. There again, don't ask me if the poor dreamer is me; I won't tell you. It's like believing in man's humanity: I used to believe in it, heart and soul, in spite of man. I no longer believe in it. For all you know, I could be telling you about the life and slow death of a man I don't know; I only know he's a human being like you and me, but his fate has been manipulated, disfigured, amputated. That's the illness."

So I can take notes without leaving anything out, I keep listening to him but I don't look at him, not even sideways. I concentrate on particular words and am surprised by his dry tone of voice. No trace of sentimentality or self-pity. And yet, with every sentence, I expect him to allude to a nervous breakdown, a depression, a botched suicide attempt caused by his illness.

He stops to catch his breath, and I take the opportunity to ask a little question, as if inadvertently: "And the kiss?"

"What are you talking about?"

"You mentioned it a moment ago."

"Up to me to talk; up to you to listen."

"But—"

"If I'm not mistaken, the last word I uttered wasn't *kiss* but *illness*."

"Fine, let's talk about it. This illness of yours, when did it start?"

"Really, Doctor, you disappoint me! Do you really think one can pinpoint the origin of a desire or the fear of seeing this desire die out? And what if I told you that this illness is older than I am, would you believe me? Better yet: Would you understand me?

In fact, by questioning me about my past, you're forcing me to make a big, exhausting effort, you're making me think out loud, and it's painful. Are you aware of this? You're driving me to entertain doubts about myself, to analyze my thought, open it up, dissect it, go back in time, far back, as far back as possible, to the last frontier, to its inception, hence to human thought in its earliest form, which would be that of the Creator. Is that what you want? And what if I told you that my thought, which you're tracking through me, goes not back and forth in a straight line but in fits and starts; it consists of shattered fragments; it burrows a path in a zigzag from one image to another, from one brain to another, from one existence to another, I'd almost be tempted to say from planet to planet, from galaxy to galaxy, from god to God?"

His speech becomes more rapid, almost breathless: "It could be, Doctor, that the difference between us is our attitude toward reason. For you, a scientist who is used to believing in reason and rationality, thinking is a noble undertaking, for it questions you while it questions itself: for isn't man 'a thinking reed,' an animal who reflects on his condition, a creature who elevates or lowers himself, imprisons or frees himself thanks to thought? That's not the way I see it, Doctor. For me, for the madman that I'm afraid of becoming or that I might already be, thinking is an unreasonable, complicated, painful undertaking that can go up in smoke and end buried in ashes. For me, thought can quickly unravel, crumble to bits, become dispersed and go offtrack: trying to cohabit with it can spell ruin. It drags me beyond myself. Like a cancerous cell disrupting an organ's function, thought chooses simple words but unpredictable routes and winding pathways, marked with poisoned arrows, to attain its goal in a crazy instability or in the monster's jaws. That's why, Doctor, not being me, you'll never be able to think like me. The words that leave my lips are not those that your ears pick up. Sometimes I search for words that refuse to come out; they remain hidden, inside, with the lump in my throat. Do you hear them? No. That's why, Doctor, through you, I'll say it and repeat it to anyone who wishes or doesn't wish to hear it: I won't allow the clarity of language to be glorified in my presence, or the beauty of its form; I will not allow the praise of refreshing sleep or redemptive thought. Both are nothing but illusions and betrayals; if madness lives within me, it has the right to repudiate them—and to announce that one can become mad out of disgust for clichés, for ready-made sentences that one feels like breaking and punishing. Did I make myself sufficiently clear?"

He stops, exhausted. Should I point out to him that what he's just said, and his way of saying it, could easily be proof that he isn't ill at all? That the ease with which he expresses himself is evidence of a lucid mind, of an intellectual power that enables him to develop, with simple words, a surprisingly limpid and remarkably well-constructed set of ideas? I might irritate him. Isn't denying the patient's illness stealing what makes his personality, hence his identity? I confine myself to humorously praising his intellectual qualities. After all, didn't he cite Pascal, the mystic, in his monologue, and Nietzsche, the philosopher?

"I have the feeling," I say to him, "that philosophical doubt is what torments you most. Am I wrong?"

"It attracts me and torments me only when the philosopher in me dominates. I resent all the people who prefer solutions to problems. Take Plato and his theory of philosopher kings. I'm for philosopher madmen or mad philosophers: for me, they are the real kings."

I wonder if he's telling the truth. I'm convinced he remembers an incident, an episode, a wound that marks, for him, the boundary between before and after. There is always a moment of crisis when reason fails. Odd fellow, Doriel. I catch myself thinking that I find him different from my other patients. Curious. In my notes, I cross out the word *curious* and replace it with *strange*.

And that "kiss" he dropped as if regretfully . . .

Occasionally now Martin will quiz me on the morale of this very special patient. Usually he respects my reticence about divulging what happens in my office; he knows perfectly well that medical confidentiality includes spouses: betraying the patient's trust is forbidden. If I keep silent, so does Martin. But recently he can't refrain from trying to make me talk. It seems that, for the first time, one of my "cases" interests him. I stand up to him, invoking the principle of the private hunting ground. I tell him that a doctor's office is not a library where, by definition, everything is available to satisfy the visitor's curiosity. And since he's insistent, I ask him to tell me the reason. His answer: he feels this patient preoccupies and troubles me more than others. I admit it, while refusing to explain why. Martin isn't happy; I realize that. I also realize this is the first time our relationship has become strained.

Excuse me, what I just said is inaccurate. Ever since our marriage, ten years ago, and even before, one subject has always made us uneasy: not having children. Yet he wanted to have children and so did I. "You're afraid for your career?" he used to ask me. "Do you really think that a good mother can't take care of her patients?" He didn't understand a thing about the situation, or at least he pretended not to. And I kept silent. A taboo subject. Not to be broached. Actually, I was lying by omission to my husband. Yes, I was afraid. Afraid of his not liking me. Afraid of remaining alone, of being abandoned for not giving him a child. I had consulted the best specialists. My mother, deeply religious in spite of the hardships of the past, had even begged a renowned Hasidic rebbe to intercede with the Almighty on my behalf. But my gynecologist had left me no hope.

Yet we loved each other. For both of us, it was a first love, or almost—let's say the first serious love. A serene love, not a tempestuous passion, devoid of social or religious obstacles. We were both born in New York, into well-to-do Jewish families.

His parents came from Poland, mine from Hungary. I went to college in Boston, he in Chicago. We met by chance in the airport during a blizzard, in the middle of the afternoon. Hundreds of travelers were rushing around looking for taxis to get home. The airline personnel advised us to call the nearest hotels. All the phone lines were busy, and whoever could get through was told, "Sorry, we're fully booked." In the evening, the waiting rooms turned into huge dormitories. Strangers fraternized, exchanging lamentations and exclamations such as "Oh, if I'd only known!" Relationships lasting one night for the most part. Mine with Martin will last a lifetime, as they say.

We completed our graduate studies at the same university in Philadelphia: his in the social sciences; mine in medicine, psychotherapy, and psychiatry. Initially I wanted to specialize in the criminally insane. We got along perfectly. He helped me find specialized works, and I helped him understand their content. Our first discussions revolved around my vocation: Why was I fascinated by history's great criminals? Probably because, under the influence of Dostoyevsky, more often than not, I saw them as ill.

Martin: "But what is it that interests you in them now, and in your prospective patients later: the crime or the illness?"

Me: "The connection between the two, that's what fascinates me. Because, for me, there's a connection."

Neither he nor I allude to what remains locked inside us, notably, the fact that this connection is closely related to our parents, both his and mine: they are survivors from *over there*. Isn't that the reason why Martin, possibly subconsciously, decided to become an archivist? So he could have access to forgotten documents covering the dark period? In those days I didn't know yet, but I found out later, that Martin's parents suffered from the same badly healed wounds as mine. That's another taboo subject now: we talk about everything, including the Second World War, but not about the tragedy that befell European Jews, called the Holocaust, for lack of a better word. We've never uttered the word under our roof. If perchance someone mentions it on television, Martin scowls, as though he is being personally attacked. He gets up and turns off the television set. After a long, awkward pause, our conversation resumes, calm and fruitful, each of us safeguarding, in our heart of hearts, a very secret, fragile, and vulnerable area belonging to our parents, whom we want to protect without really knowing why or for how long.

Eventually, I gave up my specialization. I'm busy with therapy full-time.

And with my patient Doriel Waldman, among others.


On this day I invite him to go far back in time and describe for me, impromptu, a childhood memory, any memory, dark or bright, happy or painful, or even stupid and insignificant. I suggest he shut his eyes and let his thoughts wander freely, with or without me.

"A real memory or a dream memory?" he asks, dead serious.

"A real dream can easily turn into a memory," I say.

"Would a snippet of memory or a dream fragment satisfy you?"

"I'd even settle for a fragment of a fragment."

I can watch him from an angle. He hasn't obeyed me: he keeps his eyes wide open. He talks in a low voice, a murmur, as though he wants to make me lean toward him, over him, very close. I repress a start, for he suddenly starts speaking in the third person.

"He sees himself as tiny, still a child, in the arms of a woman, no doubt his mother. He wants to sleep but can't. He is aching somewhere, he doesn't know where; it may be a stomachache or a headache. He's begging for the light touch of a warm hand to remove the weight on his chest; he prays to heaven to send it quickly, right away, for he can't bear it anymore. And his prayer is answered. Here it is, the hand he needed. He sees it with an unusual dazzling clarity. He calls to it, but it is floating in the air. He seeks it with his mouth, tries to seize it; it's close, very close, but then it crawls on the wall and higher up to the ceiling. Cursed be the fear that grips the child and separates him from the blessed hand: he will have to get up to catch it; too bad, he does it, he gets out of bed, he's afraid of falling, he falls. He is going to yell, cry for help. 'Come on, hurry up, help, can't you see I'm falling, the child is going to crash into the dark, gaping abyss'—but he's no longer a child: he has grown up and aged; he's collected a thousand offerings and a thousand miracles to give to the frenzied vagabonds lost in the forest where magic spells threaten, and he's composed a thousand songs to sow them in the sand and ash. He's become intoxicated on a thousand flowers and the magic of a thousand stupid and glorious words. He has received a thousand kisses as rewards or warnings, but he abandoned the dreaming child somewhere: forgot him, repudiated him. Then a new wave of anxiety overwhelms and oppresses him, denser than the previous one. An unknown hand slaps over his lips as if to stifle his cry. It is the hand of an old man, his father perhaps: he too seeks a hand to rescue him. The hand of the child who has grown old is too weak. He's ashamed of his weakness. And his helplessness."

Doriel stops, exhausted. Absorbed by the rhythm of his voice, I have stopped taking notes for a few minutes: anyway, the discreet tape recorder is still going. Should I ask the question that crosses my mind? Can it be to run away from shame that he has taken refuge in illness? Can it really be to escape his fear of madness that he hides inside madness? But I say nothing. My question would imply that his illness is real, and I'm not yet convinced of that. I know he's suffering, but I don't know from what.

Traces of schizophrenia?

"Doriel," I say. "What you were just telling me, what was it? A dream? A hallucination? Try to remember; it could be useful. For me and for you. Try."

"Very well, to please you, since you seem to like these kinds of fantasy tales. I'll start again. No, I can't anymore. I know; madmen repeat themselves, but I don't like to. One famous scholar doesn't like the Bible—he criticizes it for lacking the unpredictable. Well, when I talk, nothing is predictable. For example, the mother and child: I no longer remember whether I was the child, or whether the mother was my mother. You're going to laugh, but for all I know, I was my mother."

He pauses, then is about to continue but changes his mind suddenly.

"Continue, Doriel."

"Clearly you haven't understood a thing," he answers, rising from the couch. His voice has changed. It has lost its gentleness, its melancholy. It has become hoarse.

*Yes, I expressed myself in the third person. That's normal. There's a word I rarely use. It's easier to describe another person's melancholy and sorrow. Even in addressing a doctor. To talk about oneself could easily turn into exhibitionism. It's only with you that I can discard masks and my many inhibitions. Including the mask of madness? Yes, that one too. If I don't show myself to you truthfully and guilelessly, how can we expect Sisyphus's dybbuk to be happy?*

# 6

He arrives, his face drawn, as if he's just had a coughing fit or been running a high temperature.

"Power," he begins breathlessly, as though he has an urgent message for me. "I want to talk to you about power, Doctor. Contrary to what you may think, your patient's power, mine, is greater, stronger, and more dynamic than yours. More destructive, you'll say? I'll answer: more varied and changeable. Yours is confined and rigid; not mine. It moves. Yes, Doctor, the power of a man like me enables him to ignore time and abolish distances. You live in the present, whereas a man like me lives both in what he leaves behind and in what he anticipates. You live only your life, whereas I inhabit the lives of others. Like a novelist, a madman is embodied in several characters simultaneously. He is Caesar and Cicero, Socrates and Plato, Moses and Joshua. True, you have to allow for consciousness and the imaginary. Don't bring it up, please. I have both. But between yours and mine, there is an abyss. Mine bring me closer to reality; yours do not. Tell me the truth, Doctor: Could you be what you aren't? I can be. I could be you, whereas you could never be me. And God? Which of us could be God? In the Orient, at the edge of a magical forest, I asked my ascetic friend that question. He merely smiled at me. In Jerusalem, a beggar stared at me with a sad look and started singing to himself; I asked him the same question. He didn't tell me I was foolish or blasphemous but that I was crazy, like the sage Shimon ben Zoma, who broke into the Garden of Forbidden Knowledge, looked where he wasn't supposed to look, and lost his mind. And, by way of explanation, the beggar asked me: 'Since you were born, you're doomed to be. But God, our God, the God of Israel, the Creator of all living things and all worlds, could He not be? What would we do in a world from which He would be absent? We would feel miserable and unhappy. And so would He.' "

Thereupon, perhaps in order to show his secular knowledge, Doriel launches into a long philosophical discourse. Has he had his fill of Nietzsche? Now he cites Spinoza and his excommunication, Schopenhauer and his unrelenting opposition to Hegel, Heidegger and Nazism. He breaks off in the middle of a sentence and leaves me, repressing a smile that I can only describe as mocking.

I know he's suffering; I've said so. I also know he goes around with a secret hidden inside him that may be the cause of his suffering.


That evening, at the dinner table, Martin remarks: "You've been more and more distracted for some time now. Will this analysis take much longer?"

I reply that I have no idea. "What can I do? My work is sometimes a bit more complicated than yours."

"I know."

Of course he does. But does he know anything about the things that I myself know nothing about, in their essentials?


"You ask me how I live and from what? With whom and where, in what kind of housing? Or how I pay for my food? Is that what you're interested in today? Sometimes I think your questions have more to do with you than with me. Are you having problems in your married life? Are you having financial difficulties? If so, tell me, and I'll double your fees.

"I'm getting no response? Good, I'll do likewise. You know, Doctor, you don't have to be a psychiatrist or politician to blabber on and say nothing.

"Do you know how I earn my living? Please note, I didn't say 'live' but 'earn my living.' Funny word, *earn*. As though you win something by living. But in my case, that's almost true. I didn't gamble, but I won. Games of chance—that's what you probably think. Poker, roulette. You think I have the occult power not of guiding the tiny magical ball on the desired numbers and foreseeing its trajectory but of predicting the slot on which it will land and come to a stop? If you like to think that, be my guest. I know it as well as you: with their calculations, mathematical geniuses can obtain the same result. But math isn't to my taste. I don't understand it at all. Did I tell you about my occult power? About the mischievous demon who whispers, barely audibly, precise instructions in my gambler's ears: it's the eighteen, or it's the twenty-four. This demon is never wrong. Had the great Fyodor Dostoyevsky been lucky enough to be loved by him, he would have lined his perpetually empty pockets instead of making his family unhappy.

"If you really think I'm a gambler, you're going to ask me why the managers haven't collared me yet, for they're always on the lookout for dangerous intruders like me in casinos all over the world. Eh, I know you; you're dying to ask the question, right?

"Well, it's simple. I could answer that I know how to control myself. I'm content with little; I take only what I need for two or three months at a time. Not an extra cent. It's an infallible system. Every day, casinos handle astronomical sums of money.

Modest gains don't attract the croupiers' attention. Besides, I refrain from going regularly to the same gambling rooms. Yes, this is what I could say, except it isn't true. I'm not a gambler. Gambling doesn't interest me; besides, I don't need to gamble. However, Doctor, I'm prepared to take risks to help you out. One word from you and the biggest casino in Las Vegas will wind up on the verge of bankruptcy. Okay, that's the end of my fantasies; I've never set foot in a gaming room."

"Too bad. I was about to ask you when you discovered your gift, at what age? Under what circumstances?"

"That's a gratuitous question. And it's insulting. I'm not a gambler; I've told you as much. I can be accused of many faults, but not that one."

"In that case, here's another question: Why did you invent that lie?"

"To hide the truth from you, of course."

"Why are you so eager to hide it?" I ask.

"Because I prefer to keep it for later. But . . . let's elaborate a bit more on the gambling hypothesis, which you seem to like. I remember when I first discovered I had a gift. I remember I was still young, and in a train; I remember it was a mountainous region; several adults were playing cards. At one point I tried to guess the numbers the neighbor on my right was being dealt. And I guessed right. I started to smile. The plump and cheerful woman sitting next to me asked me why I was smiling. I told her, whispering in her ear. So she wanted to know if I could guess the numbers of the player facing her, a skinny, taciturn fellow, and I could. This could have been the start of a promising career."

I suggest he stop talking about his gift for gambling and instead concentrate on the plump woman on the train. Who was she? How was she dressed? Had he looked at her face? Her bust? How had he felt?

"You're annoying me, Doctor. I told you, I was young, just a boy. You have nothing but sexuality on the brain. As though at that age I was playing not with cold and lifeless numbers but with torrid, erotic fantasies."

"Did she caress you, in a simple, completely natural way, the way an adult woman sometimes caresses a child's hand, cheek, or hair?"

He replies vehemently: "No! She didn't touch me. I . . . She—" He breaks off. As though he is trying through pure fabrication to understand what I am driving at.

"Why did you stop talking? The plump woman . . ."

"Well, I can see her now. After an hour, she realized that something was fishy: the man to my right was winning all the time. And this was thanks to me. So, she burst out laughing, got up, and wanted me to sit on her left. But since there wasn't enough room, she put me on her knees. And suddenly, I felt like laughing and crying at the same time; I was in another world."

"And then what?"

"I've told you everything there is to tell."

"Everything?"

"Everything about my gifts as an inventor of cock-and-bull stories."

"And what about the rest?" I ask.

"The rest, Doctor, has nothing to do with cards."

"And how about letting me be the judge of that?"

"And what if you got off the train?"

"Personally, I'd like to stay on board a bit longer."

"The train has left . . ." I wait for him to continue, hoping to find out more.

". . . with me inside." He pauses, then continues. "Let's change the topic, if you don't mind? Yes, change the topic. Except for people like me, the topic always stays the same, since the cards and the numbers never change. But I see you have nothing more to say to me, Doctor. Is it because you think you know every-thing? Things have suddenly become transparently clear to you?

You say to yourself: My patient is a magician, and that explains everything. Magicians are usually a bit weird. In manipulating reality, they see and go too far. But remember, Doctor, I'm not a magician who guesses what numbers will turn up. Personally, I only know words. I try to control them and say, Hurry up, or else, Go back, let the next one through, for I need it. Sometimes they listen to me and obey, but more often they rebel and run away. Why? I have no idea. Go ask the dictionary if you want an explanation, not me. I can tell you what I do, but not how I do it. If I knew, if I understood the meaning of the strange power I go around with and that opens all closets—a power that could make me the most erudite man in the world, and the most lucid—do you think I would reveal it to you? These special gifts, whom did I get them from? I owe these donors, whoever they are, more than I owe you, Doctor. But you, you owe me a lot."

"What do I owe you?"

"The truth."

"Which one?"

"The one that shakes me out of myself and at the same time buries me more deeply inside, while urging me to surpass myself toward fear, in fear."

"You mention fear often," I say.

"Yes, fear of not recognizing myself anymore, Doctor."

"Aren't you being too hard on yourself?"

"Let's say not hard enough. The fact is, I wasted my life, Doctor. Yes, this life left me all alone too often, and I betrayed my solitude. I betrayed everyone."

I suggest to Doriel that he talk about love. He asks with feigned seriousness: "Love as a philosophical concept? Would you like me to comment on Plato's *Symposium,* whose aim was to praise Eros, the god of love? Sensible love or passionate love? Petrarch's love for Laura or Dante's for Beatrice? And what about

David's for Bathsheba or Amnon's for Tamar? Lovers rarely talk about love, and when they do, they talk badly, more often in the past than in the present. The moral is, philosophers are everything except lovestruck."

After a momentary pause, I tell him my area is medicine, psychiatry, and not metaphysics. If I'm asking him to talk about love or his love affairs, it's because of my calling: I'm paid to be curious, that's all. True, I prefer the classics to the moderns, until the latter become classics themselves: Shakespeare and Musset, Thomas Mann and Franz Kafka; so I know that there's romantic and redemptive love, and the other kind, born of romanticism, that inevitably ends in debauchery and decadence. Which of the two played a dominant role in his life?

Doriel adopts a light tone to tell me the fable of the woman whom he knew nothing about, except that he loved her in his own way but not in the way she wanted to be loved, which explains their separation.

"Love, very well, I'll talk to you about love. I was young, not wealthy—not yet—and fully pubescent. You're picturing the blue-eyed Maya, Maya of the missed opportunity? No. Rina or Lilith? Ayala? No again. I'm talking about Nora, who was twenty-four and divorced. But . . . what if it was Lilith, disguised as Nora? With these women, anything is possible. They know how to seduce and trap you. I can still visualize Nora. And I can still visualize myself. A lovely summer day in Manhattan. I'm coming out of the big Forty-second Street library; I've just spent hours there going through newspapers and books to find the least costly universities where qualified professors could supervise my research on the interconnections between politics and religion among Jewish scholars in Spain prior to the expulsion decree. I'm going home to my uncle's house in Brooklyn and heading for the bus stop, for I like buses more than the subway. I'm wondering if my uncle will wait for me for dinner. I hope not. I love him, but he's too inquisitive. He'll no doubt ask me the same old questions about my immediate future plans. Did I find the information I needed at the library? Did I investigate things thoroughly? Have I really decided to go to the university instead of studying the Talmud and Rabbi Bahya ibn Pakuda's *Duties of the Heart*? Who'll pay my tuition? Who'll cover my expenses: book purchases, lodgings, clothing? And really, why, oh why, couldn't I be satisfied with religious studies, like him? And get married? Too attached to my well-being and me, my dear uncle! Should I confess to him, in strict confidence, of course, that I already don't feel good about myself—that my faith is faltering? Will he leave me alone? Or does he actually want me to move out? But then with whom will he discuss the day's events? And to whom will he describe his memories of the past and of the Old World?

"The bus arrives, and, lost in my thoughts, I see it pass right by me. Bah, I'll take the next one. Here it is. I rush toward it and almost knock over a woman passenger who succeeds in climbing in ahead of me. There are two empty seats for us at the back of the bus. One glance at the woman by my side and my heart skips a beat. I forget all about my landlord and try to decipher the strange expression lighting up this woman's face, a woman bursting with vitality and sensuality. I feel myself blushing. Why is she smiling at me? What should I do? Look away and make believe I don't see her, as if she didn't exist? Fortunately, she takes the initiative. She must have a gift! 'Do you know you hurt me just then?' she says in a low voice. 'What?' I say, frightened. 'I hurt you? Me?' 'Yes, you. When you rushed toward the bus like a roughneck, you stepped on my left foot.' 'Oh, how can I make up for it?' I exclaim, dying of shame. 'I'll teach you,' she says, taking my hand in hers. I don't know what I'm feeling, but I know I've never felt it before; this is the first time.

"At a downtown stop, the young woman gets up and so do I. We get off the bus together, holding hands, and walk to Greenwich Village. We've gone just a short distance when we come to an imposing building in the middle of the block. My guide presses a button and a wrought-iron gate opens. The elevator takes us to the fifth floor. Without letting go of my hand, she takes a key out of her handbag and opens the door. As in a dream, I follow her inside. I don't understand what is happening to me or what it all means. What am I doing in this sun-lit, luxuriously furnished apartment, with this woman who is so self-confident, who gazes at me as though I am someone else, someone who belonged to her? Besides, who am I for her? She releases my hand to draw the curtains and take off her shoes. 'It's too hot in here,' she says, helping me take off my jacket. 'Don't you think?'

"All of a sudden, I'm ashamed. Ashamed of being too hot, of wearing a wrinkled shirt, ashamed of my poverty and awkwardness. Ashamed of breathing, ashamed of feeling so foolish and distraught, ashamed of not being able to blurt out the words and sighs that are suffocating me. She sits down on the couch and says; 'Come closer; let me look at you.' In her gentle and cool hands, my head is going to burst at any minute. Her burning desire spreads to my body. Her lips open mine and murmur something like: 'I don't know who you are and I don't care to know; don't tell me your name; I'll just lie about mine. Let's say it's Nora. The important thing is that moment when you'll be in paradise; I promise you a great surge of desire and happiness.' Once again, it's a first time. I discover I have unspoken sensations.

"But, at the last minute, I resist her. I'm still too repressed, tyrannized by taboos. Kissing, possibly. Going further, no. Clearly frustrated and unsatisfied, Nora asks: 'What are you thinking about?'

" 'My mother,' I say foolishly.

" 'Where is she?'

" 'Dead.'

" 'And your father?'

" 'Dead.'

" 'Your brothers and sisters?'

" 'Dead.'

"I fear her continuing to question me, but she has something else in mind: galvanizing my senses. All my bones and arteries, all the cells in my body long to respond with vigor and jubilation, but a voice within me calls me to chastity. 'I can't tell you why,' Nora says, 'but on the bus, as soon as I saw you, I guessed you were an orphan.'

"An image gives me a start: my uncle must be waiting for me for dinner! 'Can I make a phone call?'

"She points to the phone next to the bed. 'Tell him you're going to spend the night with a friend.'

"I hear the familiar voice: 'Where are you?'

"My uncle seems more frightened than angry. I lie badly; I stammer: 'I met . . . at the library . . . I met a friend . . . a lot of things to discuss . . . He invited me to spend the night at his house.'

"My uncle pauses for a minute to take in the meaning of my words. 'Okay, but you'll tell me all about it tomorrow . . . when you return. And don't forget your tefillin . . . did you take them? If not, take your friend's; don't forget.'

"Of course, I say to myself, smiling; I won't forget. I won't forget anything about this day or night.

"Nora waits for me to join her and then questions me. 'What language were you speaking?'

" 'Yiddish.'

"Outside, dusk is falling like a silent shadow. We say nothing, each locked in the past. I feel I've crossed a threshold into a new stage of life; even without going too far, I know that I've committed a major transgression in the eyes of God. From now on, nothing will ever be the same. But what about Nora, why is she anxious? I don't dare ask her. She draws me close to her and says: 'You're like a series of discoveries for me. I've never known anyone so young and innocent. And I've never heard anyone speak Yiddish.'

"I ask her: 'Why did you choose me?'

"She thinks before answering: 'Actually, I have no idea. Instinct, intuition. I could have taken another bus, and you too, you could have accompanied someone somewhere else. But . . . when I saw you, I suddenly started thinking about my life: I'm rich and still young, twenty-four; I can buy anything and ditch anything without it changing my life or my conception of life, except . . . except that my husband left me. He left me and laughed.'

"She falls silent abruptly, and since it's already dark, I don't know if she's crying, if her tears are making a noise she alone can hear. Then, just as suddenly, she stiffens. 'I have an idea. You'll think it's crazy, but listen to it anyhow, okay?' Okay. What surprise will she come up with next? With a serious expression, she starts talking, almost lecturing: 'You're young, younger than me. At my age, a woman can be proud or desperate; I'm both. But since you're here, I say to myself that I should forget my pride. So . . .' I wait for her to continue. 'Here's my idea,' she says. 'It's a heavy proposition. Stay with me.'

"What does she mean, stay with her? All day? All night? I hear myself stammering: 'To do what?'

"She bursts out laughing: 'You're so naïve; I love it. To do what, he asks. To live and be happy. Today and tomorrow and next month. Forgive me; I'm stupid. I'm just running off at the mouth. It's because I'm lonely . . . and sad.'

"Should I explain to her that the story of my solitude is much sadder? No. The Book of Job taught me that the sadness of one group of people doesn't alleviate the sadness of others. On the contrary: it adds to it.

"At dawn, she stares at me.

"She is still in bed; I'm dressed. She asks me: 'You won't forget?'

" 'No, I won't.'

" 'What will you think of me when you remember this night?'

" 'I'll think that I knew a generous, solitary woman.'

" 'And what did I teach you?'

" 'I don't know yet. Do you? If you do, tell me.'

" 'I taught you that two people can come together without loving each other. You're leaving, and what you've left me with is remorse.' The young woman's voice turns melancholy. 'Yes, my little Yiddish friend. This night will remain a moment of great sadness for me because nothing was accomplished.'

"A thought stirs my mind: If it's Lilith, she didn't defeat me. Yet she speaks well.

"I never saw Nora again.

"I have to confess, Doctor, that I missed her sometimes, especially during the first weeks. I could less have become accustomed to her luxurious lifestyle than to the easy, kind tenderness she showed me. Especially since—I'm ashamed to admit it—my uncle was beginning to weigh on me. Had he guessed what I had done on that frivolous, promising night? Was he going to rebuke me for having spent the night away from home? In the morning, he saw me put on the phylacteries. So I hadn't borrowed them from 'my friend.' Had he detected a sign, a trace of sin on my face or in my behavior? Too interested in my activities, too demanding, too religious, and above all, too indiscreet, he liked his multiple roles of godfather, protector, guardian, and supervisor. He wanted to be informed of everything I was up to, every minute of the day and night. He wasn't a petty person, but his obsession with religious practice spurred him to pry relentlessly into my private life, for which—I don't know why—he felt responsible as much as for everything else. Had I recited my morning prayers and studied the Talmud? Had I had lunch and dinner, and with whom? Had I made sure that the food was kosher? In my personal dictionary, he was listed as a harmless little inquisitor, charitable but demanding. The fate of my soul worried him as much as his own. Sometimes when I would point out to him that the concept of soul was meaningless to scientists, he used to get mad: 'So what does that prove? That supposedly intelligent people are rather stupid, for their knowledge is based on ignorance.'

"In his own way he also contributed to my immoderate attraction to both irony and the irrational. It was a winter evening. My aunt Gittel was already asleep, but we were drinking hot tea to warm up. My uncle loved to be in the warm indoors while it was ice cold in the city. 'Oh,' he said with a sigh, 'I feel sorry for scientists for glorifying the rational and atheists for being mad about cold, frosty reason. What attracts us, what elevates us to God, is what sets the brain on fire and lights up the soul.' I asked him if too much heat might not harm the soul he was so concerned about. He nodded in agreement: 'Yes, too many flames might destroy the soul.'

" 'In that case,' I cried out happily, 'long live the soul!'

"He looked worried: 'You're playing with words whose meaning escapes you, you're making fun of the sacred, you're wrong! Be careful, otherwise madness—you hear me, madness—is waiting to trip you up. It strikes and bites voraciously; it will eventually make you fall to your knees so your wild, unworthy soul can be whipped by a thousand unsatisfied demons who won't even kill you!'

"I was probably wrong to contradict him, but I couldn't help replying: 'Are you implying that the soul itself can go mad?' He glared at me and left the room to go to bed.

"Which leads me to ask you the same question, Doctor: Do you believe in the soul? And if you do, do you find it plausible that, pushed to the limit, it can sink into madness?"

# 7

"You're annoyed, Doctor, disappointed maybe; I can guess as much from your silences—they crop up intermittently. You listen to me; that's natural—you have no choice; it's your job. However, you feel I don't open up enough: I'm hiding things that you might need in order to figure me out, analyze me, and even cure me. Am I mistaken, Doctor?"

"No, Doriel. You're perspicacious. You express yourself well, too well. You steer your thoughts and sentences efficiently, with a logic that appears sound and flawless, whereas it's those flaws, those slips, that I'd like to focus on in your ideas, your memories, and your words. Try to understand: it's the obscure part of your words that can enlighten me. It's inside your private labyrinth that I can best find my bearings. Whereas you're preventing me from doing so. You're very eloquent, but most of the time, even when you're talking, you skirt around the most important things."

She's right. I'm too attached to logic sometimes. I wouldn't mind being cerebral. So my self-control works to perfection. Should I let it be disrupted? And then: To what extent am I really conscious of what I'm trying to hide from her? Let's play for time.

"You claim I'm not talking about the most important things. Give me an example, Doctor."

"Your parents."

"What do you want to know about my parents? They're dead, I told you."

"Yes. But you didn't tell me anything else about them."

"Probably because there's nothing to add."

"That's not true."

This makes me angry. "Are you accusing me of lying? Or of cheating?"

"My profession doesn't allow me to judge anyone."

"But you just—"

"I just pointed out to you that my words don't concern the truth. I simply think that you're trying to escape reality. Is it your fault? Your weakness, maybe? I'd say it's your problem, a problem that's part of what is troubling you, sufficiently so that you came to solicit my help."

"I appreciate your frankness, Doctor," I say politely, but with harshness in my voice.

She doesn't reply. She is waiting in vain for me to regain my calm. As soon as I recall my parents, I'm overwhelmed by a paralyzing anxiety.

"Some other time," I say. "We're not in a rush."

I know she has limitless patience. I don't. Why make her unhappy? I decide to tell her a few little odds and ends about my parents—and then, behold, I can't stop: "My parents died young. I didn't really know them. I'm the second of their three children. Very devoted to tradition but open to the world—they mastered several languages—my parents were always busy, always smiling. I was born in 1936 in a small town in the heart of Poland, but where there was a mixed population of Romanians, Hungarians, and Austrians. After the First World War, the deadliest war in our country up until then, people had confidence in the future. We lived in a small house in the shopping district. My father was the secretary of the community, and my mother . . . my mother . . . I don't recall what she did exactly. I think she just did everything she was expected to do. We used to see one another only in the evening. During the day, I used to go to the heder—there was a clandestine one in the ghetto. My sister, Dina, the eldest, had attended high school many years before. Little Jacob, or Yankele, had a tutor. For the Sabbath and holiday meals, we all 'helped' our mother in the kitchen. Though busy with his many obligations—helping the needy and orphans, visiting the sick—my father never gave up studying. I never saw him without a scholarly book tucked under his arm. I think I inherited my passion for reading from him. They can take everything away from us, he often said, but not knowledge. Or the thirst for knowledge. Loving the Torah is deepening it.

"I remember the Sabbath of my childhood. Many years later, even when I was tormented by my illness and tried to forget everything else, the lights of 'the seventh day' still flickered and beckoned in the depths of my memory. The beginning of the Sabbath. The celebration of its peaceful holiness. Time erected into a temple. The child within me remembers nostalgically: I used to sing as I returned from the house of prayer with my father, and when I became older, we both sang '*Shalom aleichem, malachei ha-sharet, malachei ha-shalom*'—'Peace be with you, servant angels, angels of peace'—and my child's heart used to burst with happiness.

"The following day, after the morning prayer and the meal, my father made all of us fulfill our charitable duties. Dina organized cultural get-togethers. My mother visited hospitals. As for me, my father used to take me to the edge of a forest to visit the Jewish patients in the insane asylum. Yes, Doctor. Though he was not at all wealthy and worked hard to earn a living, he took an interest in the insane, for according to him, they were more defenseless than the poor. At first, he used to leave me outside, in the courtyard or garden, while he went and brought 'his' patients sweets and fruits. During the Pesach holiday, he gave them matzoh.

"One day, suffering from pneumonia, he got up in spite of a

fever and went to visit them. I accompanied him to the door. 'If I have to stay awhile and you're afraid of being alone,' he said, 'you can come inside, but make sure you don't speak to any of them.' This was my first direct contact with this deranged world. All of them were old, or at least seemed so, even those who had not yet reached adolescence. Some of them stared into space with a vacant look; others fidgeted restlessly as if they were being bitten by insects. A redhead sat on the floor by the window, his head in his hands, roaring with laughter. Two steps away from him, to his left, a man beat his breast and mumbled incoherently. Two mustached midgets were dancing the czardas. At the other end of the room, which had windows with bars on them, a giant with the shoulders of a boxer and the head of a child signaled to me to come closer; from his jerky movements I understood that he wanted to know who I was. I didn't want to appear impolite, so in spite of my father's instructions, I answered him. He held out his hand and I took it, which was a dreadful mistake: he refused to let go of it. Terrified, I begged him: 'Let go, let go, my father is waiting for me.'

" 'One never leaves this place,' he said. 'And here your father is me. Do you hear, you little idiot? Each one of us here is your father, get it?'

"I felt overwhelmed with panic. I cried out: 'No, no!' Nodding his small head on his ox-like neck, he merely laughed louder and louder as if to say, 'Too late, too late!' And several madmen applauded. At that moment, Doctor, I myself probably came within a hair's breadth of madness. Is it the madness that would reappear later in my life? Fortunately, my father rescued me.

"Who can rescue me today?

"There's also religion, Doctor. Let's not forget the position it occupied in my life. By clashing with reason, it can prevent you from living in reality. The devotion, compassion, generosity it advocates: sublime words drawn from the dustbins of history, as Marx and Lenin would say, the most famous doctors in the field of societies-in-evolution. The rigidity of the laws, the bewitchment of the mystics: these I knew and even liked. The lyrical beauty of the lamentations was something I was steeped in. Doctor, you who belong to another world and another time, you can't understand. Jewish life in small towns—and Brooklyn was a small town, a shtetl—which, in spite of poverty, became lively spiritual centers attuned to the slightest flutter of the Lord's eyelid. Are you able to grasp the moving grace of this life nourished by an absurd hope—absurd because timeless? My childhood years in a secret hiding place, and my adolescence in the yeshiva, all those days, all those twilight hours spent turning the pages of dusty books in flickering candlelight, far from the noise and neon of the twentieth century. Should I tell you about this so that you can come to my rescue? Brought up by my uncle, I was initially the most religious, the most devout boy. Then there was a break. And the Leah episode is part of it. Okay, not too fast, Doctor. Each lapse in its own time. But I have a question for you that can't be put off: In order to cure me and relieve the burden of my dizzy spells and the excesses I'm driven to by my crises, will you follow me to that time and place? Will you be able to? Will you have enough strength?

"In my tradition, man is supposed to believe that Satan chooses as his favorite prey the just man, not the sinner. Satan is brave. And ambitious. Cunning. He deals with minor everyday sinners out of habit, between two yawns, almost without giving it a thought. He prefers to go where he isn't expected. Where the challenge means a struggle. Where victory, always uncertain, will create a sensation even in the loftiest spheres. Parenthetically, Doctor, do you believe in this theory? In fact, do you believe in the celestial figure called Satan? Well, he exists and I've met him. At first, I succeeded in disarming him through fear. Fear of punishment, in other words, of Satan himself? No: fear of God. Yet isn't He a charitable and good father? In those days, I still knew, or knew already, that God too is to be feared."

I break off. I'm sure she'll ask me if I still fear God today, and if the fear of God is essential in the Jewish religion, to the point of neglecting love of God. At least I'll have a ready answer to the last question. In Jerusalem, a novelist who was a devotee of Hasidic tales and sayings said to me one day: "Do you know why God demands that each of us love Him? He doesn't need our love, but we need it." I saw this novelist only once, and this was the only thing he said to me, but it remains etched in my wounded memory. Should I tell my interlocutor about it? She's the one who questions me.

"What became of your sister, Dina, and your little brother, Jacob?"

"I didn't see them often. But I could have gone with them where they went."

"On the other hand, a moment ago you described your childhood. You spent it with your parents. Do you see them when you talk about your childhood?"

"I see them even when I'm not talking about it."

"Tell me about it."

"I can't."

"Tell me why not," she says.

"I see them and I become a child again. Excuse me: I see my mother mostly. I see her again, exhausted in the morning after a sleepless night, and I'm in pain. I see my father looking worried, and I feel the familiar ache. But sometimes I see my mother looking radiant at the Pesach seder and I smile at her. And I listen to my father describing the exodus of our people, and I feel like singing. I catch glances exchanged between them, and though I haven't prayed in ages, I feel a prayer spring from my heart, suddenly eager to reach the celestial throne, but it expires in flight.

"I see them in the last years of their lives, and my life becomes heavy with nostalgia.

"My father had located a safe spot in a small village, too small for the German army to come to and flaunt its tanks and policemen. We were the only Jews in the region. Since you want to know everything, I'll tell you that I grew up in a lumberjack's barn—Vladek's. He and his wife, a decent, skinny, and toothless peasant woman, knew who we were; the rest of the population didn't know. I remember their son, Edek, a hoodlum whom we had to be wary of; he poked his nose into everything near his house. A member of a clandestine Zionist movement, my sister signed up in one of their Warsaw sections; she had been promised a certificate for Palestine. Jacob, or Yankele, a year younger than I, had learned not to cry too loudly. My mother wasn't with us. She had been contacted by the Jewish Resistance and become a liaison officer. Blond and protected by a fake Aryan identity card, a flawless Polish-speaker, she traveled around the country visiting the scattered members of her network and organized contacts with their families so anonymous emissaries could bring them money and news.

"The days were all alike, and the nights even more so. Twice a neighbor informed on us, lured by the reward of a kilo of sugar per arrested Jew; we were forced to desert our refuge and take shelter in a hut in the middle of the forest. We slept on straw. Once or twice a week Vladek brought us bread and vegetables. We drank water from the spring. Yankele got sick several times; Father nursed him with the medications my mother obtained for us. Father entertained him by telling him stories about his own childhood and youth. For example, the story of his bar mitzvah; it had taken place during Shavuot, the holiday celebrating the revelation on Mount Sinai. People drank sweet wine, danced and sang, and my father thought he was being fêted. Later he understood he hadn't been entirely wrong. 'Every time a Jewish child proclaims his desire to belong to the continuity of his people, we all have reason to applaud him joyfully,' your grand-father explained to me.' And he added: 'Being Jewish, especially during dark periods, is a grave matter, but it is also thrilling. Being Jewish means fulfilling oneself in more than one dimension; it's like living a forty-eight-hour day intensely and to the full. There. That's what I'll tell you too, my dear little Yankele, when you turn thirteen. And as a gift, I'll give you the benediction I received from my father and that he received from his: to be alive the day when you'll welcome the Messiah.' To avoid having some inquisitive, malicious vagabond hear him, he spoke in a very low voice and with great gentleness. And my little brother's eyes, already ageless, absorbed his melancholic voice and image, and they accompanied us throughout all our peregrinations. And in my own voice I sometimes still hear our father's voice."

"When did you see your parents for the last time?"

"You don't understand a thing. I still see them."

"Yes, I understand. But I mean—"

"I know what you mean, Doctor. My parents, yes, the last time I saw my parents in the flesh, in other words, alive, was after the war."

"And Dina?"

"I told you. Dead."

"And Jacob?"

"Dead."

"And—"

"Stop, Doctor. Don't ask me any more questions about my uncles, my aunts, my cousins. I would have loved to see them again and make them talk the way you make me talk. But for each one, I'll give you the same answer.

"Dead, dead, dead: this dreadful word, as bitter as the bitter herb of the Haggadah. After the war, it was on everyone's lips and in everyone's ears. But Dina's death was so absurd. Even today, I don't understand: Did God or destiny want to mock her and us by sparing her for over four years of occupation and danger and then taking her away from us a week before the arrival of our liberators? That morning, the sun had decided to force its way through the clouds. And Dina couldn't resist; she left our barn to bask in its warmth. An informer spotted her and cried out to her not to move. To get him away from our refuge, she started running toward the forest. A minute later, she was lying on the wet ground, shot down by a bullet. Ten days later, the informer was executed. But his punishment didn't alleviate our grief."

"And your little brother?"

"My parents left him in the care of a Christian family."

"He died of an illness?"

"No. A neighbor informed on him, and the family that had taken him in preferred to give him back to us. Then my mother and Dina took him to Warsaw. To the ghetto. The famous teacher Janusz Korczak admitted him to his house. I can imagine the hour of separation. I'd give a lot to know what my little brother thought and said at that moment. I'll never know."

"And your parents?"

"Why are you hounding me? You'd like to hear me pronounce that same word again—the same word always? I won't."

"Why not?"

"Because we're talking about my parents. They deserve another word. A special one. A word belonging to them alone. Try to understand, Doctor: I wasn't with them. I didn't see them die. I became an orphan without knowing it: I was too far away, on the other side of the mountain. And ever since, I know it."

Thérèse keeps silent for a long while. Then, after hesitating slightly, she speaks, her voice a monotone again. "For you, these memories are dreadful. I can understand perfectly well that you don't want to dwell on them. But we must delve into things more deeply. So let me ask you this: Could you be refusing to use that *word* because you feel guilty about them? Guilty because you weren't with them to the end?"

"You're very insistent, Doctor. But be careful; don't go too far."

"What effect does it have on you?"

"It hurts me." In order to check my anger, I draw a deep breath. "You forget that I was a bewildered, lost little boy. What I did or didn't do wasn't for pleasure or on an impulse. Could I foresee the accident?"

"If you had known, if you could have—"

"Leave me alone, Doctor. I don't know what I would have done. Would I have been so foolish as to run to catch up with them in death?"

She waits for me to calm down.

"When you think about your father, about your mother, *what* comes to mind?"

I don't reply right away. Calmly I take several deep breaths and reflect; that's what I need. I should tell her I think about the life I had and shared with my parents. That, yes, I shouldn't feel so unhappy, since they didn't die in a camp but in a free country. That, at night, I try to walk them to the car, and imagine the rest. I see them alone. And sometimes, in a hallucinatory state, I see myself with them *over there* and I suffocate.

"Doctor, listen to me closely. Get one thing straight: there are some things you'll never understand. You didn't live their life, but I carry it around within me like a trace of blood. And their death like a burn."


EXCERPT FROM DR. THÉRÈSE GOLDSCHMIDT'S NOTES

In the evening, at the dinner table, I have trouble eating. My mind is elsewhere. Sad, troubled. Where do my thoughts lead me, and to what end? My husband, discreet and considerate, talks about his work at the library: there's a greater demand for books on war than for novels. He comments on the news. The election campaign in America. Bloody incidents in the Middle East, famine in Africa, political convulsions just about everywhere. Civil, religious, cultural, economic wars: it never stops. Oh, may the century come to an end; it is high time.

"Did you know," he said, "that the Hundred Years' War actually lasted a hundred and fifteen years? Nowadays wars are shorter, or is it the same war going on and on, with occasional periods of peace?"

I listen to him absentmindedly and try to dodge the question: "That's a subject for historians; let them sort it out."

"But war also interests psychiatrists. Didn't you tell me that all wars originate in the souls of those who wage them?"

"But is it reason that ends them? I think so, don't you?"

"To be sure, anyone can start a fire, but few people know how to put one out. Didn't Plato say that it is only for the dead that war has an end?"

Lost in my thoughts, I don't fully grasp the meaning of the remark and merely say, "War is always a disease."

Martin sets down his fork and knife and scrutinizes my face. "And your special, not to say privileged, patient isn't its only victim. If you're not careful, we'll become its victims too."

I pull myself together. "What do you mean?"

"You're absent again. I know where you are and with whom. You've changed since you've been treating him."

So I tell him about my last session with Doriel.

"It's going badly. I don't feel I'm getting anywhere; I'm at a virtual standstill. Oh, on the surface, there's progress. He talks, he talks without losing his temper too much. An occasional outburst. But on rereading my notes, I realize that we're going nowhere. Today he told me that I'd never understand him or, more specifically, that I'd never understand, period. And I think he's right on that point. I wonder if I shouldn't admit defeat and call it quits."

"Good idea!" Martin exclaims, nodding. "You've been irritable lately. With me, but also with yourself. You're not pleased with what you're doing, and you're very hard on yourself. You're edgy, withdrawn, and you seem to be struggling so as not to drown."

I don't contradict him. Honesty forbids it. A perspicacious and lucid observer, Martin is quite right. Confronting another person's madness entails a risk; I'm perfectly aware of that. I don't know where I'm heading anymore. Do I know where I am? Am I still bound to my husband by an intelligent, generous love? Is it still the fertile and happy love of the past? I make an effort to hide my inner turmoil.

"What you're saying, Martin, is probably true. I suddenly feel inadequate. But just as I like to fight standing up, I'm trying to dream with my eyes wide open. To give up now would be a betrayal and a self-betrayal. You're responsible for the works of writers, whereas I'm responsible for human beings. I feel responsible for their right to think, act, and live intelligently, without harming others or themselves. That's why I believe that if we sometimes have to respond to laughter with laughter, we should certainly not respond to the absurd with the absurd, or to the incomprehensible by giving up."

"First of all, you're underestimating my work. I'm responsible for human beings too: the authors and their readers. Second, I still feel responsible for you. What about you, do you still feel responsible for me?"

Automatically, I stroke my forehead, as I always do when I feel disconcerted. How can I answer without hurting him?

"It's not the same thing, Martin. All of this is becoming more and more complicated. All I know is, if I call it quits, if I give up this case, I'll have to give everything up. For good."

Martin nibbles his lip, something he rarely does. Confused

and perplexed, he asks: "Give *everything* up?" He sounds as though he is putting his entire life and all his anxiety into that word.

And suddenly harmony is restored between us. Silent, I find myself thinking that for each human being, the other person is not just a pathway but also a crossroads.

# 8

"For months and months now we're trying to get to know each other better, Doctor. Where are we at this point? I don't know what I told you anymore, but I do know what I concealed from you. Did I say anything original to you about man's destiny? About love? Am I capable of it? Did I describe the love of a real live woman, hidden away between the spring and the diviner? And life—what is life? I have no idea. But how are we to live? That's the real question. Is it worse to live in isolation, bumping into every corner, against every passerby, against every wall, or to live in a downy, misty space lacking consistency, where everything is blurry and translucent? As for life, Doctor, I think I've drunk it down to the sediments. Did I tell you often enough that I'm not happy? Did I tell you why I remained a bachelor? Did I talk to you enough about faith? I see it as a test without end, a confrontation. I fight, and I no longer remember why. I often think I'm just an interlacing of cracks opening up on fear. Is that why I didn't want to become a father? There's a passage in the Talmudic texts that forbids man to have children in disastrous times. And it explains: If God decides to destroy the world, who are we to oppose our will to His?

"However, would you like me to tell you about the experience I had, a short time before my bar mitzvah, in the house of my first teacher? His name was Reb Yohanan. He was nicknamed 'the Miracle Maker.' It happened on the day of his wife's funeral.

"I remember her: timid and very self-effacing in her own home. Rivka was mute and expressed herself with head and hand gestures. She never complained and refused to be pitied; she thanked God for her fate, laughed when anyone told a funny story drawn from biblical or Hasidic sources, and was sad when the occasion required it. Was she really mute, or was she afraid of adding her voice to the voices of men?

"The couple had two children, a rebellious boy, Noah, who became my friend, and a sickly daughter. Noah didn't go unnoticed: high-strung, dissatisfied, he seemed to sense that there was something unfinished about him. His ailing sister, Beyle, could stay in bed for days on end. From time to time, but rarely, she would half open the door to the study room, glance at the young students with a panicked look, and immediately shut the door again. Did her father see me as a potential son-in-law? In that modest household, I was treated with consideration, I would even say with tenderness.

"The calamity struck on a day when Rivka, alone at home with Beyle, had a heart attack. On returning from the morning service, Reb Yohanan and I found her inert, lying on the floor in the kitchen. The ambulance came quickly, and we took her to the hospital. But it was too late. The physician told us quite clearly that it had been a matter of minutes; she could have been saved. 'It's my fault,' Reb Yohanan replied. 'I shouldn't have left her.'

"The family gathered at his house during the week of mourning, eating hard-boiled eggs, symbolizing the ever-turning wheel of life, and hearing the customary phrases, 'May the Lord console you among the bereaved of Zion and Jerusalem,' and not hiding their grief. The house was full of people from morning to night. Some came to take part in the prayers, others to bring food, since work is forbidden during periods of mourning.

"Bearded, slow in his gestures, his eyes doleful, Reb Yohanan seemed to be coming out of an unspeakable hell, and kept blurting out the same few words: 'It's my fault.' These words resonated inside me many years later in completely different circumstances, as though they had been specially made for me: Yes, it's my fault. And though I could keep telling myself that who will live and who will die, and how, is decided by God alone, up there, during the High Holy Days, I nonetheless clung to the idea that in some inexplicable way I was to blame.

"The visitors talked mostly about Rivka. Had she been unwell? Had she complained of any aches? Being reserved and silent, how could she have explained to the doctors any pain or discomfort she might have felt? As I wasn't a close family member, I didn't have to obey the *shiva* laws, laws of incomparable sensitivity and compassion, centering on the bereaved person, who must at all costs be protected from fatigue and indiscretion. I drew up a chair for one caller and gave a glass of water to another. I became a kind of spokesman for the family and tried to answer the visitors' questions as best I could. You see, Doctor, talking about Rivka provided consolation; I was participating in the events and the rituals, and integrating them into a time frame and a frame of reference.

"Some callers came for Reb Yohanan; others had been close to Rivka. There were several people who had spent time with the couple when they lived in Rovidok, before the war.

"Thanks to them I discovered this small town lost in the Carpathian Mountains, and I became very fond of it. Christians called it 'the White Church' and Jews 'the Black Church.' A traditional town; you can probably picture the familiar landscape from your readings. So could I. I listened with curiosity to the old people's descriptions of life in the past and managed to reconstitute an entire community that I didn't know. Its wealthy and its poor, its schools and shops, its anxieties and joys. I would have given anything to take part in a marriage over there, a rabbinical wedding. I would have given anything to be present when the newly written Torah was brought to its place of honor in the sacred ark, ushered in by a jubilant crowd. A Sabbath with the famous Magid of Tolipin, a stormy public debate about a man suspected of belonging to the Shabbathalan or Frankist sect: a mix of memories and comments—wasn't it sheer madness?—I listened to them with envy. Life there conformed to the rhythm of the Jewish and Christian holidays. Yom Kippur was just as important as Christmas.

"During that week of mourning, I also learned that my teacher and his wife had been in Auschwitz.

" 'Reb Yohanan,' said one of the visitors, 'do you remember? You had a crazy but brilliant idea. You went from one block to another begging the Jews not to forget what day of the week it was. On Saturday you wished us *"Gut shabes"* like before.'

" 'And our walks after the war, Reb Yohanan, do you remember?' another person asked. 'On our return home, the two of us wandered in the deserted streets and ruins looking for relatives and friends. Those were hard times, almost as harsh as the war itself: the houses, now uninhabited by Jews, were occupied by Ruthenians, Hungarians, Ukrainians. You were asked to perform miracles, and you replied that you were helpless, stripped of your powers. You used to tell me that our sacred books mention souls who return to wander on earth because they're not wanted in the heavens yet. So they're doomed to keep company with the living, who don't see them, don't feel their presence, who laugh, sing, and work, and deny them the right of sanctuary among them. Sometimes I wonder, you used to say, whether my soul isn't part of this group; I wonder whether I'm not already dead. And whether our survival here is nothing but the dream of our dead.'

"This shed a new light on my teacher. I never could have imagined that he influenced so many lives.

"But Lord of wars and mysteries, how had he managed not to sink into melancholy and insanity? And if I did succumb, is it my fault, my fault alone?

"Rivka and her husband were part of the last convoy to Auschwitz. I was told—yes, during that week of mourning, I was told of the miracles her husband had had to perform in order to save her. I couldn't understand how, as a mute, she managed to survive the daily hardships and the Birkenau selections, she who was physically unable to utter a single word in response to the questions to which all the prisoners were subjected.

"And yet.

"A very short woman wearing a wig and soberly dressed gave me an explanation in her shrill, high-pitched voice: 'Oh, you want to know if I knew the Rivka for whom we grieve? Yes, I knew her. We were together. What would you like to know? Did she ever mention my name to you? Oh, excuse me, I forgot, she couldn't speak, the poor woman. But I can tell you, she was unique. A unique consoler. She suffered more than we did, endured more pain and humiliation than us, and yet it was she who helped us stand firm. She just had to look at us and smile. She made us laugh by gesturing like a Purim clown or a circus acrobat. I sometimes lost the very last spark of hope; it was she who succeeded in rekindling it. One day, I was frightened for her; we all were. It was during that terrible selection of October '44. We were lined up naked. At the door stood the team of our judges and executioners. Like all of us, I had wasted away and become weak. If they take my number, I'm lost, I thought; Rivka too. If they ask her a question, any question, her age, for example, she's lost. I was as distressed for her as for myself. I thought: Reb Yohanan, if you're still alive, and even if you're not, I implore you, you who perform miracles, save your wife. I prayed that we'd both become invisible. I passed. They didn't stop me. Rivka was stopped; the SS doctor asked her something. We all held our breath. She didn't lower her head in front of him. She replied by shrugging her shoulders. The SS doctor said something else to her, and I was petrified that he was going to notice her condition. But suddenly she moved her lips. I had to cover my mouth to stifle a cry. Perhaps my eyes had deceived me? Had she talked? So her saintly husband had succeeded in saving her? The important thing was that she had passed the selection. Later, I asked her what she had thought of at that moment. Of God? Her parents? The danger hanging over her? She began laughing, whereas I began crying.'

"Admit it, Doctor, they were both crazy. Yes, Doctor, there are times when you have to be abnormal if you want to live normally in the hell of men. But let's return to Reb Yohanan and his bereavement. On the last day of *shiva* he received the visit of a Hasidic rebbe. Tall, thick eyebrows, haughty bearing and confident gait, he stopped for a moment by the door as if he was inspecting the premises. Escorted by two vigilant young secretaries dressed in black, he walked in and addressed my teacher with the traditional benediction. He took a seat opposite him and, following custom, waited for Reb Yohanan to say a few words before speaking.

" 'I knew Rivka's father very well,' he began. 'We came from the same village. We were friends and partners. Yes, partners. We had made an agreement: he promised to support me so I could devote myself to studying and teaching, and in exchange he would get my share of paradise. The document was signed before two witnesses. We were young at the time, adolescents, but Rivka's father never forgot his commitment. Even during pogroms, he tried to help me. When I lost my strength, he gave me courage. When I felt my reason falter—my reason, mind you, not my faith, which remained intact—he spoke to me with kindness and set me straight. When he was stabbed by a hooligan and knew he was going to die, he summoned me to his bedside. He was ashen, drained. I had to lean down with my face close to his to catch his words: "In a little while, I'll be crossing the threshold and entering the world of truth. It's time for me to free you of your vow. I pronounce our agreement null and void." I objected, but he silenced me and whispered in my ear: "I have one favor to ask of you. Promise me you'll watch over my daughter." I promised him: "At the slightest danger, she'll have only to remember our agreement and my promise, and she'll be saved." '

"Later on, Doctor, I recalled this visit. Did I hear correctly? Had the illustrious rabbi come just so my question about Rivka's survival would be answered? I also recall he waited for a *minyan,* ten men, so he could say the Minha prayer. Noah recited the Kaddish and the family sat on stools to listen to the ritual words of consolation for the last time. The *shiva* was coming to an end. The rabbi paused in the doorway and gazed at us with an inspired look. Reb Yohanan blew his nose, the other visitors stayed still, and I asked myself, and I ask you now, Doctor: Against a world invaded by madness, should we use the faith of our ancestors, or our own madness?

"Actually, Rivka wasn't mute. Reb Yohanan himself told me on the last day of *shiva.* Why did she make believe she was? There's a whole story behind that too. Many years earlier, when she was a young bride, some harsh words had escaped her, words that were too critical of a neighbor whose behavior had displeased her. The next day the neighbor fell and broke her leg. In expiation, Rivka took a vow of silence and kept it to the end of her life."

## 9

At the beginning of the next session, the therapist asks me in a natural, quasi-indifferent, almost technical tone of voice, "For you who are so preoccupied by the suffering of men, isn't it the same suffering? Aren't the ancestral faith and your illness two sides of the same experience, the same trauma and the same memory, one the light and the other the shadow?"

Obviously, she has a knack for sending me back to my own questionings, and using those to drive me on further and further in my quest, demanding that I deepen it and dwelling on its failures more than its repercussions. Suddenly, for no reason, she reminds me of the woman on the bus and her solitude, of Leah and her elusive beauty, of Maya and her blue eyes with their dark shadows. Maya knew so many things. Where is she now?

"You're right," I say. "As always. Apparently I need you so I can understand my own ideas better."

Once again, my thoughts turn to Maya. For the time being, it's still Maya. You're different, Maya. I don't know why, do you? I only know that you are. Different, special. I love to be with you. I love your being here. When you're here, I love even the walls that separate me from the prison that is the world of men.

Maya, as usual, doesn't agree; too bad, but she refuses to talk. A voice within answers: The world is not a prison and the other person is not your jailer. Remember, Doriel, you like metaphysics more than psychology. The magic of the other is that he allows you to define yourself, though he doesn't limit you in your choices. Actually the other is your freedom more than your confinement.

The therapist doesn't hear this voice. She asks me questions, but I'm talking to the young woman with blue eyes.

I feel close to you, Maya. I like your melodious Yiddish and the idea that your knowledge envelops mine and reassures me. This makes you smile? You know me mostly in my hazy madness, even when I have doubts about your power and the means that would enable me to resist it. But do you know who I am when I'm not myself?

Maya replies that she does know, but she would rather hear me say it. As for the therapist's impossible, inaudible questions, the mad storyteller within me answers.

"I am Doriel, the lookout. This has nothing to do with Maya or anyone, but in the past, in ancient Judea, my role was to wait on the mountaintop for the appearance of the new moon. When I saw it, I cried out in a voice that could be heard from one end of the country to the other: '*Barkaï, Barkaï!* The first moonbeam is here; it brings light and warmth!' Nowadays, I feel like saying something completely different; I feel like being less confident and yelling through clenched teeth, 'Lookout, where are you? Say, watchman, how far into the night is it?' But the lookout is blind. And the watchman, mute. Yet the experience of their ordeals doesn't sway their judgment in any way. Do they at least know how far into the night it is, that night encumbered with the omens and warnings that we carry within ourselves, that night that welcomes us until it crushes us with the burden of its ghosts? Could I be one of them? And what if I am my own ghost, and as such immortal? But isn't being immortal no longer being? But then which one of us is mad, my ghost or me? And who will help me understand when I am truly ill: Is it when I *know* that I am or when I don't know? At least, Doctor, tell me whether you, thanks to your studies, your education, and your experience, whether you would be able to discern the dividing line. You nod; I can guess as much; I sense it. You're going to tell me that, to your great regret, mad thinking and thinking that isn't mad but that gallops at full speed and strays into lands that have no horizons are so close that they often meet, become superimposed, and end up merging. But then, where are we going? What will become of us? Who will protect us? Who will possess the truth, and how will it fit into our existence?"

I pull myself together; I'm losing my footing. I'm talking to the doctor, and it's Maya who answers me. And now, while writing, I'm talking about Maya, and it is no longer she who is listening.

I address a psychoanalyst, and it is a loved, departed woman who becomes my interlocutor. Is this madness? The obliteration of boundaries, the suppression of all ties? But, for the love of God, where are we? A terrifying thought occurs to me; I try to chase it away, but it keeps returning: Who will help me break the bark that is strangling me? And extinguish the black sun that blinds me? Who will tell me who I am? I know that I'm not you and you're not me. But careful, for the love of God, don't tell me, don't try to convince me that the other is my opponent, my enemy, and that this enemy is me.

# 10

The psychiatrist is very interested, probably much too interested, in my mother and my relationship with her. Naturally, she's gorged herself on the works of Freud and Freudian literature. For her, Freud remains the Moses of a people imagined and governed along her conceptions. In short, she's convinced that my "problem" lies in my conscious or unconscious conflicts with my mother, for she lived far away from me for too long and had an untimely death.

"You're on the wrong track, Doctor. You'll see. But, fine, I'll talk to you about my mother."

Thus does the patient start to describe his childhood; and he notices that he is not short of words.

He remembers his mother; he remembers her lips, her breathing, her warmth, her tenderness, her laugh. Her courage too, of course. She was a heroine, his mother. Legends had been spread about her feats of arms during the German occupation.

"You'll never guess, Doctor, the name she had in the Resistance. 'The Madwoman,' that's how she's listed in the Polish annals. Blond, beautiful, and strong, with piercing gray eyes, she had an Aryan identity card, and her daring aroused her comrades' admiration. A volunteer for the most dangerous missions, she eventually seemed to somehow guarantee their success. She relayed messages and plans of clandestine actions; occasionally she also delivered arms. On more than one occasion, she escaped the Gestapo traps and the prying eyes of the Polish informers. Didn't she fear death? Above all, she feared torture.

"I recall an evening at their house, after the liberation, when my mother's former comrades gathered to celebrate a decoration my mother had just received from the Polish army, whose envoy was a colonel in full uniform. The table, covered with a white tablecloth, paid tribute to the guests. A variety of dishes, numerous bottles; there was enough food for an entire battalion. Everyone drank a lot, laughed noisily, and my mother was not outdone. Glasses were raised to honor the fighters, dead and alive. None was forgotten or overlooked. 'Remember the attack against the train filled with soldiers and ammunition?' Glasses were emptied at one go. 'And the execution of that traitor Franek, do you remember?' Another glass was emptied. Two or three guests were collapsed on the rug; I never would have thought that my mother was capable of putting away that many drinks without passing out. My father didn't really participate in the celebration except in a minor way, and had the colonel not come up with the idea of entertaining the guests by getting me drunk, no one would have noticed my presence. The sole subject of conversation was my mother: her train trip from Warsaw to Kraków, from the Białystok ghetto to the Lublin ghetto. Her walk with the emissary sent by General Bór-Komorowski, the leader of the insurrection in the capital; a secret meeting with another emissary sent by Mordecai Anielewicz, the commander of the Warsaw Ghetto uprising. A thousand and one nights of flight, challenge, combat.

"Suddenly, a solemn silence fell, and the colonel turned to me. 'Do you know, child, that your mother was admired and loved by all the patriots, men and women, who fought under my command? Do you know that one day a bastard collaborator informed against her to the German police? When she was arrested, they found coded messages on her. She was tortured with inconceivable cruelty to get her to cough up names and addresses. But she kept her mouth shut. All those you see assembled here at the table took part in one of our most brilliant operations: we helped her escape. Drink up, child, drink to the glory of your mother!' I could hardly stand on my feet, and my father got up to protect me: 'He's too young, Colonel! One sip of our good vodka and he'll be rolling under the table! Don't turn him into a drunkard!'

"I looked away from my mother. The word *tortured* was stamped in my mind. In order to retain it, I imagined my mother as a ferocious and victorious warrior, and I felt better."

After a pause, Thérèse returns to the attack. "Continue. What happened next?"

"What happened? The first signs of an insidious anti-Semitic groundswell were becoming apparent in the country. The new regime set about de-Judaizing, albeit surreptitiously, the politics and history of Poland. The same colonel who had glorified my mother was ordered to play down her past as a Resistance fighter, 'rather nebulous' now, according to him. A German document, discovered recently in the archives, mentioned her name and reported her courage, described as 'criminal,' of course, by the Communists. Odd, all of that. They even went so far as to insinuate that because she had managed to escape from prison she had probably disclosed to her torturers the names of the patriots who were arrested in a subsequent operation. A Zionist envoy came to see us one evening and advised us that these events should be a lesson: 'You're no longer wanted here; it's time to go to Palestine.' It was completely illegal, but the Brikha, the mythical clandestine Jewish organization, would take care of everything; it had efficient branches in central Europe as well as in occupied Germany and Austria. My father was hesitant but my mother was enthusiastic.

"Such is the irony of fate, Doctor. If we had stayed in Poland instead of going to France, my parents might still be alive. As for me, I was intrigued less by my mother's elation than by my father's hesitation."

"What about Jacob?"

"My little brother? I think I already told you. He was dead by then."

"When? How?"

"You want me to repeat the story? One of my father's relatives knew Janusz Korczak. He got him to take Jacob into his house of children. Everyone knows that Korczak and all his little lodgers died in Treblinka.

"Do you miss your brother?"

"What kind of . . . indecent question is that? Of course I miss him."

"Tell me about him."

"No!"

"Why not?"

"Because it's none of your business."

"Everything is my business—everything that concerns you. I have to know everything."

"My little brother doesn't concern you."

"But he's part of your life, isn't he?"

"Don't make me angry, Doctor. My little brother deserves to be left in peace."

"But you think about it sometimes—"

"Be quiet, Doctor. Jacob is dead. He died far away from us, separated from me, an atrocious death. If you keep insisting, I'll get up and leave."

A long silence sets in.

"And what about Dina?" the doctor finally asks. "What happened to her?"

"There too, I told you. The Resistance. The underground. She was arrested and tortured. Put in a train going east. Escaped. Came home to us, in the village. Murdered by a bastard. A bullet in the head. One week before the liberation."

Thérèse turns the page of her notebook, then says, "You haven't said anything about your mother yet."

"I haven't? What more do you want? I told you that she is no longer with us."

"Tell me about your *deep* relationship with her."

She really goes too far. After being obsessed by my little brother, now she's obsessed by my mother again. Not my uncle, aunts, or father. The conversation is turning into a debate, the debate into a confrontation. She needs remembered incidents in my relationship with my mother; she demands details, even minor, frivolous ones. Did I really love her? Always? Only out of duty? Did I ever have arguments with her? If I did, over what? Did I find her beautiful? Seductive? How did she dress? Did she wear makeup? Did I ever see her in the middle of the night? How did she kiss me, on the forehead or on the cheeks? Do I still see her in my dreams? And what effect does it have on me when I wake up? No hint of sensuality? I'm beside myself with anger. Who does she think I am? Does she think I'm suffering from perverse senility? I barely lived with my mother. We lived apart for more than three quarters of my childhood; she had other business, as they say, namely, chasing Germans from Polish territory. My flare-up has no effect on my therapist. Calm, as usual, she points out to me that if I become irate, it means she has touched an obscurely alive and sensitive area of my memory. I resent her; I resent her teachers in psychoanalysis for bringing all problems, enigmas, afflictions, and secrets of human nature back to sexuality. She explains that she is duty-bound to follow all trails, even those that are paved with badly healed scars. I tell her to go to the devil.

"Exactly," she says. "I'll take you there." And immediately she adds: "I noticed a touch of annoyance when you described your mother's activities in the Resistance. Am I wrong? Wrong to deduce that you would have preferred she remain with you and your father? And share your long winter nights, your dangers, and your fears? Be hungry like you. Be in pain like you. Is it so inconceivable to think that a child would want to keep his mother next to his crib and his bed no matter what?"

"I'll let you determine what a child wants or doesn't want. But what a Jewish child wanted or feared in occupied Poland is something you'll never know. Don't try to violate her right to silence, Doctor. Even by putting the blame on me."

"You seem angrier and angrier."

I feel my blood boiling. "Yes, I am; how could I not be? You're taking a path that leads to dishonor, but don't try to drag me onto it! I'm warning you: you'll do it without me!"

"You're using a new, strong word—*dishonor*," Thérèse says. "I don't understand. What dishonor are we talking about, yours or your mother's? Do you reproach her for having abandoned you, you and your father? Or for something worse?"

I feel overcome with anger. "Now what are you driving at? I have no idea what you're alluding to, or what theory you're referring to. Why are you people so eager to make us feel guilty? Do you intend to repeat the lies of the Polish anti-Semites? How dare you?"

"In the Resistance, your mother didn't live alone. She had comrades, and not just women. Did you think about this later? Did it ever occur to you, even in a confused way, in your subconscious, that she might have met an exceptional man whose courage and strength she admired? And that maybe—"

In my indignation, I stand up to look directly in her face. "Stop! That's an order! My parents loved each other! They were a magnificent couple! If you dare pursue this angle, if you think you'll solve my personal problems by accusing my mother of I don't know what ugly, indecent thing, I'll leave you immediately—but not without having spit my contempt and rage in your face. Is that really your ultimate purpose?"

She shuts her notebook without saying a word.

As for me, I leave without even glancing at her, and with a bitter taste in my mouth.

*Don't hold it against me if I divulge too many details to you about my "conversations" with my therapist. Some of these will seem unpleasant to you. I don't hold it against her. She's doing her work, whereas I'm not doing mine. She told me several times that her aim was to "puncture the abscess." Whereas I'm trying to stop her. For her, it's like dealing with a boil. But we're dealing with something else, with an ailment for which no physician can give a precise diagnosis. What are we dealing with, then? I still don't know. But I know you have something to do with it—you, whom I love as much as my life. Perhaps one day, in a joint effort, we'll discover it, you and I. One day.*

Unhinged, perturbed, terrified: that's how I feel since my last visit to Dr. Thérèse Goldschmidt's. Could she have succeeded in sowing doubts in my mind? I try to recall and relive the period of my family's reunion in the summer of 1944. I describe it for her, though halfheartedly.

Were we happy? Absolutely, I swear it. Well, as happy as parents could be with their son after a tragedy has taken away those close to them, dead without burial. Did my parents love each other? Absolutely, I swear to that too. They loved each other as is possible only with human beings who have waited too long, with every last bit of strength in their body, to assert their faith in each other. Admittedly, there were sometimes heavy sorrowful or tense silences between them. These occurred most often in the evening, at the dinner table, or when we listened to music, if one of us accidentally mentioned Jacob's name, or Dina's, or if my father quizzed my mother about life in the underground. Once I heard him whisper, as if to justify himself: "If it hadn't been for the child, I would have gone everywhere with you, always, you know that." Later, when I remembered this, I realized that a child can be not just a source of joy but also an accumulation of obstacles. Had my mother been unfaithful during the war? I believe with all my heart that the reply can only be no. She loved me; she loved us too much; she had too much self-respect to jeopardize that love. However, an incident kept in the background, absurdly, resurfaces in my memory. And when I think about it, it makes me blush. It was in May 1946. A beautiful spring day. We were in our country house near Tomaszów. I was playing on the lawn. My father was resting under a blossoming locust tree, and my mother was reading, stretched out on a deck chair by his side, when the doorbell rang and gave them a start. Who could it be?

"Go open the door," my father said to me.

A young, well-dressed man, holding a bouquet of flowers in one hand and a book in the other, smiled at me. "I know who you are; you're Leah's son."

"How do you know?" I asked, stunned.

"Oh, I know a lot of things. It's my profession. I'm a journalist. Go and announce my presence to your parents, please."

"But . . . what's your name?"

"Romek. Tell them that Romek would like to see them."

"Do they know you?"

"Your mother knows me."

With that, he followed me to the garden. My father saw him and put down his newspaper. My mother jumped up from her deck chair and walked toward him, holding out her hand. "What are you doing here, Romek?" she asked. And, turning toward my father, she said pompously: "Come and see, a friend from the Resistance has come to visit us. He's a journalist. I told you about him."

My father stood up and shook hands with the visitor, with a courtesy that was not devoid of warmth. "All my wife's comrades are welcome in this house," he said. And after a pause, he went on: "But I didn't know you knew our address." Romek answered that Polish journalists have a reputation for being well-informed. My mother stammered a few words that I didn't grasp, but I saw that she was ill at ease. And my father too was embarrassed; that was unusual for him. I wasn't mature enough yet to know that adults are more secretive than children. We sat around the small table under the locust tree, and my mother went to fetch some cool drinks. It was very hot. The conversation began, a polite, almost banal conversation.

"I read your articles and editorials," said my father. "I prefer those that aren't about politics."

"Me too," Romek replied, with an air of feigned seriousness. "Unfortunately, everything nowadays is political, even the weather."

"Except for the fact that politics changes more quickly than the weather."

"Sometimes I wish I knew which of the two is most predictable."

"If I had to wager, I'd bet on the weather," said my father.

"And me on politics," said Romek.

"And we would both lose," my father said. "I wonder if we haven't already lost."

Romek stiffened. "What are you referring to?"

"As a journalist, you must be aware of the bad winds blowing in our country these days. May I be frank with you? You seem to be close to the authorities. Too close. If I were you, I'd be careful."

My mother returned with some lemonade. A brief silence settled in, interrupted by the chirping of birds too lazy to be flying. It was time to change the subject.

"If I understand correctly," said my father, "you worked in the

Resistance with Leah. In a way, you know things about her life that my son and I still don't know."

"Of course not," Romek protested. "We fought side by side, that's all. We confronted the same enemy, but not with the same temerity. When it came to daring, no one could equal Leah. Compared with her, even at the end, I felt like a beginner. In fact, that's what brings me here today."

My mother, who hadn't yet uttered a word, looked up, intrigued. Romek focused his gaze on my father: "I had the idea of doing a story on your wife, for the radio and my newspaper. She deserves it and so does the nation."

"And what would you tell?" asked my father.

"Her life story. What she fought for. Her patriotic idealism—"

"For example?"

Romek, who hadn't yet touched his drink, took a sip. Because he was thirsty? Or because he needed time to think? At random, he began to describe some dramatic episodes in which my mother had played a prominent role. The German officer she had lured into an ambush. The military pharmacy robbed in broad daylight (the Resistance was short of medicine). The speech given to her unit when it was preparing for the Warsaw insurrection.

"Oh, what a speech! What inspiration! What persuasiveness! You're too young, you probably don't realize it, but when your mother talks, she knows how to command obedience. She knew how to find the words that would inspire the fighters on the eve of the action. I remember some of the appeals she made in a calm and solemn voice: 'You know as well as I do who our enemies are. Bloodthirsty barbarians, bent on occupying our lands, destroying our homes, murdering our children. You've seen them at work; now they'll see what we're capable of. You'll show them your anger and you'll be justified. You'll deny them the right to pity and to life just as they denied their victims. If, to restore our honor, we have to kill or be killed, will you accept the terms of our oath?' And they all cried out at the top of their lungs: 'Yes, we accept them! Yes, we'll fight! Yes, we'll kill those who killed our people and humiliated us! Yes, we'll save our honor!' That's the story I feel like telling, but that's just one example among so many. The street fighting during the insurrection—she was there, on the front lines, under the machine-gun and heavy-artillery fire, intrepid, tireless, nursing the wounded, who blessed her as though she had the power to save their lives. So, what do you think of my project?"

My father quickly glanced at my mother. "What's your opinion?"

She stared straight ahead. Tense, lost in thought, she seemed to want to run away from the portrait Romek had just painted.

"Leah," said my father.

She pulled herself together.

"It doesn't appeal to me at all," she said finally. "War heroine? No, that's not a role for me."

"Don't you think it's our duty to bear witness for the sake of history?" Romek asked in a low voice.

"I did my duty by fighting; let others do theirs by bearing witness."

"But if we stay silent, others will speak in our place and say anything. They'll distort the truth—"

"They've already started," said my mother, interrupting him.

"And they'll fabricate even more," Romek went on. "The anti-Semites will call us liars, cowards—"

"Some already are," my mother said, interrupting him again.

"All the more reason to speak up loud and clear, to shout, intervene, set the record straight, take action . . ."

"What's the point?" asked my mother, losing her temper. "They'll always outnumber us; they'll always be more virulent and powerful."

The journalist lowered his voice again and went on in a near whisper: "Leah, I don't recognize you. You're Jewish; I'm Jewish. You are what you are, and me, I'm a journalist. You express in acts and I in words the loathsome, unspeakable things we lived through. We did so many things together in the name of truth, for the memory and honor of our people. And now, you refuse to fight, whereas I'm doing what I can. Who knows if tomorrow I'll still be able to. Are you in such deep despair?"

"Yes, I am," said my mother in a very low voice.

And suddenly I had the painful feeling that they were alone, she and Romek, since they were conversing in a language that rose before us—my father and me—like a wall.

How can I possibly not talk about these events?

EXCERPT FROM DR. THÉRÈSE GOLDSCHMIDT'S NOTES

Last night, I didn't sleep. I wonder if I'm not on the wrong track. Yet I saw Doriel's angry outburst as an encouraging sign. And particularly in the garden scene. In his unconscious relationship to his mother, the little boy inside him had remained tormented. We'll have to dig even deeper. After all, that's what analysis is all about: reality gushes forth like blood.

That day, in the family garden, Doriel must have noticed something serious, even shocking, whose significance had remained buried if not hidden inside him for years. Why was his mother so reserved, indeed ill at ease, in front of her former comrade-in-arms? Why had she stayed silent for so long and not taken part in the conversation between her husband and the journalist? Did that mean that, during the war, the two former Resistance fighters had been much closer—more intimate—and not just members of the same clandestine movement? At first sight, this was a plausible hypothesis. Two youths who are often living together, taking part in the same tragic events, initiating the same exploits, confronting the same dangers, and facing the possibility of prison, torture, or death, can easily abolish the boundaries that would separate them in normal times. Is an affair, even a brief one, unthinkable, inconceivable, and to be refuted with no further consideration? If so, war literature would find itself quite impoverished. When hatred wreaks havoc in the hearts of men, and death is busy filling up the cemeteries, faithfulness can attain its limits and frailties. Under these circumstances, in the eyes of the fighters, eternity is measured in days and hours; they might as well make the most of it.

This is probably the coded event that the analyst within me is looking for. At about four in the morning, I got up to go to my office and consult my notes. Martin joined me a short time later, bringing two cups of coffee.

"You're having trouble sleeping? Because of your privileged patient again?"

"Privileged but difficult, the most complex and resistant patient in my career. As soon as he gives me a key, he changes the lock."

"This must appeal to you," said Martin. "You hate things that are easy."

"True enough, but the distance between too easy and too difficult can be enormous, which is the case here."

As I was talking, I was leafing through my notes with one hand and stirring my coffee with the other.

"Here it is, the session when I gave him a bit of a rough time and drove him into a corner. I forced him to remember a painful episode: his mother's reunion with a possible or probable lover in his and his father's presence when he was a little boy. Of course, I expected him to react, but not so violently."

I described to Martin Doriel's behavior when he had calmed down. When I questioned him as to what he presently thought of Romek, he shrugged and said, "Oh, nothing, nothing special." And since I was insistent, he flew into a rage again. No longer in control of his movements or his language, he jumped up, trembling all over, eyed me scornfully as though I was his mortal enemy, began beating his chest, and stuttered some incoherent words: "He's a bastard, a traitor, a swindler. As soon as I saw him, I hated him; I'll always hate him, to the end of my days. He showed up with his hands full of thorns and an empty heart. Guilty of rape, he isn't human. You don't steal the mother of a child who is in hiding and pursued by a thousand policemen. I repudiate him as a human being just as he repudiated my father. I despise him for the contempt he showed my entire family. I curse him, but curses don't scare him, and justice even less. Now I understand some things better. His attitude toward me later. His generosity. His bequest. To make amends, to atone, that's what he hoped. But he demeans everything he touches. He wounded my mother and humiliated my father. As soon as I think of him, I feel humiliated too. He should have been ashamed. And you too. You want me to feel unworthy. You want to bring me down on my knees, my head bowed. I never should have come!"

"I'd never seen him in such a state," I said. "I tried in vain to calm him. The gentler I became, the more he unleashed his rage against the world and destiny."

"Do you think," Martin asked, "that he looked where he should not have? That he imagined the worst? That in his fantasies he saw his mother and her lover locked in an embrace, in the midst of—"

"I have no idea. Anything is possible. After all, he has a vivid imagination."

"You should be pleased nevertheless," Martin said. "You touched him on the spot that hurts him most. You just have to keep it up. At least now you know where you're going."

"No, I don't! That's the problem. Ignorance. It's odd, but the more I proceed with this case, the more I feel I lack knowledge and experience. With every new session, I feel less confident and less successful at figuring him out. I don't even know what he's suffering from anymore. And in what way his illness might be concealing an act and project that so elude him that they make his life a living hell."

Martin stood up. "I'm going back to bed," he said. "Aren't you? One piece of advice: don't get bogged down in his madness."

Disconcerted, I looked through my notes again. What did Martin mean? Was I really in danger? What danger? That of allowing my patient's transference of his love for his mother to me? And of his making me lose my reason, my intelligence, my sense of reality? Worse: Could I be in danger of cutting my ties with my surroundings? Of becoming estranged from my husband?

# 11

*I sleep badly. More and more so.*

*Do I have the right to disturb your sleep—you, whom I love?*

*You, who have always been asleep and will be forever?*

*I await the dawn, which will make all the demons return to their hells.*

*And images to their asylum.*

*And first among them, the image of that gray morning of the funeral.*

A huge crowd was there. I remember. Hundreds, thousands of men and women had come from the neighboring areas, and even from Paris, to accompany me to that cemetery near Marseilles. All of them angry with the English, whom they blamed for my parents' death. That was absurd, and they knew it. My parents had died in a car accident in the mountains. My father was driving and the car skidded. Her Majesty's government had nothing to do with it. But it was because of England's policies that Jews like us had to get across borders clandestinely and bribe policemen and the captains of barely seaworthy old ships to get to Palestine illegally. It was because of the English that a new pitfall awaited us at every turn. Hence the wrath of the crowd. Women cried, men shouted, rabbis prayed, orators spoke—not about my dead parents but about the right of our people to have a state, a homeland, a sanctuary. I didn't cry. Had my tears dried up? No, there was another reason: the rejection of reality. And maybe the first sign of a crack in me, of illness. I didn't believe that my parents were no longer with me. In spite of everything I was told, in spite of what my uncle Avrohom kept telling me while trying to teach me the difficult burial Kaddish, something within me refused to accept that it was my parents, my father and mother, who were to be buried before my eyes. "Cry," said my uncle. "Etch this gray and dark day in your memory just as it will be engraved here on this stone. Later you will think about it and your joy will no longer be unmixed. Cry, my child. You're an orphan now and will remain one all your life." In front of the open tomb, I had trouble reciting the prayer for the dead. The crowd thought it was because I was choked with tears. Actually no tears ran down my cheeks. And for a long time I felt at fault for my lack of sorrow.

The consequence of this tragedy was that I didn't leave for Palestine.

My uncle Avrohom was against it from the beginning. And not for political or economic reasons but for purely religious ones. Like some anti-Zionist rabbis, he declared that tradition prohibited hastening the course of events: when the Messiah came, he would establish the Jewish state according to the law and the spirit of the Torah. Not before. For him and his group, whoever violated this Talmudic precept was in fact excluding himself from the community of believing Jews. This attitude prevented disciples of their persuasion, living in Poland, Czechoslovakia, and Hungary, from being saved by accepting certificates allowing them to settle in the Holy Land.

There were stormy discussions, both public and private, between Avrohom and the heads of the Brikha, the Zionist organization that opened frontiers and the doors of international offices as by an illusionist's magical gesture. I heard them shout without understanding their arguments. "But his parents were preparing for the Aliyah with their child. What right do you have to go against their wish?" yelled one of the Zionists.

"If they were still alive," said Avrohom, "I would have persuaded them."

This lasted for hours, night after night. The Zionists had called on their own religious teachers, whereas Avrohom received the support of his. The leader of the Zionists, a tall redhead, acted as if he was addressing the United Nations.

"After what our people have gone through, at a time when the survivors of the worst tragedy no longer know where to go for a bit of rest and respite, you're going to tear this child away from his larger family?"

"And what about God in all this? The God of Israel? Have you forgotten Him?" asked Avrohom.

The redhead: "You dare to invoke God? Here? Now? But where was He when we needed His kindness, His justice, His power?"

Avrohom: "He was with us. Like us, He suffered! Like us, He had had enough of the murderous secular humanity!"

The redhead: "You must be joking! A God who is the prisoner of child murderers! And you still believe in Him!"

"Ungodly person," Avrohom said, beside himself with anger, "leader of the ungodly, you're blaspheming! And you want me to entrust my nephew to you? Never, do you hear me? Never! If you want a Jewish state, return to the faith of our ancestors; apologize to them for having deserted them! Implore them to intercede for us on high, and you'll have your national home!"

It was discussed in the Yiddish newspapers, whose over-politicized readership got carried away for one side or the other. Here and there, rioting broke out between demonstrators and counterdemonstrators. No one had thought of asking me where I wanted to go. I didn't count. You'd almost think I existed as a mere prop, as a propaganda tool. But what if they had asked me? I think I would have opted for Palestine, but I'm not sure—I had no family there; I didn't know Hebrew. In fact, I had no will or consciousness. Alarmed, I floated in the air, with no friends, no ties, no security net whatsoever. In a way, I was absent, as if dead. Dead with my parents. Finally the authorities intervened. They decided that since Avrohom was my uncle, he had the law on his side. He took me to the United States, whereas I had left Poland to go to Haifa and Mount Carmel.

And because of that too, I don't know why, I felt at fault.

I often discussed religious faith with my uncle. Naturally, he wanted to give me the same education he received as a youth in Poland. A yeshiva in Brooklyn agreed to instruct me free of charge. But I wasn't ready. Avrohom insisted and I resisted. So he begged my aunt Gittel to argue his case. He knew that I liked her. There was an understanding between us that was hard to define. Discreet, timid, she had a gentle voice but a gaze that could become stern on occasion. I liked to watch her light the Sabbath candles. She told me to come closer, and for the first time, she stroked my hair.

"Your uncle treats you like a son."

"I'm not your son," I replied. "I had parents. They're dead, I know. But I'm still their son."

Her smile was so fragile that it moved me. "I didn't say we were your parents; I said you were *like* a son."

I lowered my head silently. She went on in the same intimate tone of voice. "Your parents are dead and I don't know why. Maybe we have no right to look for a reason."

"Would you be angry if I looked anyway?"

"No, I wouldn't be angry. But your teachers will show you how and where to look. And most important, until when, so you don't go beyond the limit."

"Do you think they know?"

"They probably know the question."

"Do you know it?"

"Yes, I do."

"Tell it to me."

"Why were your parents killed? Why did the Lord—blessed be His name—punish them? For what sins?"

"And the answer?"

"I told you, I don't know." She remained silent for a few moments. "I think that in the eyes of the Lord there's an answer; there must be one. But . . ."

"But what?"

"There's worse. Let's say they were punished for having sinned. But why were you punished? That I'll never understand."

She fell silent, and I noticed a tear running down her hollow cheek.

It was because of my aunt, and for her sake, that I agreed, though halfheartedly, to go to the yeshiva.

Wasn't that madness?


From my few years of Jewish studies—intense at first and too drawn out in the end, though never sufficiently fruitful—I retain a mixture of curiosity, weariness, and momentary bedazzlement. I remember my classmates better than my tutors. The latter, for the most part, were too interested in my literal studies and not enough in the frustration growing in me day after day. For them, only the distant past contained the meaning of life. The fleeting present was its shell or bark and to be rejected. The same applied to politics and fashion—puerile enterprises to be looked upon with disdain. Fortunately, my friends and I talked about everything. Current events, sports, vacation. Girls? Allusively, perhaps. Like the bygone prophets, I experienced the wrenching distress of living in two worlds. I can imagine you nodding: yes, the therapist must be right; *schizophrenic* is the suitable word for him. Like the sad and courageous Mr. Job, I cursed the day I was born. I resented the one responsible for dropping me down on this earth where everything begins in doubt and ends with the victory of death. Would I have preferred to be born somewhere else, in another family? Let's say I would have preferred not being born at all. But what about the soul, as the great teachers of the tradition would say, what about that? After all, it can't keep wandering in the invisible higher spheres until the end of time. That was its problem, not mine. I refused to suffer the consequences of the acts of my distant ancestors. Abraham didn't ask me whether he should obey the Lord and sacrifice his eldest son to Him. And King Ezekiel didn't ask my opinion before deciding to go to war with the Babylonians. And Don Itzhak Abrabanel didn't consult me as to whether he was right to go into exile rather than convert. My past had been their present; they alone were responsible for it, as far as I know. Well, I wanted to be responsible only for my present.

I don't know what my aunt and uncle wanted me to become. (I'm not talking about the years that followed my meeting with Romek's brother, Samek; I'm talking about earlier, when I still had money worries.) A community rabbi, like their elder son, Shmouel? Copy editor in a publishing house of holy books? Son-in-law of a wealthy financier like their youngest son, Yaakov? The sons treated me like a privileged member of the family. I got along well with them. On holidays, they joined us for the services and the meals. I liked their young sister: petite, agile, with a ringing, slightly provocative laugh, Ruth had a biting sense of humor, though it wasn't offensive. Under other circumstances, if she hadn't been engaged to a brilliant Talmudist from a California yeshiva, I could have fallen in love with her. I had the impression she resembled my mother slightly from the youthful photos I had seen of her. I felt closer to her than to my paternal uncle. When Avrohom looked at me, he saw someone else, or in any case he didn't just see me alone. His eyes told me so. He constantly tried to find someone on my left, on my right, or in back of me. Was it my dead parents that attracted his attention? Sometimes I had a feeling he knew a secret that concerned me. Late one evening, when we were alone at the dinner table, he seemed about to reveal it to me. At the last minute, he changed his mind. I had to wait until he died to find out more.

I had strange relationships with my classmates, particularly the first year. Sometimes I was too assiduous, sometimes much less so. I was already unstable and subject to unpleasant mood shifts. At the very beginning, probably to please my aunt and uncle, I devoted my days and evenings to prayer, meditation, and the study of the holy texts. "You need a friend," Avrohom used to say to me. "You're not supposed to study alone in a yeshiva." I found one: Jonathan. He was my age, clumsy, awkward, and looked permanently lost. In what way were we different? He adored the teaching of the laws and their interpretation, whereas I preferred the midrashic legends and their spare, concise, succinct style. Sometimes, in the evening, after dinner, we met at the study house. Inspired hours, shared dreams under the sign of friendship.

"You and your stories," Jonathan used to say to me in a tone of feigned exasperation. "You know too many of them; you become attached to them; they've already imprisoned you. Eventually they'll be the ruin of you. Stories are dangerous; even the most beautiful come with arrows, and you don't know that you're the target."

"You're exaggerating. My stories don't scare me at all. They come from anywhere, from somewhere or nowhere, and I catch them, that's all. Do you remember Rabbi Nahman's captivating words? He compares the *yetzer hara,* the spirit of evil, to a man who lives with a clenched fist. People think he's hiding a treasure inside it, and they try to pry it open. A long struggle ensues and the man finally opens his fist of his own will; it is empty."

"Another one of your parables," said Jonathan. "Can't you live and express yourself like everyone else? Why do you try to be different, always distant, wrapped in a world that others don't have access to, not even me? You need only touch something and it catches fire. You just say good evening and the words take on I know not what mystery. Am I your friend or not? I'm afraid for your soul and also for your mental equilibrium."

In fact, Jonathan was right to worry about the salvation of my soul. But if I am endangering it, it isn't because of my stories. There came a time when I inevitably realized that I was wasting my time and, above all, my raison d'être by remaining on the yeshiva benches. Little by little, I realized that some rabbinical laws, though full of meaning for those who love them, leave me shockingly indifferent. Deepening the commentaries of rules concerning old-fashioned, antiquated rites, considered relevant even though the temple had been in ruins for centuries, its altar demolished, its priests scattered, its cantors idle and silent, the questions and moral dilemmas they posed no longer brought much stimulation to my mind.

Several classmates and I—though not Jonathan—started going to the occasional daring film and reading forbidden secular books: novels, literary and philosophical essays, and various subversive works verging on Bible criticism. Was it the fault of my teachers? More likely it was my own. An inevitable crack in my faith? A badly healed childhood wound? My mind awakening to the practice of doubt? Excessively strict habits becoming shaky, old uprooted customs becoming loose and irresolute; more and more, I was drifting away, as they say, from some aspects of our ancestors' religion.

You know the arguments. How can one believe that the universe is no more than six thousand years old when there's scientific proof showing the opposite? How can one keep on thanking God for His blessings when His creatures are killing one another off in His name and proclaiming they love Him? And why would my prayers and praises be so important to Him? Whether I recite them or forget to recite a few, why would that so affect

Him that he would inflict reprimands and sufferings on me? How is one to love a God who needs so much flattery? Was I already vulnerable, a victim of my questionings and my doubts?

And besides, let's be frank. As always, as in every story, there was a woman. Yes, in spite of the stifling ultraorthodox ambience in which I was growing up, indeed perhaps because of it, my adolescent body found it difficult to resist desire. I blushed when my cousin Ruth talked to me. One day, we were alone for a short fifteen minutes. She had come to see my aunt Gittel, who had not yet returned from the market. Distraught, prompted by a sense of unknown danger, I felt my heart thumping as if it was about to burst. Ruth didn't notice. She asked me what I was doing. I replied that I was getting ready to go out.

"To go where?"

"To the study house," I lied.

"Is it that urgent?"

"Yes," I replied. "They're waiting for me."

"Who is waiting for you so urgently?"

"Jonathan."

"He can surely wait."

"No . . . Maybe . . ."

"Stay with me a little while."

"Wh . . . why?" I stammered.

"What a question!" she answered with a mischievous glint in her eyes. "Just to keep me company."

This was my first time alone with a woman. We remained standing in the middle of the room, close to the table where I sometimes did my homework. She looked at me in her usual way, smiling. And I had no idea where to go to hide my feeling of helplessness. More than ever my body asserted its rights: my chest, my eyes, my legs, my hands, my every limb wanted to participate in my inner upheaval. As for Ruth, she was relaxed and natural. "I hope I'm not disturbing you," she said.

"No, of course not."

"Are you always alone at this time of the morning?"

Why this question? "Yes. Often," I said, "when Aunt Gittel goes to market."

"So, every day?"

Why this question? I couldn't understand. "Yes, I think so."

Should I remind her that she had a fiancé? Aunt Gittel's appearance put an end to our conversation. But now I know that my break with the teachings of the tradition coincided with the onset of the agitation I felt in my cousin's presence.

EXCERPT FROM DR. THÉRÈSE GOLDSCHMIDT'S NOTES

Doriel Waldman's crises and their language. Semantic jargon? Bouts of paraphasia?

"Do you like to eat?" I ask.

"The bark more than the tree," he responds.

"Do you like to drink?"

"The tree is thirsty and I swallow the rain."

"And then what? What happens next?"

"Time pursues the words; the words fall to their knees."

"Who is your enemy?"

"The face of the faceless person has stolen mine."

"What do you hate?"

"Two times three equals a baby's smile."

"Do you like to read?"

"The clouds drift away and I'd like to follow them."

"Do you like music?"

"Oh, the vagabond who winks at me is nuts."

"What about painting, are you interested in it?"

"With my finger I am the clouds and I become a cloud."

"And the rain, do you like it?"

"The angel that is tracking me down is black and dazzling."

"And the devil, what does he look like?"

"Finally two times seven equals fourteen."

"That's correct. How did you get that?"

"It's so simple, Doctor. Three times Sunday and four times Tuesday equals fourteen."

Should I have a neurologist colleague examine him? A doubt crosses my mind. What if this is just a game for him? The patient starts laughing; he isn't exhausted, but I am. Perhaps because I don't feel like laughing.

# 12

At times, in an involuntary and unpredictable way, everything spins around and becomes dislocated in my mind. At the slightest little thing, and often for no apparent reason, I weep without shedding tears and I roar with laughter. I'm lonely, terribly lonely, though a crowd surrounds me and hems me in. I see men eat when they're thirsty and drink when they're hungry. They walk around naked in winter and too warmly dressed when it's stiflingly hot. The old men play with hoops and the children pray like old men. And the words in my mouth no longer like one another; dissonant, disfigured, bloody, they refuse to be grouped together. Taken in isolation, each one has a meaning, but together they have no meaning. As a result, I'm no longer stretched out on the therapist's couch but on the wing of an eagle that is carrying me to treetops high above the stars. Behind me, a huge crow is trying to catch us. He is holding my head in his beak. I feel like screaming, but no sound comes out of my tight throat. I feel like keeping quiet, and I hear myself speaking but in the language of birds. I ask the crow why he's pursuing me; he replies in the language of humans that I'm mistaken, he's the one fleeing, not me; I'm pursuing him. I ask the eagle where he's taking me, and he replies, in his own language, that he's bringing me to the place where all languages fuse into a beautiful, beneficial flame. I tell him I don't understand, so then he ruffles his wings and threatens to get rid of me if I keep bothering him with my childish talk. I challenge him: let him dare separate himself from me, let him dare; without me he would die. To punish me, he flutters and lo and behold he falls, while I keep flying like a king through the distant skies.

Frowning and looking absorbed, Thérèse is taking notes quickly so as not to miss anything. After a pause, she asks: "As you see it, which one is you: the crow or the eagle?"

"I don't see any difference."

"Come on, seriously. Don't tell me that the two birds are alike."

"No, I won't say that. All I'll say is this: for me it's the same whether I identify with one or the other."

"Do you like birds?"

Her question is a slap in the face. She has a knack for touching a hidden wound.

"There was a time, Doctor, when I loved birds. Actually, I envied them."

"You see? We're on the right track. It might lead us to an explanation of your . . . illness."

She's getting on my nerves. I'm talking about birds and she about illness. If she persists along these lines, I'll say good-bye. What's the use of wasting my time, lying here like an idiot?

"Shut your eyes," says her voice, and I can't decide if it's the voice of the eagle or the crow.

"Okay, my eyes are shut."

"What do you see?"

"Good God, are you kidding me? What can I possibly see, since my eyes are shut?"

"Where are you right now?"

"In your office, if I'm not mistaken."

"Think about the birds and tell me where you are. And why you envied them."

Okay, she succeeded in bringing me back to the Polish village where I lived with my father. I see myself in the house that sheltered us. Most of the time, we had to remain inside. The tiniest slipup could attract an informant's attention. Summer, of course, was more dangerous than winter. People stayed outside longer and could be strolling around anywhere. Also, our host, Vladek, forbade us from going near the windows. "You never know who might see your reflection or shadow," he said. But one morning we had a visitor anyway: a bird dropped in unexpectedly. He stood at the window ledge and watched us, very intently, as though he had no other occupation in life. A strange thought popped into my mind: he's a traitor, an informer; he wants his reward. That's the kind of world we live in; birds too are our enemies. In spite of Vladek's warning, I went up to the window and told the bird he was disturbing me; I begged him to leave us alone: we've done you no harm—be nice, little bird, go away. But instead of flying off and joining his flock, he smiled at me. So I told my father that I envied this creature. Looking up from the book he was engrossed in, he stared at the motionless bird, who stared right back.

"Because he's free?" my father asked.

"No," I replied. "I envy him because he isn't human."

I stop talking. The therapist doesn't reprimand me. She puts away her notepad and says today's session is over: "We'll try to find your birds again next time."

Next time? The birds have never left me.

Their gazes are our prayers.

*It is your gaze I like. It appeals to me. I am writing to it. I'm convinced, foolishly, that my words are inscribed in it. One day I'll read them back out loud. For you. To see you smile. And I will tell you—no, I'll tell you now: don't be too frightened of what will happen to us. I'm telling you about my past so you won't be frightened.*

Those years of isolation, anguish, and exile, as you call the years I lived in that Polish village, you're asking me to describe them to you, is that it? The village noises used to come to us from afar: drunkards singing, neighbors quarreling, the moans of beaten wives and children, the drumroll preceding official decrees. Sometimes, all of this seems to me just one long night broken up by my mother's brief appearances. Like my father, I read a great deal, often with him. And I was even more silent, on our land-lord's strict orders. Noise was another one of our enemies: to avoid making any, I acted mute for days and nights, especially when Vladek had visitors, so much so that I sometimes was afraid of having lost the power of speech. If I'd been asked what I planned to do on the day of liberation, I would have answered: shout, shout with all my might, tell the world that I'm me, and though the world may be deaf, I'm not mute.

During that whole time, my father took care of me. I don't know who taught him to sew the buttons on my shirt, to prepare cold meals, to nurse the colds I used to catch at the first winter winds.

He also watched over my education. Whispering in a calm but fervent voice, he taught me some Yiddish, Polish, and Hebrew texts. He read to me in the evening, by the light of an oil lamp. And when we were too afraid to light the lamp, he told me stories in the dark, stories in which the innocence of children and the madness of the sages helped God save His Creation.

Too long or too short, the seasons affected my mood. How does one live through a stretch of time where nothing happens? Between sleep and wakefulness, no event came to sustain my memory. In the beginning, to keep busy, I counted my respira-tions and blinks. Then I began to dream with my eyes open. I succumbed easily, too easily, to depression and anger. The songs of summer, the snowfalls of winter. The purity of spring, the autumn mud. The days came and went, chasing or embracing the fugitives of the night.

I remember, with nostalgia, the solitude shared with my father. I then feel gripped by a powerful though subtle emotion. He had only me, and I had only him. When I think of the succession of hours and nights, I see the traces on his face. The hunger that racked my stomach was his as well. He was the beginning and end for me. My unspoken dream? Becoming a child again so I would not have to suffer the shame of adults.

I remember a summer day when we were almost arrested. We were in the attic because our host was expecting relatives. "Be careful," he warned us. "Don't move. Don't talk. Wait until the people are gone. But if a kid wanders into forbidden territory by chance, give him a thrashing and knock him unconscious. Got it? Afterward, I'll teach him to forget."

Unfortunately, what he feared did come about. While the adults were feasting, a little imp came nosing around in the attic. I have no idea what he was looking for. Maybe he suspected something. He came in, sniffed left and right, poked the straw next to the door, and left.

We had a narrow escape.

"What would we have done if he had discovered us?" I asked my father.

"We would have beaten him."

"To death?" I whispered, holding my breath.

"No. Only enough to make him forget."

Then he added: "I could never kill. And surely not a child."

What about me, I thought in my foolish little head; could I?


"I know, Doctor, I'm aware of it: I talk a lot about my father and not enough about my mother. Don't conclude from that that I didn't love her. Don't try to put everything on her back or mine. Don't go searching in me—a person who hasn't studied Freudian or Lacanian theory—for complexes that exist only in your convoluted therapist's mind. I'll have you know I loved my mother and still love her. But, what can I say, the war and the accident amputated my life. Is it my fault that I lived for too brief a time with my mother? You ask me whether I feel I didn't see her often enough during the occupation? Indeed, she didn't visit often. And when she did, it was only for a few hours. She stayed one night, never more. Each time, she arrived late in the evening, exhausted. She knocked at the door, using the agreed-on signal: three knocks, then two, then four. She stopped at the doorstep to look at me before turning to my father. Whether summer or winter, she always wore the same coat and the same dress. At each visit, she seemed smaller and frailer. She kissed us both, me on my cheek, my father on his neck. I saw her cry only once. Sitting apart in a corner, my father was quizzing her about her activities; she explained that she wasn't allowed to tell him: if he was arrested, he might speak under torture. The Resistance would have to bear the consequences that it was best to avoid. My father reproached her, smiling: 'So if I understand correctly, you're hiding some things about your life from us, right?'

"My mother burst into tears: 'You suspect me of not being faithful to you two,' she said, sobbing. My father managed to calm her, but for a long time I resented him for having made my mother so unhappy.

"I feel you're listening more attentively, Doctor. What interests you? My mother's grief or the worry I shared with my father? Don't tell me you sense a crack in our family life. And because of my mother's possible misconduct? I forbid you! True, I sometimes look like I'm losing my temper. But it's because you provoke me. I have no idea what you're driving at, what misdeed you're trying to uncover, and by whom. But I order you to stop this indecent game; I won't play it anymore. You'd like to know whom I'd like to protect, my father or my mother? Well, I'd answer that they both deserve my protection, and besides, it's none of your business."

I raise myself on my elbows and glance at the therapist quickly; she seems pleased with herself.

She is smiling.

Later, I learned many things about my parents. Of the two, my mother impressed people most. She knew what had to be done and how to do it. She was decisiveness itself. Most often, my father didn't even try to argue. No doubt because she had worked in the Resistance and he had not. But why had she? Because she was blond and attractive. She could easily pass for Aryan, whereas he, with his brown hair and sad brown eyes, looked more Jewish. But it was my father who found the peasant Vladek who agreed to house us for an exorbitant rent.

I remember the good man. Actually, Vladek was good only when he received his zlotys. He had a wife and two children, a boy and a girl. I never saw his wife full-face; I only heard her through the wall. As for the children, I used to see them playing in the courtyard. It was they who were the greatest threat to us; they were capable of unintentionally discovering our subterranean cubbyhole or the barn we used as a hiding place. For me, being little, this wasn't so painful; but for my father, it was. He was crouched for hours, and it was hard for him to move his head. For me, the silence was intolerable. In fact, after the war, my father remained slightly stooped, whereas I remain haunted by the silence.

We would hide in the storage room only when policemen, Germans, suspicious people, or nosy neighbors were in the area, no doubt searching for Jews like us. I've forgotten why, but this happened particularly in the spring.

One day, again I don't remember when, I saw an incident that could have turned into a disaster. Vladek appeared and started to argue with my father about raising the cost of our accommodations. "You have to understand," he said, "your presence here endangers us all, my wife and my children too." My father replied that he wasn't rich; he had just enough money to honor his commitment, no more. The peasant was annoyed: "And what if the war lasts for years, will you be rich enough to continue paying me?" My father answered that the war wouldn't last much longer; the Allies and the Russians were more powerful than Germany. The argument continued in this hostile vein until Vladek shouted: "If you don't accept my conditions next month, I can't guarantee anything." It was clear: he was going to throw us out or inform on us.

By chance, my mother came to see us two or three weeks later. My father told her what had happened. Though worried, she reassured him: "Leave it to us."

My father asked: "Who do you mean by 'us'?"

As always, she gestured to convey what she used to repeat over and over: "It's best for you not to know."

The important thing was that the peasant stopped making demands and threats. Later I learned what had happened: a comrade in the Resistance went up to him one Sunday as he was coming out of church and whispered in his ear to leave us alone. "If you start again or if your lodgers fall into the clutches of the Gestapo, we'll set your house on fire with you and your family inside it. You know we mean it."

The comrade in question? Romek.


"Some human beings are born old. Others live and experience anguish and happiness before being born. Then they forget everything and spend their lives trying to remember. That's sort of what's happening to me, Doctor. Oh, I know what you're thinking: Lo and behold, my patient has gone stark raving mad! But I know that; I knew that long before you. Otherwise, what would I be doing here, stretched out on your uncomfortable couch like a lazy fool? However, the sentence I just cited isn't my own, it's from the Talmud. And I find it suitable, except for the last part: I try to forget sometimes, whereas you do everything to tear down the walls of oblivion. Who will win the fight? All I know for sure is the loser will be me.

"I've been a loser since the day I followed my parents' coffins to the little country cemetery overlooking the sea near Marseilles. I was eleven years old. It was during the High Holy Days of 1947. The weather was still beautiful. Avrohom held my hand. The place radiated peacefulness. The wind rustled the fir trees, informing the golden leaves that the cold would be returning; trembling, they seemed to say to the wind: give us some respite, go away, allow us to enjoy the last rays of the sun. Sometimes the wind brushed against my face too, but I couldn't understand its message.

"One week after the funeral, in other words, after the *shiva,* there was a ceremony during which my name was mentioned more often than my parents'. When they spoke, the Zionist leaders thundered against the English: 'It's because of them and their anti-Jewish politics that this innocent little boy is now an orphan,' shouted Giora, their leader. A friend of Avrohom's, wearing felt hat and caftan, beseeched the Lord to take me under His protection, for wasn't He 'the protector of widows and orphans'? This time again, the event ended with my reciting the Kaddish.

"The sky was light blue and reassuring. There was no wind that day. Appeased, the earth had welcomed my dead without wounding them; they had been wounded enough during the accident in their smashed-up car. Avrohom had stayed by my side every second during the week of mourning. Now time was going to become a thing that had to be weighed, examined, questioned, and that we would try to tame and love.

"When the week of mourning was over, I got up like an invalid in need of crutches. Avrohom questioned me on my recollections. He wanted to know everything. Everything about my parents, whom he had never met. Were they practicing Jews? Were they happy? When did they laugh heartily and when did they think things over in a low voice? I described such moments as clearly as I could, but I didn't mention the incident that had made my mother cry.

"And I regret I told you about it, Doctor."

"Why, Doriel? Why this fierce desire to leave a minor, insignificant incident shrouded in secrecy . . . except if it conceals something that frightens or shames you?"

Suffocating with anger, I remain silent until the end of the session.

"It's been almost three weeks since you last came to see me. Is it because you've been feeling very well or very ill?"

"I don't see anyone. I'm not myself."

"I see you. Does that bother you?"

"An old man treading on his violin strings, that's what."

"And he doesn't slip?"

"A child smiles and the rain answers him."

"And he doesn't get wet?"

"A young woman becomes old, and the earth turns around her mangled body."

"And she doesn't weep?"

"An acrobat goes down on his knees to pray, and the funeral continues."

"And the dead man lets it go on?"

"A beggar collapses under the weight of his desires."

"And he still has hopes?"

"The gods become angry, and the soul starts singing a song that makes the grass grow."

"And the skies become clouded over?"

"The sun goes out, and the madman becomes drunk on its deadly rays."

"And what do you do to find peace again?"

"I feel my destiny crumbling away."

"And what else?"

"Someone is walking backward and I feel drained."

"But you came back. That's good."

"Came back from where—who can tell me? Someone who wasn't with me, where is he now?"

# 13

Jonathan was my friend. A friend in whom I could confide my doubts and fears. But at one point, the complicity we shared vanished. What came between us? This will make you laugh: neither the ambition to succeed nor the intentional transgression of the daily commandments, but God—it was God Himself who suddenly intervened between my friend and me. And once again, a woman played a part as well.

One morning, contrary to her habit, Ruth burst into the dining room without knocking. I was there poring over an obscure passage in an ancient text; the passage was giving me trouble, and this irritated me. It concerned the suffering of the Messiah that only man could cure, in every generation. Jonathan and I had already discussed it the day before, and I said to myself that we would do well to discuss it again in the afternoon. A recent article on mysticism's predominant role in modern thought and fiction might be of help. A complicated hypothesis that was not necessarily convincing: noting the failure of Western culture as an ethical response, men living in the Auschwitz era inevitably turn to the other side, the side of mysticism. The unspoken attracts them more than the clearly articulated. They postulate that the mystery of the end is conditioned by the mystery of the beginning. Pure wisdom resides in the before, not the after. In trying to smash the very tools of literary expression, we formulate, on our own level, the Kabbalistic conception of shattered vases *(Shevirat HaKelim)* that accompanied the Creation. Such is the dreadful power of man according to a German mystic of the early Middle Ages; he can use it to understand and to stop understanding, seize the being locked inside the moment and also liberate him without realizing that this twin approach is always about his own self. He has been given the power of getting a step closer to heaven, but he can't prevent heaven from receding.

When I was interrupted by Ruth's arrival, my thoughts became muddled. Yet, unconsciously, I was waiting for her. Lately, she had been coming to her parents' house several times a week and always when I was alone. Usually she stayed near the door, as if to preserve a certain distance between us. This time she came closer, stood by my side, gazed at me fixedly, and asked if she was preventing me from studying. I was about to mumble, "No, not at all," but then said, "Yes, very much so."

She gave a faint smile and said, "That's good," in an almost inaudible voice, so intimate that it sent a shiver down my spine. She leaned toward me and whispered, "Let's see, what book are you so completely engrossed in?"

I stammered a few incoherent words; my chest felt crushed by an iron fist. I scanned my mind for an appropriate reply—to no avail. I felt myself blush as if my teacher had guessed that my soul was dangerously close to the precipice. In another second, Ruth's beautiful face would be close to mine. My breathing stopped. What would she do or say? One question, she asked me one tiny question: "And where does love fit in?" She wanted to know my thoughts on the subject. Nothing more. I felt clumsy and ignorant. What answer could I make up? True, love was mentioned in the texts I was studying, but only one kind of love. God commands us to love Him. But a woman? A woman can be innocent yet bewitching. As I wasn't answering, she pursued her cross-examination in a more and more pressing voice: "Have you ever loved, I mean loved a woman, a woman like me?"

I'm done for, I said to myself; I felt I was going to be spirited away by the thousand and one demons populating hell. Fortunately, I heard the front door. In a flash, Ruth stood straight and changed her expression to welcome her mother: "I was waiting for you," she said. As for me, I plunged back into my book, hoping that all this had been nothing but a dream, soon to be dissipated, and whose effects would remain invisible. The two women retired to the kitchen. One second later I went out to meet Jonathan. Would he be able to guess what had just happened to me? I decided not to tell him anything.

But in the course of the afternoon, I interrupted our study and asked: "What do you think of sin?"

"Which sin?"

"Any sin. At which point does a thought gone astray or a repressed desire become a sin?"

"For example?"

In order to avoid mined territory, I answered: "The existence of God. Imagine someone who begins to doubt, who is afraid that he is losing his faith but continues to practice the mitzvoth; is he a sinner?"

"I don't know what to answer. To live without faith is inconceivable to me. God is God and He is everywhere, both in the stars and in the dust. How can one imagine His nonexistence?"

"But if God is everywhere, hence in our acts as well, and in our thoughts, how can our instincts, our failings be explained?" I asked.

"One day, we'll study Maimonides, the Prague Maharal, the philosophers. For the moment, I'll say to you that in my opinion God knows all the answers. Or better: God is the universal answer to all questions."

I remarked to myself: there are men who have a thousand things to conceal; I have only one. Then Ruth burst into my mind again, and I decided to change the subject.

The next day, I sat down to work again alone in the dining .

room. But I realized that I was waiting for Ruth. And it was while waiting for her that I lost my innocence. It's so simple and obvious: as a result of waiting, I forgot God, and He too is supposed to be waiting for us.

Could He have forgotten too?

At that point, the door opened and Ruth entered, holding a basket of cherries. As usual, she remained standing, a faint smile on her lips. Aware that I was blushing, she lowered her eyes. I felt distraught, unrecognizable to myself. Every limb in my body disowned me. However, Ruth continued to look at me, while her smile became more marked and pensive. I felt like telling her that I thought she was beautiful, as beautiful as the biblical Sarah and Rachel, Jacob's beloved, King Solomon's Sulamite, my only points of reference when it came to beauty, but I didn't dare. I felt like telling her that she moved me, but I didn't know how to. The pregnant silence became unbearable. It was she who broke it. "What are you thinking about?"

Should I admit that I was thinking about her? That I'd thought of nothing else but her since the day before?

"I'm studying."

"What are you studying?"

"The Midrash."

"What part of the Midrash?"

"The problem of redemption."

"I knew it was a promise; I didn't know it was a problem."

"It's both."

"Isn't it one or the other?"

"Oh, that would take too long to explain," I said.

"We have time. My mother went to see a sick friend; she won't be back until the afternoon." She stopped, breathing quickly. "We're alone," she said.

All of a sudden, I was overcome with panic. Imperceptibly, Ruth's face came closer to mine. Stupidly, stammering, like a lunatic, I started repeating what Jonathan and I had learned those last few weeks: the goal of man isn't just to free himself of the evil that threatens him and entraps him; he must also end the exile of the Jewish people and all peoples by hastening the arrival of the Messiah. How is that to be accomplished? Nothing is easier: by restoring to Creation, through moral acts, its original equilibrium, in other words, its purity.

She gazed at me at length and started to laugh.

"And here I was, convinced you were thinking about me!" she said. "And what if I told you that I need to free myself too?"

I held my breath; it's better to keep silent. And Ruth went on. "You and your friend, and my father, and your teachers, you think you're the only ones who want to save the world? There are people who claim you're on the wrong track. I was told about a young Polish Jew, before the war, the son of a rich merchant, who worked toward the same goal. He was a Communist."

"I don't understand: Jewish and a Communist? Can the two go together?"

"It seems that in the past, yes. This young Jew came home one evening and just declared that God did not exist and that the world would be freed when all men realized it."

"Ridiculous," I said. "For any society, denying the existence of God can only bring about even greater oppression, brutality, cruelty—"

"I agree with you. Only—"

"Only what?"

"If God's existence implies that we must obey His laws and if these laws forbid me to love, what should I do?"

What did she expect from me? That I cut myself loose from the discipline that binds me to Moses? That I free her from her ties? From her fiancé, perhaps? I was more naïve than she, and weaker. Immersed in matters of the soul, I knew nothing of the mysteries of the body, mysteries that she must have known. Here she was leaning over me, and I didn't know how to behave. I didn't stand up and run away. She was very close and I remained seated. She came closer still, and my head burst. She extended her hand to me. Since I didn't react, she seized mine.

"We're alone," she whispered in my ear. "Alone in the house. Alone in a world that tells us not to be afraid." Still whispering, she pressed her lips against mine. "We're mad," she said, "and that's good. Let's give thanks to this holy madness. It offers our bodies their due by making us free and triumphant."

A thought stabbed me like the blade of a knife: if this continues, I'll have to suffer the trials of hell. But it didn't continue. It was Ruth who put an end to the ordeal. She released me and began to laugh.

"You see? Heaven isn't up there; it is here, and I can create it, with your body and mine." She continued to laugh and handed me a few cherries. "Taste them; they too come from heaven," she said.

Then she straightend up, ran her hand through her hair, and headed for the door. As for me, I was gripped by the old sensation of being abandoned. I thought of Ruth's parents. Being cursed by them or by God, I didn't know which would be worse. I only knew that I would be. I'd crossed a threshold, violated a taboo, and nothing would ever be the same. I was both the judge and the man condemned. I lost not only my innocence but also my self-respect.

And a voice rose within me, the voice of a madman waiting in ambush, already seized with panic: "Lord, may my guilt not tarnish you."

"Well, Doctor, think about this question: Can man become mad because of God? You're not answering? Here's another one: Can man choose his madness?"

"Madness and choice," says Thérèse, "an odd combination of words. I wonder why you've used it. And why when speaking of Ruth."

"I have no idea; it just came to me."

"Without thinking?"

"Yes. Without thinking."

"By mere chance?"

"Yes. Pure chance."

"The mind doesn't work by chance, believe me," she says.

"Mine does."

"Because it's exceptional?"

"I don't claim there's anything exceptional about me; I'm not narcissistic."

"But you've just attributed an interesting dimension to chance."

"Interesting? For whom?"

"For both of us."

"Not for me," I say.

"Does my being interested bother you?"

"No. But still I'd rather change the subject."

"Because it concerns Ruth?"

"No. Yes."

"Ruth is part of your illness?"

"Possibly. I'd rather not dwell on it."

"She hurt you, didn't she?"

"By doing what?"

"By making fun of you. By first trying to seduce you and then rejecting you?"

"That's not how things went, not that way."

"So how?"

"I told you. Let's change the subject."

———

She asks me additional questions and repeats others in her professional, impassive, impersonal voice, as though she is filling out an administrative form; nothing I can say will make her change her rhythm or tone: a human machine, that's what she is. I withdraw into a gloomy silence. What drives her to submit me to this cross-examination? Who does she think she is? I know this kind of exercise. I no longer answer her. She brings it up again during subsequent sessions. I don't understand her obstinacy. Why is she so interested in this silly and humiliating adolescent episode? She clings to it; it's impossible to get her to drop it. As for me, all I want is to forget it. She wants the opposite. She wants me to go back in time, relive the seduction scene, and rummage around the dark and dirty areas. Might she be a bit lascivious, this charming therapist who requires payment for the pleasure my past provides her?

During our forty-fourth session, a few minutes before the end, she succeeds in catching me off guard—even worse: in shaking me up. She puts the question to me calmly, as though it is about the weather.

"There's a little detail here that escapes me: Are you sure of the truthfulness of your Ruth story?"

"I don't understand what you mean."

"I'm talking about your memory. Surely it isn't perfect; no memory is. Do you really believe that the experience you described corresponds to reality?"

"I still don't understand what you're driving at," I say, trying to contain my anger.

"This can happen even to people who are healthy psychologically. With the years, the past becomes blurred. We forget real events and 'remember' dreams or imaginary episodes."

"And you think . . . I lied!"

"I think your memory may have lied to you. Isn't it useful

and important, both for you and for me, to consider all the possibilities?"

She stands firm, whereas I stick to my guns. She insists; I don't give in. Yet, deep down, doubt creeps in. A victim of my present-day certainties, could I be mistaken about my past? Could I have taken my desires for shared promises? The therapist sees more clearly inside me than I myself. After several weeks, guiding me with a word or silence, she succeeds in making me rediscover the truth: there was nothing between Ruth and me. Our very last meeting, similar to the previous ones but shorter, took place in an uncomfortable, uninterrupted silence. There were no insolent questions or abstract answers. There was Ruth's beauty, which I acknowledged, admired, and loved, that's all. Had I desired her body? I'm not even sure. I think she shook my hand on arrival, but with a lowered gaze. Was I too shy or cowardly to take the initiative? Had I kissed her, would she have pushed me away and reminded me that she was engaged? There's no way of knowing. I was close to very few women in my life. Yet I'll always remember Ruth and our innocent relationship.

But . . . if there had been nothing between us, why did I portray myself as guilty? Why did I invent this role for myself?

She has driven me mad, if I wasn't already so, my brilliant, irascible therapist. With a wave of her magic wand, my knowledge has seeped away and my memory has grown dim. Swept up in a dreamlike whirlwind of aggressive dancers and shy warriors, oscillating between laughter and agony, the noise of the ocean and the tranquility of mountaintops, once again I lose all sense of identity. I talk to myself and can't decide whether I am the person talking or the person listening, the person who believes in God or the one who doesn't. Hounded by dark, demonic forces, I am running without making headway or even moving—as though I exist outside space and time. At one moment, I know that dawn is approaching, but right afterward I correct myself: it is midnight.

Shortly after the real or imaginary incident with Ruth, I left my family and its excessively strict environment. So as not to see Ruth anymore? More likely so I would no longer be exposed to the temptation. I knew that the next time around I wouldn't know how to resist. I gave my uncle Avrohom a more or less plausible explanation: I was about to turn twenty; at this stage in my studies, I felt a need to deepen my knowledge by going to a Bene Beraq or Jerusalem yeshiva. Sitting opposite him at the table, my hands on my knees, looking lost, I answered his questions. Still anti-Zionist, he wanted to be sure that I wasn't going to the Holy Land in order to fight the Arabs.

"They say there will be war over there," he said.

"No doubt."

"Do you want to die?"

"No."

"To live?"

"No again."

"What do you want?"

"I don't know. All I know is I have to get away."

"Is it an escape?"

"Maybe."

"An escape *from* or an escape *to* something?"

"Maybe both," I said.

"You won't get involved in politics over there? You promise?"

"I promise."

"Or in business?"

"I promise."

"You're going solely to study the Torah, agreed?"

"Agreed, Uncle Avrohom."

"And nothing else?"

"Nothing else."

"Are you going alone?"

"Alone."

"For how long?"

"For as long as it takes to fulfill myself in my studies."

"That can take a lifetime."

"I realize that."

"When do you plan to leave?"

"In a few weeks or a few months. I haven't set a definite date."

"And who will pay for your trip? I'm not very wealthy."

"I know, Uncle Avrohom."

"Bah, we have time to think about it. With God's help, we're bound to find a solution."

"Yes. With God's help."

Avrohom reflected for a minute, stroked his beard, and said, "I'm sure that up there your parents are proud of you."

And me, recalling my failed affair with Ruth, I said to myself: I'm not so sure.

As for the sessions with Thérèse Goldschmidt, they continue. And they're going rather badly.

EXCERPT FROM DR. THÉRÈSE GOLDSCHMIDT'S NOTES

"I can't go on," I say to Martin. "I'm at the end of my tether." I inspect my nails with a vexed expression, as I do whenever I'm dissatisfied.

"Can you talk about it?" Martin asks.

"No . . . Yes . . . if you want. After all, you aren't a stranger."

"Is it your Doriel burden once again?"

"Yes. I realize I can't possibly help him. He escapes me."

"He refuses to cooperate? He clings to his illness, is that it?"

"He's an unhappy man no longer seeking happiness."

I stop speaking. I fear saying things best kept unsaid.

Afterward, we go to a nearby movie theater. A political film: a denunciation of war and the ruling classes. And especially authority.

Usually, when we come back after a movie, we like to sit at the kitchen table and discuss it while savoring our herbal tea, which is supposed to help us fall asleep. Then we recall cousins and friends whom we see only rarely: a neurosurgeon who lives in California; a professor of contemporary history who teaches in Arizona. Not tonight. Doriel alone preoccupies us. It is he who has made me sullen, instilled in me the seeds of self-doubt, made me unsure of my judgments and inferences.

"What happened today? A new incident? Something unusual?" Martin asks.

"No, nothing unusual. That's just it; everything is going the way it usually does. I ask questions in order to prod his memory; he goes along, responds, but never follows through. I invariably feel he stops at the threshold, as in front of a wall, as though he feared flying up to heaven or crashing into an abyss. So he makes me want to scream."

"But isn't that the daily bread of psychotherapists? You're all looking for the key that will open the fortress where the enemy—the pain or illness of the soul—is hiding? And haven't you told me over and over again that this key is located in a box that is double-locked? That one must constantly find a key in order to lay hands on the next one?"

"What can I do? I'm racking my brain to find an answer, even a temporary one."

"Have you thought of handing your recalcitrant patient over to a colleague?"

"I don't know . . . Have I told you that he talked about the successor of Besht, the founder of the Hasidic movement? The great Magid of Mezritch used to say that when you've lost the key and are standing lost and powerless in front of a locked door, there's only one solution: to break down the door."

"Marvelous advice!"

"Heavens, you're not going to suggest . . . I use force! Is that what you've learned in the books amassed in your library? That violence is an option even for mental diseases?"

"It's you who mentioned the Hasidic master . . ."

"I don't mean violence. When a soul is involved, one should be able to break into it gently. With the proper word. A gesture, a sign, a look. A handshake. A silent pause, why not?"

Martin lets me think for a long time.

"If only," I say to him, smiling, "I could make him admit that love is part of life and that one can demand it without being ashamed."

"Isn't he too old?"

"Of course he's growing old. Like everyone."

"Like us?" asks Martin.

"What are you driving at? Honestly. We're younger than Doriel. Okay! Granted! He's old. A bit."

"Don't tell me you're afraid of growing old."

"I'm not saying I am. But what about you, always so calm in the midst of your books, so sure of your powers—could you be afraid?"

"Yes," says Martin. "I'm afraid sometimes. Afraid of living a diminished existence, like a useless object. To feel my body go on its own, without my soul. And conversely: afraid of finding myself abandoned, deserted, betrayed by my reason. In short, afraid of dying before dying."

"That's perfectly natural. For someone with your intelligence, no longer being able to control your thoughts and desires would be the most atrocious ordeal. But . . ."

"But what?"

"Don't forget our pact. We swore to watch over each other,

you over me and me over you, to make sure we're spared that humiliation. But if I'm no longer here, who will take care of Doriel?"

"There's really no one in his life?"

"No one. Except maybe one of those women who, until proof to the contrary, belongs to the world of his pipe dreams. He lives with her. He talks about her as though she still exists. And the more he talks about her, the more I'm convinced she has never existed. If you go by what he says, she has the smile of a frightened child."

"Well, then, it's simple: let's find his lady love for him; she will teach him to smile. A small personal ad in the papers would do the trick."

"Don't make fun of him," I say.

"I'm not making fun of anyone."

"Then don't make fun of her."

"Sometimes, dearest, you don't catch on at all: maybe she's making fun of him. And of us too."


"Doctor, before describing my experience in Israel, perhaps I should talk to you about abandonment. This feeling has accompanied me and oppressed me, even in the heart of Jerusalem, where I lived most intensely with my memories. Actually, it has weighed on me since childhood, since I was separated from my parents. *Separated* seems too weak a word. Torn away, rather. I never should have left them. I should have clung to my mother's hand, to my father's arm. I shouldn't have let them die without me. I know I'm wrong, that it wasn't my fault. I was too small and they were too determined. I know that the Angel of Death always triumphs over the living, past and future. But that's where you're mistaken, Doctor: knowledge doesn't help man find the vital answer, or genuine peace. There is a level where love of God and self-knowledge serve no purpose."

# 14

In Israel, where I finally went years later, I visited more than one yeshiva, questioned more than one rabbi, and took more than one ritual bath, hoping for a miracle. In pious Bene Beraq, near secular Tel Aviv, and in the suburbs of Jerusalem, I attended classes that were invariably dazzling, given by erudite teachers. I quickly realized that the knowledge I had acquired during my studies in Brooklyn was very meager. I had much to learn. But that wasn't my aim. Was it the need for a change of scene more than a craving for the new? Plagued by a vague feeling resembling guilt, I searched for a school or a man who could teach me repentance. Was guilt already part and parcel of my condition? A puritan to the fingertips, I was still obsessed by Ruth. I hadn't touched her and now I wondered if it had been because of timidity, fear of scandal, or uneasiness about transgressing the laws. And with every woman I passed, be it in a park or on a bus, I saw Ruth looking me up and down. It's foolish and senseless, I admit, but once I even recognized her in the face of a man. I didn't know where to run to: Where can you hide from your own self?

In Safed, the city of the Kabbalists, I went to pray at Rabbi Itzhak Luria's grave. I sought his advice. In Jerusalem's Old City, I communed in front of the Wall and into its countless cracks I slipped many pieces of paper with my request; I implored King David, as one who had known the taste of sin, to show me the path to remorse, forgiveness, or at least oblivion. One night I noticed a man alone next to the Wall. He was silently gazing at the starry sky, which seemed within close range and protecting the sleeping city by enveloping it in peacefulness. Suddenly the man burst out laughing. I moved closer to him, wondering what could amuse him while he prayed in front of the remaining vestige of the Second Temple. And I realized that he was an old man; he was sobbing and laughing at the same time. Then, while I stared at him fixedly and wondered if he was laughing and crying for the same reasons, I burst out laughing as well, loudly and merrily. I thought: the world he lives in is not mine; his prayers are unknown to me, but my tears and his will stream—who knows?—until the Lord's black-gold chalice overflows, the chalice He holds in His right hand for as long as His people are still in exile. I laughed because his face, though contorted, was Ruth's eternally youthful face.

Now he sensed my presence. His eyes still gazing up at the sky, he asked me: "Where are you from?"

"From far away."

"What are you doing here?"

"I am seeking."

"What are you seeking?"

"I am seeking a way of overcoming my baser instinct."

He meditated for a long time; then, still without looking at me, he asked, "Are you married?"

"No. I'm a bachelor."

"Why?"

"I don't know."

"We must find you a wife. Do you want me to take care of it?"

"Why not. On one condition."

"Which?"

"I don't ever want her to question me about my sources of income or, generally speaking, about my past."

"Or else?"

"Or else I won't marry her."

He looked at me and said, "You're in great danger, young man. May the Lord protect you." Then he burst out laughing, pressed his face against the Wall, and turned his laughter into a prayer where there was no place for Ruth.

And no place for me either.


A month after my arrival at the Lydda airport, I lived in the dorms of various Talmudic schools, where I also ate two meals a day. My needs were more than modest, and thanks to Samek, Romek's brother, my pockets were always full. I could have stayed in the best hotel in the country, but I would have been ashamed. I knew that my uncle Avrohom would not have approved; he would have been afraid that the food wouldn't really be kosher. And then he was in the habit of saying that it was a mistake, not just a sin, to show one's wealth. What was the point of arousing envy and pride?

I had no trouble enrolling in a Jerusalem yeshiva where one of the tutors, originally from Szatmár-Németi in Transylvania, was my uncle Avrohom's childhood friend, even more fanatical than he. He belonged to a sect close to Neturei Karta; virulently anti-Zionist, it still hasn't recognized the legitimacy or existence of the state of Israel. Its official, everyday language was Yiddish. You felt like you were in one of those vanished towns in a remote part of central Europe. I understood this from the very first Sabbath; at the morning service, the cantor didn't recite the prayer for the protection of Israel and the victory of its defenders. They lived in a prewar time. Seeing my astonishment, Haïm-Dovid, the rabbi's son, gave me the usual ritual argument: for us, Jews believing in God, the existence of a new Jewish state is contrary to tradition and rabbinical law, hence, as we see it, a sacrilege, both immoral and illegal.

I strolled with him one Saturday afternoon in the narrow,

dark little streets of the Old City, where the stones themselves tell the story of the only people of antiquity to have outlived antiquity. I asked him if his group was close to the Arabs. Yes, absolutely. Better one Palestinian state than two states living side by side. And all of this in the name of the Torah and in its honor! I couldn't believe my ears: Didn't he know that whoever uses the holy scrolls to kill becomes an assassin? I remembered the arguments between Avrohom and the Zionists in Marseilles. But in those days, a sovereign Jewish state didn't exist yet; now it did, and its existence was in constant danger. And did Haïm-Dovid trust an Arab state more than a Jewish state? Yes, absolutely. This was a ready-made answer, spoken in his drawling accent and as simple as daylight.

Dressed in his threadbare caftan, almost in tatters as though he had always worn it, Haïm-Dovid couldn't talk without caressing his chin, though it was beardless, and punctuating his words with a peremptory "absolutely." Will it rain tomorrow? "Yes, absolutely." Is your ailing father feeling better? "Thank God, yes, absolutely." For Haïm-Dovid, the most trivial facts fell within the province of the absolute. Should I join him and stay in this yeshiva? "God willing, absolutely." I asked him why; I needed to be persuaded. He didn't avoid the question.

"Elsewhere, you're in danger of losing your footing completely. You can't imagine Satan's power. He wears many masks. Here, it's the heresy of the Zionists. They will surely try to lure you away from the straight and narrow path."

"Are you crazy? Satan, here? In the Holy Land? In the city of David and his prophets?"

"Where do you expect him to be? Satan doesn't care about cabarets; there people don't need his help. Absolutely. It's in a yeshiva, a setting of prayer and study, that he prowls to catch his prey. Do you want to know how he goes about it? I'll tell you: he uses easy patriotism, politics, and even the obsession with security to achieve his ends. What are the politics of this country if not Satan's modern tool?"

Obviously, the arguments between Avrohom and the Zionist leaders in France were perpetuated in Jerusalem. And here I thought that Israel's opponents could carry on their fight only outside Israel. I told this to Haïm-Dovid, who did everything to enlighten me on this point. "You were wrong, and it's time you realized it. If you want to save your soul, stay here, with us. Otherwise . . ."

"Otherwise?"

He hesitated before adding: "Otherwise you'll end up like my brother. Absolutely."

This was how I learned that Haïm-Dovid had an older brother whom he preferred not to talk about. He told me only that he had changed his name. This aroused my curiosity, and I wanted to know what had become of this absent brother. Haïm-Dovid shook his head: no, he wouldn't tell me anything else. And he changed the subject.

Before coming to a final decision, which would put an end to weeks of hesitation, I thought it might be a good idea to consult the school head, the *rosh yeshiva*. Without making an appointment with a secretary, I showed up and knocked at his door. As no one answered, I opened the door and entered. The rabbi was sitting at a table piled with scholarly books, some leather-bound and others in shreds, and seemed so engrossed in study that he didn't notice that he was no longer alone in the room. This was the first time I was seeing him from so close. I was surprised not by his spiritual radiance but by his physical strength. By some odd optical illusion, when seen from afar he seemed thinner and of medium height. But in his office I could see, even though he was seated, that he was tall and robust. He had broad shoulders, and his heavy head was buried in his powerful hands. I felt vaguely disappointed. I had expected an elderly ascetic for whom the body is an enemy to be starved or at least an obstacle to be mastered through fasting and insomnia. But the rabbi seemed to be in good health, in too good health. Well fed, well rested. If he had worries, they left no trace on his brow.

Suddenly, he looked up and asked, "Who are you?"

I told him.

"What are you doing here with us?"

"I came to study."

"What, in your uncle Avrohom's circle there's no more studying? There are no more yeshivas in Brooklyn? You had to cross the ocean and come all the way here to study the teachings of Hillel and Shammai and Abbaye and Rava?"

"Inside these walls, I thought, the Torah is taught differently . . ."

"Well, young man, you're not wrong to think that. In general, except for a few protected places, study is *different* in this blessed country corrupted by nonbelievers. What I mean is this: it's the *sitra ahra,* the impure side, that hovers over students and their teachers by deluding them, deceiving them, and leading them astray from the Torah of truth that is ours . . ."

He went on in this vein, in a monotonous voice, condemning everything that is called happiness, life, and the obligation to live in Israel: secular society, the intellectuals, cultural and artistic events, morals, political figures, the world of finance, the military, the cult of nudity and pleasure. These were nothing but sins and sinners, and ungodly beyond redemption. But what about the faithful who attended synagogue every day? They were also guilty of a thousand transgressions. And what about the young students crowding the schools? Lost in the eyes of the Lord. And the little children? Punished and unfortunate through their parents' fault. He stopped to blow his nose, and I took advantage of the opportunity to ask him timidly, "But,

Rabbi, for you, the fact that there's a Jewish state welcoming hunted Jews counts for nothing?"

"This Jewish state should never have been born. Its creation is an offense against God. Our wise men prohibited it; that's in the Talmud. To be worthy of it, we were supposed to wait for the messianic times desired by the Lord, blessed be His name. All haste is unhealthy and doomed to failure. Here nothing was learned from the Bar Kokhba episode in Roman times; his rebellion cost thousands and thousands of human lives. But our political leaders, the Zionists, were impatient. They were yearning to play the statesmen. They wanted their own state so they could violate the holiness of the Sabbath, turn innocent children into pagans, and ridicule the lessons of life given us by our teacher Moses. That was their true goal. To prevent the final redemption, and estrange the people of Israel from the God of Israel." Anger distorted his face, and the violence of his words left him winded.

I asked him, "Would the rabbi have preferred the Jewish community to live here under Arab domination?"

"Yes. In the past, Islam was more hospitable toward us than the Christians."

Was that true? Embarrassed for not having studied medieval Jewish history sufficiently, I quickly returned to the present. "The rabbi seems to forget the millions of Jews who want to live in safety on the soil of their ancestors *right now.*"

"They should have stayed where they were from in the Diaspora. Not only is the 'return to Zion' an error, it is also a tragedy."

"Isn't the rabbi aware that there are countries where Jews are still in danger? If they remain where they are, they risk suffering and violent death."

"I don't wish that upon them," the rabbi replied with a long, sorrowful sigh. "I pray for them every day."

"But then, Rabbi, what should they do? Wait?"

"They should pray. They should remain Jewish. I prefer a Jew who dies a Jew than a Jew who lives like a renegade. Your uncle Avrohom, who is as close to me as a brother, doesn't he have the same view as I?"

"I hope not, Rabbi."

"But you're not sure."

"True enough, Rabbi. I'm not sure."

His expression became solemn, and he gave me a long, hostile look, possibly, too, in order to gauge the extent of my ignorance. Slowly, a strange sadness came over him. "Don't stay with us," he said. "You don't belong here. You won't find anything here. Avrohom was wrong to send you to me. My son shouldn't study with you. One day I'll be told that you've followed in the path of Haïm-Dovid's brother. To the edge of the abyss. And I won't be surprised."

He bent over the large book he had been consulting before my arrival. A sign that I was dismissed. A pity. I would have liked to continue our conversation. To tell him that while in his presence listening to his arguments, I felt oddly guilty for not feeling guilty enough. I wanted to question him about my classmate's brother. It was too late now. Too bad. The next time?

I left him reluctantly.

A few days later, at nightfall, we went to the Wall, Haïm-Dovid and I, simply to talk about various things. Didn't his father forbid him from seeing me? Apparently not. Or was it conceivable that he chose to disobey the rabbi? Why not? After all, we were friends. I knew him better than most of the students. It was with him that I took occasional walks in the evening, admiring the sunset on the hills and the domes of the Old City. I loved and still love that time of day. Young Talmudists make their way toward groups of praying men. Beggars bless us; I empty my pockets to fill theirs. Yesterday's shadows stand out against the walls and invade the memory of the passersby and the fantasies of the ghosts. Sometimes, when Haïm-Dovid heard the muezzin calling the faithful to prayer in the al-Aqsa Mosque, he plugged his ears, but not I. I loved it, and I still love to absorb every rustle of the wind through the trees, the moans of those in despair, the languorous song of the disinherited and the wanderers. Even when I'm not in Jerusalem, I am mad enough to live in its memories by integrating them with mine.

In Jerusalem, in those days, I liked to be alone, truly alone. I hadn't been afflicted by madness yet, as you might think, or by a curse, as my friend Haïm-Dovid would think, but for reasons I myself don't know, I aspired to keep my distance from people, no matter who they were.

I hadn't yet come to a decision about the near future, but I was still living at the yeshiva. Haïm-Dovid wanted to know why I had gone to see the rabbi and what my conversation with him had been like. So he didn't know what his father thought of our friendship. I frowned.

"How do you know I saw him? I didn't tell anyone."

"Oh, in an environment like ours, everyone knows everything. And quickly. Absolutely quickly and absolutely everything."

"You say people know—but be more specific: What do they know exactly?"

"They know the two of you talked for a long time."

"Absolutely?"

"Hmmm . . . for a long time."

"And what else?"

"The *rosh yeshiva,* may the Lord grant him long life, isn't pleased with you," he said.

"And do you know why he isn't pleased? Indeed absolutely displeased?"

"No, we don't know why."

"Are you sure?"

"Absolutely." Then after a hesitation, he said, "The *rosh*

*yeshiva,* may the Lord grant him long life, doesn't owe anybody any explanations."

"And no one receives his words in secret?"

"Not I, in any case."

Should I tell him what the rabbi had told me about his brother? Why upset him?

"Tell me, Haïm-Dovid, what's your brother's name?"

He gave a start. "Why do you want to know?"

"No idea. Just like that. You mentioned him the other day . . ."

He scowled. "I shouldn't have. Forget what I said."

I couldn't overcome my curiosity: Why this rejection of his brother? What sin had he committed to incur the blame of the rabbi and be repudiated by his own brother? I decided to be frank. "I owe you the truth, Haïm-Dovid. The rabbi mentioned him as well."

"What did he tell you?"

"He warned me not to be like him, not to follow in his tracks; otherwise . . ."

"Otherwise?"

"Otherwise, I too will wind up at the bottom of the abyss."

"Come with me," Haïm-Dovid said in a tone that was suddenly resolute.

Cutting our way through the crowd, we approached the Wall. There my friend took a sheet of paper out of his pocket, tore it in half, wrote a few words on both halves, and inserted the two pieces into the cracks in the Wall, while murmuring a psalm.

"The first is to save my brother, and the other one is to protect you," he said.

And once again, after a hesitation that made him sigh as if in pain, he added, "My brother is cursed. As for you, try not to imitate him; it would be madness on your part."

He told me about the path bestrewn with traps and challenges taken by Béinish, his older brother, whom he had admired and loved.

He had gone mad, as I would later. An irate madman. Rising up against established authority and the discipline of faith, rebelling against the rigorous laws inherited from our ancestors. To put it plainly, a rebel against his father and the blazing symbol he embodied.

Yet, during his adolescence and throughout his studies, Béinish had made his parents and relatives proud. Tall, slender, generous, he was a fast learner, remembered everything, quickly knew his way around the most obscure Halakhic sources, and during the services, he showed a piety and fervor that aroused satisfaction and pride in his tutors. He wasn't known to have a single weakness or fault. Perfect in everything, rigorous in his spirituality, eloquent in speech, he could match the renowned scholars of the neighboring schools and was never conceited about it. Naturally, on the day after his bar mitzvah, his parents received calls from the most illustrious families having young girls to marry off.

Everything was going well. At sixteen Béinish was engaged. The young girl, Reisele, came from a great and wealthy Szerencsevaros family, and her father was known for his charitable deeds as well as his devotion to the Torah. Everything took place as in the past in central Europe. The two families prepared a wedding that would stand out for its festive splendor as well as the fervor of its religious ceremony. Three orchestras made the guests throb with joy and melancholy; seven troubadours vied for the honor of entertaining the gathering with their humor, acerbic and tender, sharp yet never aggressive. About fifty rabbis went out of their way for the occasion. The most illustrious among them, the venerable Rovidok Rabbi, a descendant of the famous Magid of Kraków, had the voice and face of a biblical prophet; he danced the ritual dance with the young bride, each of the two holding a corner of the handkerchief. Beggars came from every part of the country for the paupers' feast. Sumptuous meals were distributed on every day of the weeklong festivity. The gifts the couple received would have delighted both present-day kings and queens and the kings and queens of old. A neighboring community offered the young groom a rabbinical position with a library, a study house, and an enviable salary. The father of the bride, for his part, very much wanted the couple to come and live in his palace for three years. But Béinish preferred to stay at his parents' house. His father-in-law didn't take offense: "My son-in-law—may God protect him—doesn't like luxury; for him, knowledge is the supreme value." And everyone was overjoyed until it all fell apart.

Scarcely two years after the wedding, a curse struck the little world of Béinish's family. It was Monday morning. Reisele, in tears, burst in on her mother-in-law, a letter in her hand. After scanning it quickly, the mother-in-law rushed to the rabbi to show it to him. "God has punished us!" she cried out in a hoarse voice. "Read this. What evil have we committed for Him to punish us this way?"

Unaccustomed to his wife having this kind of outburst, the rabbi remained calm. He read the letter once, twice, then shook his head: "What is this? What is he saying? I don't understand, I don't understand." In fact, it was incomprehensible to everyone. The young husband had simply disappeared. Yes, disappeared without leaving a trace, other than this letter with which he broke his marriage ties. Like a thief, he had fled during the night, taking only his tefillin and a change of clothes. What? Béinish was separating from his family? Béinish was divorcing? Béinish was deserting his home and repudiating his relatives? Why? What was happening to him? Béinish was acting on an impulse, he of all people? Some Hasidim, bred on superstition, declared: "It's a dybbuk; he's haunted by an evil spirit." This the rabbi didn't really believe. But then how could he explain it? And where was Béinish? Kidnapped by gangsters? Was he still alive? Should the police be alerted? To that, the response was immediate: "Whatever you do, let's not have the police around here." Among these people, everyone managed without requesting help from the impious and hostile authorities. But then what should they do?

First, keep it secret: this "scandal" would just delight the Zionist "enemies." But how could leaks be avoided? Béinish was too well known and very much solicited. Up until then, people saw him every day. Recently—in fact, since his marriage—he had seemed more taciturn, sullen, and withdrawn, and he avoided conversations and public meetings as much as possible. But there's a big difference between this and running away.

Haïm-Dovid was young at the time but mature enough to understand that his family was going through a serious trial, both painful and embarrassing. He remembered it with a sharpness that was still vivid: the faithful in whom they could confide, their grim expressions as they came and went; the improvised consultations behind closed doors; Reisele's tears; the *rebbetzin*'s sighs. And the rabbi's silences. Dense, oppressive, impenetrable, they sometimes lasted for hours and days. How could he forget them? And his father's outpouring of tenderness toward him, the younger son, when he took him on his lap and stroked his head as a way of consoling himself for an irreparable loss.

"Even today I can't explain why Béinish, the brother I admired and also envied, deserted his home and family," Haïm-Dovid said, closing his eyes as if this could help him find his words. "For me, for all of us, this remains a painful, taboo mystery. Absolutely."

As he broke off, I couldn't help asking him: "Was he unhappy with his wife? Didn't he want her to bear children so his name would be perpetuated? Didn't he love her? Or perhaps he loved her too much?"

"My father might know the answer. I don't."

"And what about Reisele? Where is she now? What became of her?"

"After the divorce, she became a recluse."

"What do you mean? Invisible from one minute to the next?"

"She suddenly ceased to exist."

"And what did the physicians say?"

"They said it was . . . psychological. A word I didn't understand but that was meant to explain it all."

"And for how long did that last?"

"Even today, she still lives in her prison, separated from the world of normal people. She listens and doesn't answer. She listens and doesn't hear. She listens and doesn't cry."

"And Béinish?"

Haïm-Dovid stiffened. Everything about him seemed to freeze: the suffering on his face, and the anguish. "He is lost. For us, he is lost."

Actually, I thought, it was the simple and ordinary story of a breakup. With the family, with intimate friends, with the austerity of faith. But also of an opening to another life and its challenge to intelligence: those were the steps in the new life of the young prodigal son lost in unfamiliar vineyards.

"Can you imagine?" Haïm-Dovid added. "In his madness, my brother even joined the army. He completed his military service. And I've heard that now he's a member of the security services or Mossad, may God punish them all, each according to his sins."

For Haïm-Dovid, his rebellious brother was insane. But was he himself normal? Isn't fanaticism, which restricts reason and blinds it, a kind of madness, and the kind that threatens not just one specific individual but a whole community?

This was probably when I decided not to stay much longer at that yeshiva. Honestly, I thought, the rabbi and his people go too far in their rejection of Israel. I can't be their ally. My uncle Avrohom would never have cursed Jews, not even those whose opinions and commitments he fought. He never would have wished suffering, humiliation, or death on them. After all, these soldiers were defending the only country in the world where every Jew can feel at home. You can deplore their negligence, the error of their ways in the area of religious practice, without going so far as to pray for their defeat, which would lead to the demise of Israel. Even today, I think I made the right choice. I'm willing to be different from others, but not in the same way as the members of that sect. I'm willing to suffer, but not to make others suffer.

"Haïm-Dovid," I asked before parting from him, "what is your brother's new name?"

"Why do you want to know?" he replied, looking irritated.

"I'd like to meet him."

He told me his name—Tamir—but regretted it immediately. I didn't realize my curiosity would anger him.

"And what if Béinish just wanted to live by himself?" he retorted abruptly.

At that point I said to myself that Haïm-Dovid, like his family, regarded his brother as ill. But if Béinish really had chosen to live by himself, perhaps I was wrong to want to meet him. What could I get out of it? An understanding of his solitude? Solitude is a battered woman who has neither the strength nor the desire to love anymore. Solitude is a starving child who dreams of a stale piece of bread. Solitude is a beggar who hasn't slept a wink for days and nights, perhaps since he was torn from his mother's womb.

Like madness, solitude is fear.

A solitary man is a man who is afraid. A man who is afraid is a solitary man. When solitude enters me, it becomes me. Solitude emerges unexpectedly when only the body belongs to me, but also when I belong to the body all alone. Solitude changes consciousness into a prison, a jail that I am afraid of leaving.

Afraid of not understanding anything, afraid of understanding everything. Afraid of loving and afraid of not loving anymore. Afraid of forgetting everything and afraid of not forgetting anything: mangled bodies left lying about the battlefield, the slow and implacable death pangs of the survivors. Afraid of experiencing hunger, afraid of having no thirst for anything anymore. Afraid of dying and of living. Afraid of being afraid. Afraid of being alone when no one is here anymore. Afraid of being alone when the loved one is here.

There exists a fear that is not yet death but that is no longer life.

"For you, is what you call madness a way of entering solitude?" Thérèse asks.

"I'm not a psychiatrist; I don't know how to define madness."

"You've been with me for a long time, haven't you?"

"Yes. Under analysis, as they say."

"Do you feel lonely when you're with me?"

"I talk to you; you listen to me. Should that make me less lonely?"

"Less insane?"

"Or more so?"

"That's exactly what I'd like to know."

"May I answer with a question?"

"Go ahead."

"In fact, God is lonelier than His most solitary creatures, for He can't *not* be. Could it be that He too is insane?"

"If you think you're shocking me, Doriel, try again. I'm not a believer. What about you?"

"I don't know anymore. I once was. As Haïm-Dovid would say, 'absolutely.' Now things have changed; sometimes I think I'm insane because I still have religious faith, sometimes because I no longer do. Did Nietzsche believe in God before sinking into madness? His last work is titled *Ecce Homo,* 'Behold the man': What man was he talking about? The God-seeking man or the man who shuns God? Perhaps the man who thought he was God? What does a person believe in when he no longer believes in anything? You who have explored the multiple faces of madness, what do you think of mine? Is it tied to a need or to a fear of the veils that solitude spreads over my eyes and heart?"

We often talk about the layout of places, but for me the problem revolves around my memories. I don't know how to organize my thoughts, and even more simply, where to rest my eyes; they are always losing their place. Which means that I am more and more astray in my own life. An unhealthy and malevolent blending of notions, terms, pictures: What meaning can be drawn from a sentence that is necessarily devoid of meaning? But, on the other hand, could the absence of meaning have some other meaning? And what about the ever-changing layout of words? Sometimes a comma travels: it runs, runs between the words, and is impossible to catch. Is the comma insane too?

As a rule, Thérèse Goldschmidt doesn't like the word *madness.* She always goes to great lengths to avoid it. She prefers *illness, mental fatigue, psychological deficiency or instability, neurosis, depression,* and countless technical terms.

"In spite of the time we've spent together," she says, "it is too soon in our common endeavor for me to tell you you're cured. We still have a long way to go."

"What you think of as too soon might be too late for me."

"Too late? So long as the heart is beating, it isn't too late."

"You aren't a cardiologist, as far as I know."

"The heart has its own illnesses, and some are psychological in nature."

"What are you referring to?"

"To illnesses linked to the life of the human body. Yes, we should bear in mind that the body has its own life, with its rights, its needs, and its mysteries. Take what is called desire, for instance. It doesn't often come up in our conversations. Why?"

"I have no idea."

"I'll be direct: Do you ever desire a woman?"

"Didn't I tell you about Ruth?"

"Did you really desire her? I mean, desire her enough to want to know her in the biblical sense?"

"What on earth are you thinking of? Yes . . . no . . . never . . ."

"The truth, Doriel, tell me the truth. You aren't all that young anymore, but did you ever live with a woman, even for one night, or for one hour, and feel the fulfillment of desire and the surprising discovery of happiness?"

"I refuse to answer."

"But . . . it's the rule—"

"I couldn't care less about your rules."

"Therefore I conclude that your answer is negative."

"You don't know a thing."

"But I need to know."

"Listen. In my tradition there are certain things it's indecent to talk about out loud. And whatever concerns eroticism is one of them. Would you be surprised if I told you that according to our wise men, God Himself doesn't look at what happens in the bedroom?"

"Let's leave God where He is. Would you mind if we returned to Béinish?"

EXCERPT FROM DR. THÉRÈSE GOLDSCHMIDT'S NOTES

This very night, as usual, Martin and I exchange our impressions of the day that was coming to an end. At the library, in an old rare book, a researcher found manuscript pages by Paritus, that strange philosopher who had frequented Benedictus or Baruch Spinoza and twice met Don Itzhak Abrabanel, the exile from the Iberian Peninsula.

"And what are they about?" I ask.

"About the mystery of the original light," Martin replies, "the one that allowed Creation to take shape. Paritus wonders about its origin: it had to have been hidden somewhere other than in the universe. But where?"

Of course I'm interested in my husband's work. I ask for explanations, details, interpretations, and reward him with a nice smile, both generous and promising. For him as for me, Paritus is a familiar figure. I've read fantastic stories about him in different narratives. We don't know much about his life, except that he wanted it to be secret. An intrepid traveler, he journeyed to many countries in Europe and Asia, visiting Jewish scholars and trying to interest them in his work. At one time, I considered writing a study of him, from the psychiatric point of view, of course. My curiosity never faded. I turn to Martin.

"Are there any new facts in these pages that could shed more light on this legendary character of yours?" I ask.

"Possibly. He describes the tragic and disconcerting fate of a woman abandoned by her husband, an *agunah;* he talks about her rights and hardships—"

"Really? What a coincidence! Just today, Doriel mentioned a similar case—"

"Maybe it's the same one?"

"No, the case Doriel cited happened a few years ago, not several centuries ago."

"Oh, you know, with Paritus, nothing is impossible."

"Stop! The story I heard today was about the brother of my patient's childhood friend."

"And was his name Paritus, by any chance?" Martin insists, smiling. Then he grows serious again. "And how was your session with Doriel?"

I shake my head, wondering if I can go into detail without betraying my patient's trust.

"Your unhappy patient, how is he doing? Still as recalcitrant? Unpleasant maybe?"

"He used to be; he's less so now. In fact, at one point, not so long ago, I asked him if that was his temperament, if he was always so arrogant and unpleasant."

"What did he say?"

"He said only with me. With other people, he's rather courteous, amiable."

"Do you see this special treatment as a compliment?"

"I have no idea. But . . ."

"But what?"

"I made a discovery that might explain quite a few things," I say in a hesitant voice. "Just imagine, my patient, perhaps because he's suffering from religious and other inhibitions, has never slept with a woman."

Martin represses another smile. "At his age?"

"Yes. At his age. It would seem that women frighten him."

"They remind him of his mother?"

"That's possible. An avenue worth exploring."

Martin agrees with me and adds, laughing heartily, "I wonder if your discovery couldn't apply to our dear Paritus too."

# 15

This day, for some reason—or maybe for no obvious reason—we talk mostly about happiness. I am more relaxed, Thérèse preoccupied. I tell her about my visit to a Communist writer who became a Buddhist, and she has trouble concentrating. I notice and change the subject, convinced that she is going to interrupt me. But since she remains silent, I stop talking, let the silence grow heavier, sit up, gaze at her intently, and ask: "Where are you?"

I have never seen her so absent.

She gives a start. "My mind is elsewhere; please excuse me."

"You don't seem yourself today. What's bothering you?"

She shrugs, tries to smile, then sighs. "Oh, it's nothing. It'll pass. In fact, it already has. Where were we? Oh yes, your writer friend."

I don't bat an eye. I nearly corrected her by pointing out that the writer in question isn't *really* a writer and certainly not my friend, but I don't feel like talking about it anymore. Some other time, not now. My main interest now is this woman's change of mood; for the first time since we've started seeing each other, she hasn't been listening.

"Tell me, what's wrong?" I ask. "Suddenly I saw your face cloud up in a way I'm familiar with: inattention close to distress. You who know so many things about me, you have no right hiding from me what's troubling you."

Thérèse waits a minute, as though she is weighing the pros and cons, and finally gives in.

"Okay, it concerns my private life. I don't have children. There. While you were talking about some people's attraction to Buddhism, an unrelated thought suddenly wormed its way into my mind: he has a friend and I don't have children."

"First of all, he's not my friend; second, you could still have children."

She tries to smile but succeeds only in wincing to hide her embarrassment. "What if we talked about Israel?" she asks me.

I feel sorry for her. Who would have predicted it?

Béinish had agreed to meet me in a Tel Aviv café near the beach. He was sitting in a corner of the terrace, spotted me, and signaled me to join him. I asked him how he had recognized me; he answered with a hand motion and a shrug. As if to say, I don't do my kind of work for nothing.

Around forty, well dressed in a gray suit, white shirt, and dark blue tie, he looked like a diplomat, industrialist, or high-ranking government official. I tried to picture him as an adolescent, with a black felt hat and sidelocks, holding a prayer book or a bulky volume of commentaries under his arm. I also tried to picture the bridegroom being led by his father to the marriage ceremony to unveil and cover his intended bride. But not a trace was left of his religiosity or former life.

"My name is Tamir," he said, without taking his eyes off me. "You wanted to meet me," he added warily, in Hebrew, of course.

"Yes, I did," I answered in Yiddish. "It's not so much your experience as the story of that story that made me want to meet you." He listened to me with, I suppose, professional curiosity.

"Go on," he said. "I understand Yiddish."

Go on? Not easy. Actually I had no plan or goal in seeking this meeting. Should I quiz him on his abrupt break with everything that was part of his youth? On the motives that had led him to reject our ancestors' tradition? On the gulf he had created between himself and his family? On the impression he gave of no longer being interested in them? What had happened to make him act in a way that he himself would have previously thought unthinkable? Had he become a renegade or madman overnight? Indifferent, perhaps? He would reply that it was his affair, not mine. In other words, his private life was none of my business.

"Are you happy at least?" My mouth blurted out these words: it was impossible to take them back. I had the feeling that they were like a slap in his face, for he turned as crimson as the flame of a simmering inferno darting into the forest in the dead of night.

"Why would you be interested in my personal happiness?" he asked, looking gloomy.

I could have told him that I was interested in everything, or that what I was particularly interested in was the quest for happiness in the life of a heretic, but I didn't want to provoke him further.

"I'm interested in it," I answered, "because your happiness, if it exists, is built on other people's unhappiness."

"How do you know? Who told you? And what gives you the right to meddle in something that's none of your business?"

"My apologies," I said, lowering my head, embarrassed. "I'm a friend of your brother's . . ."

"Haïm-Dovid? You know him? He talks too much. He always did, even as a child. A deaf and blind fanatic who thinks he's still living in the Middle Ages."

After a brief silence he spoke again: "How is he? I suppose he's engaged to a nice Jewish girl from a good family? In the hope of starting a large and above all pious family. And . . . my parents?"

I kept silent. I was afraid he would ask me if they were happy.

Should I tell him his father never so much as mentioned his name? That he had disowned him?

He seemed to be making an effort to blot out that period of his life. "You still haven't told me why you wanted to see me," he said. His tone of voice had changed from wary to impatient and unpleasant. I was taking up too much of his time.

"The break," I answered.

"The . . . what?" he asked.

"I'm curious . . . The break with your family, with their past, which is also yours. I'm struck by its abruptness. And by its finality, too. What provoked it? What made it irrevocable?"

I had other questions to ask him; they were buzzing around in my feverish head, creating an infernal nucleus that took my breath away. I gave him a sidelong glance. He too seemed about to let slip something that he kept buried deep inside. Was it sorrow, or remorse, perhaps? Should I tell him that I was sorry I hurt him? That I thought it best to change the subject? It was wiser. It was less risky to talk about myself.

"Like you in those days, I feel I'm going through a crisis," I said. "That's why—"

He didn't let me finish explaining; he lost his temper. "You're having doubts and you expect me to make them vanish? Is that it? You're obsessed by serious questions and you'd like me to give you the answers? Maybe you think that when you break with faith everything becomes clear and transparent? That the path opening before you will lead to a radiant goal that will warm your heart? That's why you saw fit to disturb me? Well, then, you're just a pathetic fool, and I resent you for wasting my time."

He got up and acted as if he was about to leave, while I stayed seated, motionless. Did he notice that I had tears in my eyes? He sat down again and stared at me for a long time. Patrons and passersby glanced at us in surprise. I heard a woman with unruly brown hair say to her friend, "They look like two brothers who are quarreling; the elder is . . ." The end of her sentence escaped me. What was Tamir driving at? He checked his watch quickly, nodded, and said in Hebrew: "You don't speak the so-called holy tongue at all?"

"I do, a bit."

"Are you prepared to make an effort?"

I was.

"It's late. I'll make a phone call and cancel an appointment. Stay put. It will only take a minute."

I was anxious. What if he didn't return? But he did.

And he brought with him the depiction of a past as dislocated as mine.

"I was suffocating," Tamir said, sipping a cup of black coffee. "That's the word that best describes how I felt in my parents' house. My mother's silent looks, the overly rigid rules my father imposed on me. The constant and haunting presence of God in my life. With every step, I ran into Moses and Maimonides. I couldn't take it anymore. I needed more air and breathing space. Burdened by my body and my self, I began to feel self-hatred and self-disgust. I yearned for sleep as a refuge and the possibility of sinking into oblivion."

His head bent forward, his eyes gazing at a faraway point in space and time, Tamir lit cigarette after cigarette, seeming to struggle against the grief or remorse, if not both, bottled up in his memory. Then he turned to me before resuming with a shrug. "A while ago you used a word that made me start: *break*. It's a hard word, a strong word, but it is fitting. And it hurts. It is brutal. It's like throwing salt on an open wound. Furthermore, in my case, I should use it in the plural."

The story he began telling me didn't surprise me. I had vaguely expected it. Like him, others before him had experienced the same periods of doubt, the same heartbreak, the same crises ending in rebellion. The literature of the emancipation and the Haskalah are filled with such stories. And they abound in the literature of other cultures. A religious youth, crushed by the pressures of his faith and his expectations, feeling cramped as if he is in a cage or cell, reaches the point when he can't take it anymore: yearning for the unexpected, for new discoveries and escape, he tears himself away from familiar places and faces in order to start a new life and a new adventure, somewhere else.

For Béinish, the accident that caused his first break occurred a month after his marriage, one morning after he had left the study and prayer house. He was crossing the street, lost in thought, when he was hit by an army vehicle. He regained consciousness only in the hospital, where he underwent several operations on his head and cervical vertebrae. His visitors included his parents and his fellow students, of course, but also Peleg, the young officer who had been driving the car.

"You can't imagine how sorry I am," he said in a hoarse voice.

"It wasn't your fault; it was mine," Béinish said. "I should have looked before crossing the street."

"What can I do so you'll forgive me?"

"Nothing. You're not responsible."

The officer was clearly distressed. "Are you sure?" he asked. "Isn't there anything I can do for you?"

"Nothing . . . but I'll think about it."

Peleg returned the next day, and the day after; he returned every day, until the morning when Béinish told him he was going home. His father had already signed the necessary insurance documents. "We could see each other again in a café . . ."

"Impossible," said Béinish. "I've never had food or drink anywhere but at home or at the yeshiva. In fact I've never set foot in a café."

"Can I come and see you at home?"

"What a question. Of course you can; you'll be more than welcome."

"You're not afraid that your father will throw me out? After all, look at me: I'm not a Talmudist. I'm not even a practicing Jew."

He's right, thought Béinish. The officer is clean-shaven and doesn't wear a *kippa* on his head. He'll shock my family, that's for sure.

"But why do you want to continue visiting me?"

Peleg smiled. "After all, I feel a bit responsible for your condition."

Béinish protested. "Stop feeling guilty. It's not your fault. I've already told you that, and you know I'm right. So . . ."

Peleg looked at him without replying but seemed disappointed and sad.

"Fine," said Béinish. "We'll see each other again. But in the park, not at home."

In the evening, he talked to his father about it and was surprised by his answer. "Let him come here. Though he has no religious faith today, he might well have it tomorrow. Perhaps he needs you. Help him. Saving a soul is a big mitzvah. It's a true good deed."

Naturally, things took a different turn.

At first, out of respect for his new friend's parents, Peleg never entered the house without wearing a *kippa* on his head, borrowed from a religious soldier in his unit. They talked about everything and nothing. Peleg preferred current events and Béinish the ancient texts.

"I'm interested in events," Peleg said one day, "insofar as I can have an effect on them. As for you, can you change the biblical stories?"

"Why try?" asked Béinish. "God Himself can't change the past. But the past remains alive and active in time. By studying it I can understand what is happening to us."

"And does that satisfy you?"

"What about you, does it satisfy you to work at trying to

change the present when you don't even know how much longer we'll be alive?"

"Philosophically, you're right. Defining the present isn't obvious; but for a living being, for a suffering sick person, for a man in love, the first time he kisses his beloved, the present certainly exists, and how!"

"It becomes a memory almost instantaneously," said Béinish. "Hence, for all practical purposes, it no longer exists."

"And in the Bible, what exists?" asked Peleg.

"Nostalgia," Béinish replied.

"Nostalgia for what?"

"For the beginnings. For origins. For what preceded time. And what sheltered it. The first moments. The first cracks. The first signs of failure for the Creator in facing His Creation's downfall. The sorrow, the distress of the Master at worlds unworthy of His vision. That is what I seek and what I find in our still-relevant ancient great texts."

"Relevant?" Peleg was surprised. "What connection do you see between all that and the anguish and heartbreak of every Jewish family whose children are doing their military service? Don't tell me that the Bible talks about terrorism!"

"It talks about conquest."

"But not about victory."

"Yes, it does," said Béinish. "Or rather the commentaries do. Victory over oneself. The only valid victory."

"And what about Samson?" asked Peleg, revealing his meager knowledge. "Don't talk to me about his spiritual or moral principles."

Béinish didn't want to discuss Samson. Too great a womanizer, the warrior wasn't his hero, even if he had defended the community valiantly against the Philistine enemy. In order to redirect the conversation, he asked, "What does the Bible mean to you?"

"A treasure trove of episodes, of possible and impossible stories. Beautiful and sad, funny and not so funny. One day, when I'm retired and this country will be living in happiness and peace, I might reread them. For the time being, I have other worries."

His worries were those of Israel. Threatened by too many enemies, its security was far from assured. The neighboring countries were becoming stronger militarily, and Israel didn't have the means to maintain a state of permanent vigilance.

With time, Béinish ended up sharing his friend's convictions. He left the world of the Talmud, where everything was open, for the world of the service, where everything was secret and where Peleg played a major role.

I saw Tamir again several times. He quizzed me on my habits, my knowledge, my tastes. At first I attributed his curiosity to his desire to learn more about his family. Wrong: it was purely professional. I understood this only at the end when, to my surprise, with a serious if not solemn air, he told me he wanted to recruit me. I told him that he was crazy.

I knew Béinish's story, but I did not yet know Tamir's story, and there was no reason for him to talk to me about it. So then why was he trying to make me into a secret agent?

"It's simpler than you think," he explained in a voice that had become impassive again. "You're an American citizen, you have an American passport, you're not involved in politics, you're neither a Zionist nor pro-Israel, you're young and intelligent; it's normal for you to travel around the world. In other words, you have the perfect cover and wouldn't attract the attention of the authorities."

"You're flattering me," I replied. "But really, can you seriously see me as a Mossad agent? I haven't read a single spy thriller—"

"A good agent is precisely someone who wouldn't be taken to be a spy. All I ask is that you think about it. The life of a good number of Jews, here and in certain Arab countries, may hinge on your decision."

Several days later he suggested I meet a friend of his by the name of Laurent in a Tel Aviv café.

I don't know why, but I expected to come face-to-face with another madman.

# 16

Laurent and his deep gaze: it warmed and calmed everything it enveloped. The bird in flight, the windswept tree, the sunlit rock.

Tall, slender, impeccably dressed, he had everything to live happily among the living. But the dead, who refuse to be forgotten or pitied, prevented it. They too know madness.

"Come," he said to me, "let me treat you to a drink."

"I stopped drinking long ago."

"A coffee?"

"Okay. A coffee."

Laurent stared at me with his gentle, understanding gaze. "Why did Tamir want us to meet?" he asked.

"Ask him."

"No, I'm asking you."

"I have no idea. I can't answer for him."

"Don't try to lie to me."

"I'm not lying. I really don't know what Tamir would answer."

"What could his motives be?"

"Let's wait until we see him again. He'll tell us."

"Why wait?"

"I don't know you well enough."

As if it is possible to know anyone, I mean really know, in a few minutes or even a few years. But if I waited longer, would I know him better? Does that mean knowledge at first sight may exist just as love at first sight exists? And if the other was merged with me, everywhere and always, as mad as I was and still am, would I know him slightly better, notwithstanding the rare sunny spells that cause more harm than good?

"As for me, I was waiting for you," said Laurent. "Perhaps just to chat. I know your name."

As though that was enough. As though a few casual exchanges could reveal anything about what defines a human being, his shortcomings and virtues, his instincts and his will to master them, his exuberant joys and silent nightmares: all these riches, all these signs, all these secrets—how could a name contain them all, except God's, hence by definition a sealed name, forever unknown, in other words, unusable and ineffable?

In response to my silence, Laurent talked. "You're Doriel. That's what I was told. But is it your real name?"

At that point, I said to myself that we were going to become accomplices. Usually, people leave their names anywhere, on a piece of paper or on people's lips. In the past, during the occupation, names were at war with one another. There were those who fell, others who got back on their feet. They were all loaded with stories. Being a good Jew, Laurent knew that the Bible is filled with names. Each one is a biography, a memory fragment. God gave Adam the power of naming, thereby marking the beginning of the human adventure, with its unpredictable, improbable, yet true developments.

Laurent had everything that women find attractive. First of all, he was slender and dynamic, well dressed, and as handsome as a movie actor. Second, he was an intellectual; he was refined, with a deep understanding of the world and an insatiable, lofty curiosity. He was also attractive to men. But I ask you, how can one possibly be attractive to everyone, to Tamir and me, to the rich and poor, to the learned and the ignorant? He had all the ingredients for a happy life. Here again, I ask you, how can one possibly be happy in a world that will one day plunge into violence and hatred, in other words, into the black hole of history? Well, Laurent didn't plunge. When I met him, he was running a pharmaceutical company. He was admired, liked, respected, even in political circles. Was it just that he lacked madness? Vanity of vanities, all is vanity; all is madness, and honors more than the rest. But how had he wound up in the Israeli intelligence?

He was born of Polish Jewish parents who had immigrated to France and worked twelve hours a day so he could have a good education. His education in the best secondary school in Paris was interrupted by the war. His parents were deported. He and his younger brother, Maurice, both members of the same underground Communist network, miraculously escaped the roundup of Jews in the Vélodrome d'Hiver.

And afterward?

Feverish days, harrowing nights. Companions vanishing in the night and fog. Imprisoned, tortured, shot.

And afterward?

The liberation. Happiness regained? Laurent skipped over events too numerous to go into. His parents? His brother? He jumped to the present.

Laurent was in love with Jacqueline. They were both proud of their children, Tili and Cécile, who were proud of them in return. In other words: he had nothing short of a perfect career, with no gray areas.

He related all this to me in a natural tone of voice without any boastfulness. Apparently, he was eager to convince me that he was leading a happy life in a sunny environment. But what had he found in this country where highs and lows came in quick succession? Something about his behavior bothered me. Was it his voice? When he spoke about his life, he seemed to be describing another person's fate.

"Laurent," I said to him several days later. "I hope you won't mind my being indiscreet, but—"

"But what?"

"Tamir wanted us to meet. We don't know why, but now we know each other and we will soon separate. And if I leave you without asking you the question that's on my mind, I'll have the feeling of having abandoned you."

"I'm listening."

I told him I had a special relationship with what is called depression, and more specifically, thanks to my sixth or seventeenth sense, with those who fear it or invite it. He looked at me with a faint ironic smile but remained silent. I told him I wasn't making fun of him, that when someone was unhappy and felt drawn by some demon or other, he sent out a signal that I detected like a kind of ultrasound. To use a mystical metaphor, I explained, it was like an abyss always attracting another abyss; I felt concerned. And today this feeling came from him.

Laurent looked at me without blinking, as if I had just escaped from a lunatic asylum. "I'm listening," he said.

"Me too, Laurent, I'm listening. I'm listening to what you hear and what draws you and causes you to slip and stumble."

That evening we were sitting at the same table in the same café, watching the patrons who came to celebrate bittersweet, unexpected victories, or to drown in whiskey defeats that could have been graver and delusions that tore them away from those who loved them.

I said to myself that in the eyes of destiny we are all voyeurs or beggars, for it is not in our power to choose other skies that we could populate with other spectacles or other gods.

Laurent stared at me with a wan smile on his lips. A mad thought, like uncontrolled grass caressing the foot of a tree, went through my mind: And what if we were close, not because of our melancholic personalities, but because he and I, each in our own way and perhaps to a different degree, were—how do you put it—afflicted souls?

"Are you still friends?" Thérèse asks me.

"No."

"How would you define your relationship?"

"He was my companion during a brief but important moment in time."

"Moment?"

"We saw each other four or five times; then I lost touch with him."

"Yet he remains present in you. More so than the many others you must have come across. Could it be because you see in him a resemblance or difference that troubles you?"

"Did I envy him? Did I fear him? Let's say he intrigued me. He made me feel disconcerted. He lived such a full life, the opposite of mine. Did he know the anguish of error, of doubt? Listening to him, I told myself that I was born too late."

"That's all?"

"No. I also told myself that he had been lucky to be able to rebuild a life. To give it meaning. To make those he loved happy. When I compare myself to him, I feel useless. I didn't do anything, didn't build anything, didn't obtain anything. Great events didn't touch me; lofty ideals didn't attract me. Compared with his story, mine seems dull, childish, and more or less futile."

I am fascinated by what I learn of the different episodes of World War II, the deadliest and most insane war in history. Those recounted to me by Laurent were the ones that Tamir wanted me to know about. They made an impression on me because they made me think about my mother and sister.

Like them, Laurent, my new friend, had been active in the clandestine struggle. Was that why I had felt close to him? Because, like my sister and mother in another country, Laurent had fought against the cruelty of the German occupier? Laurent was his nom de guerre. Idealist, daredevil, volunteer for the most dangerous missions. In spite of his youth, or perhaps because of it, he didn't wait for orders to come down. Embodying the spirit of personal initiative, he acted as he pleased. It was a question of impulse. When there was a good opportunity, he made sure not to miss it. Though they congratulated him on his successes, his superiors criticized him for his impetuousness: Didn't he know that all armies, even secret ones, had a hierarchy that had to be respected, or else his comrades might be endangered? He knew it, but his desire to defeat the enemy was stronger.

From time to time, I used to interrupt him. "Laurent," I would say, "you should write about all this."

"What for?"

"Because it's fascinating, that's why."

"What if it is? Don't tell me that everything that is interesting in life must be written up."

"Not everything, but some things."

"Which ones?"

"Those that help man progress, discover, fulfill himself."

"How are these things recognized?"

What could I answer? Romek had wanted to persuade my mother in the same way, using the same arguments. In vain. Should I press him? Laurent had already launched into another story.


"And now, as I describe him, Doctor, I ask myself: If all these events had happened to me, rather than to him, if I had been

Laurent, would I have let myself be swept up by my secret demons?"

"And what if, precisely, you had been him?" asks the doctor.

What makes her suddenly break her silence? "Why are you asking me this question, Doctor?"

"I don't know. It just popped into my mind unexpectedly. I'm thinking of our last conversation . . ."

"Well, no, I never thought I was Laurent. Are you disappointed?"

"Not at all. Continue."

"No, Doctor. First I'd like to know why you're trying to rob me of my identity. I have a right to know."

"Far be it from me to think of depriving you of your identity. Quite the contrary, I'm trying to help you to better define it so you can protect it against what's undermining it. The illness you're suffering from—as opposed to love, which protects and celebrates identity—can distort identity and bring about its loss and disintegration."

Should I answer that love . . . But the session is about to end. Thank God. I know my therapist well enough to anticipate what will come next: eroticism, love in my life, my mother's love, why I speak so little and so badly about it, and why I say nothing about women, if I have known any in my life, and if not, why. So will I forever be deprived of the joy of the senses that can only be kindled and enhanced by a woman's body? No, no, Doctor, I'm bathed in sweat; that's enough for today. In fact, excitement is bad for me; I can no longer control my words. My thoughts remain clear, but suddenly my sentences become muddled, buzz around in my head, come to a standstill, unite and intertwine, past and present merge, as human beings do, Laurent and I becoming one single self, in order to better hate ourselves and hate me, repudiate ourselves and condemn me.

Laurent, my alter ego? I repeat: his past has nothing in common with mine. In those days, time itself showed overwhelming signs of true madness.

Winter. Gray sky. Snow flurries. Icy roads. One long shiver. The homes on the long avenue de Paris are silent. The patrols are menacing, their heavy steps pounding the pavement, careful not to slip. Laurent is telling me about Rheims, on a December evening in 1942.

It is like a war film. I like war films, though I loathe war. I like them because they end with the triumph of Good over Evil. I like the pace of these films. Each shot, each word, each sign brings us closer to the death of some and the joy of others. Victory is patient. It bides its time. As for death . . . In these films, death is ubiquitous.

"That night, the entire city was shivering from the cold," said Laurent.

And from fear.

He had just left Maurice, his brother, who was living with an old friend of their father's, a former railroad engineer. As they shook hands, Maurice said, "You'll be careful?"

"Of course," Laurent replied. "I'll be back home tomorrow afternoon, as usual. As for you, stay here."

As he made his way to the bus station, Laurent began to feel anxious. It was a vague anxiety, and he had trouble pinpointing its cause. Usually his comrades admired him for his composure. So why this anxiety? He had no idea.

Would Dumas, his immediate superior, show up at the meeting place? And what if he, Laurent, was nabbed in a roundup? Would he hold his tongue when confronted by the Gestapo or the militiamen? And what about his little brother, stubborn as a mule, would he do something foolish? As it happened, it was Laurent himself who would.

And not just him. The noncommissioned German officer who

stopped him made a mistake too. Emerging out of the darkness, he focused his flashlight on Laurent's face, blinded him, and said in a low voice: *"Papieren."* Laurent slipped his hand into the pocket of his overcoat and pulled out the fake papers that identified him as a nice French boy studying at the Protestant Institute. *"Du sprichst Deutsch?"* the German asked. Remembering some Yiddish words he used to hear at home as a child, Laurent answered without thinking, *"A bissel,"* a little. No sooner had he pronounced these words than he realized his mistake. The noncommissioned officer was going to arrest him. It wasn't serious as such: his papers were good; the identity card, made by an employee in the Rouen police headquarters, was authentic. More serious? If the German brought him to the police station, he'd be searched. And in his pocket was something that could get him a death sentence: a gun taken from a soldier killed during an attack organized by Dumas a week earlier. Regaining his sangfroid, Laurent said: "I'll show you something that will convince you." He slipped his hand into his pocket again. In a split second the German was sprawled out on the snow, his flashlight still lit. Laurent bent over the body, grabbed the weapon from the German's hand, and calmly walked away without turning around.

Fifteen minutes later, he was with Maurice again. "Listen, little brother," he said, "I've just killed a German." While he hid the two guns, Laurent went on: "You must leave immediately. Very soon, the whole neighborhood will be sealed off. The army, the police, and the Gestapo bastards will search the houses. It's best to be elsewhere before they come around with their dogs."

Fortunately, they knew shortcuts to another part of the city. They found a way of getting to Paris. They took the subway to the Châtelet stop. Maurice joined their parents, who had been taken in by the wife of a neighborhood shoemaker, while Laurent contacted Dumas's liaison officer. They met in the Luxembourg Garden at lunchtime, when a great number of students clustered around the ornamental lake, seeking a bit of warmth and friendship. Laurent was ordered to go see Dumas. It was urgent. A phone call confirmed the appointment for the next day, in the late afternoon.

Broad-shouldered, wearing a leather jacket, badly shaven, with the look of a tired manual laborer, Dumas had already been informed.

"So it was you?" he asked, averting his gaze.

All the security rules had been followed. The place: a café near Les Halles. It was their first time there; the spot was reserved for exceptional occasions. Dumas had checked that there was nothing suspicious in the vicinity. Laurent had joined him a bit later. It could have been a chance meeting of two employees. Dumas stood to the right of the counter, a sign that there was no danger. The only other patrons besides the two of them were habitués. A tramp, frozen stiff, half drunk. A worker exhausted from the day's labor. Two women wearing heavy makeup being entertained by an overdressed man. They were all chatting in low voices. As though they were hoarse. A bluish light enveloped them in an unreal color. "So it was you?" Dumas asked again.

Laurent was surprised. How had his superior heard the news, and through whom? On the radio? Laurent had listened to the morning broadcast: the usual mix of triumphant news from the front and propaganda, nothing about the killing.

"So it was you?" Dumas pressed him, looking straight at him.

"Yes," Laurent replied, "it was me."

"Why? Did you forget? No personal attacks. Not without orders from above."

"I had no choice."

"Explain."

"He was going to arrest me. I was armed."

"Was he alone?"

"Not really. There was surely a patrol in the area."

Dumas didn't hide his displeasure. "You should have run away," he said. "You're young. You run fast."

"The Germans would have caught up with me."

"You were wrong to walk around armed."

Laurent didn't answer. He knew that Dumas was right. Clandestine operations required ironclad discipline. Any transgression was severely punished. Acting on your own endangered the network. Would he be expelled from the movement? For him, this would be a humiliation worse than death. "I'm sorry," said Laurent. "I really had no choice."

"I believe you, but I'm not the one who'll decide your fate."

"Then who will?" He was immediately sorry he had asked the question. He knew very well that no answer would be forthcoming.

"Does anyone know where you're staying?"

"My little brother, Maurice."

"He belongs to the movement?"

"Yes."

"He'd better go live elsewhere. You too. In a few hours the red posters will be up. They're probably ready by now. There will surely be reprisals. The Germans won't lose any time launching a manhunt; you can be sure of it. We'll probably pay dearly for this operation. Remain invisible, impossible to find. And wait for a signal from me."

He put a few francs down on the counter, nodded a vague good-bye, and left without shaking Laurent's hand. Out of caution, Laurent waited a quarter of an hour before leaving, his head filled with guilt and anxiety.

The red-and-black poster. Violent and unambiguous words. Blind fate will strike innocent people. If the Rheims killer isn't delivered to the German authorities in the next forty-eight hours, ten hostages will be executed.

Confined to his room, Laurent didn't see the poster, but he knew its content from the radio. He tried as hard as he could to stifle his tormenting feeling of guilt—all the more so since his conversation with Dumas had left a bitter taste in his mouth: he hadn't expected such strong criticism. But now he had to ask himself, What right did he have to put the lives of ten Frenchmen on the line for the life of one German? His new landlord tried to calm him: "Stop agonizing over this, and accusing yourself. It's war, my friend. If anyone should be blamed, it's the Germans." Laurent listened to him but didn't reply.

The day went by slowly and painfully. The names of the hostages hadn't been revealed yet. Laurent wondered if he knew any of them. A schoolmate? A friend of Maurice's? Suddenly, he felt a stab in his heart: What if Maurice was one of them? He had had no news from him since yesterday. Atrocious images came to his mind, and his head felt like it would burst. His brother drenched in blood, lying on the pavement, dumb with pain. And what about his parents? He jumped up and rushed to the phone. Five, six, seven long rings. Finally someone picked up—the shoemaker's wife, who set his mind at rest.

The next day the hostages were listed on the red-and-black poster. Ten names, ten faces. Condemned to death as criminals, saboteurs, and terrorists. They were to pay for the killing of the German noncommissioned officer. They were to die because Laurent thought he could spill the blood of a German without risking his own, could take the life of one of Hitler's soldiers without sacrificing the lives of innocent people. In other words, with impunity, eating and sleeping quietly. Who was the executioner of the ten prisoners? He was, Laurent—that's what the red-and-black poster clearly implied.

He went out to see for himself. He read each name slowly, stopping to think before going to the next. A Lithuanian tailor. A foreign Jew. A Polish medical student. A Jewish immigrant. A young worker of Romanian descent. An undocumented Jew. A political journalist of Hungarian descent. A foreign Jew. The names were probably fake. But not the faces. Laurent knew the journalist, Yancsi, who was also a poet. They were both Communists. They had both haunted the same circles close to the party. His accent made people laugh. He liked to sing and applaud himself. The Romanian, Yonel, had a captivating smile. Women couldn't deny him anything.

Yonel would never smile again. Yancsi would never sing again. All because of that noncommissioned bastard, Laurent said to himself. Why had he come to France? Why hadn't he stayed in Munich or Frankfurt, with his family or his beer-drinking scar-faced comrades? It was his fault, not mine. And the execution of the hostages will be his crime, not mine. Laurent kept saying this to himself, but without conviction and with no sense of relief. When death strikes, no argument can soothe a broken heart.

And where was compassion in all this? Love for one's fellow man? Fidelity? Betrayed hope? And truth? What roles did they play? And where did they belong in this world of terror?

He couldn't get his mind off the hostages, as though he sought to accompany them in their solitude. But were they alone? Admittedly, every human being meets death alone. But in the minute before, they would be together. Standing in front of the firing squad, wouldn't they all keel over at the same time? Offering their last gaze at an indifferent world, like a testament, proud of their solidarity, proud of not going alone?

Laurent couldn't sort out his thoughts. Would he have preferred to be with the hostages rather than free? It would have been more logical, more just. In truth, wasn't he really responsible for their agony and death? The Germans? They would be punished. They would lose the war; there was no doubt about that. They would be defeated, crushed, humiliated. The joy and freedom of the world would be their punishment.

And what about me in all this? Laurent asked himself. Will I be alive on that day?

That evening, a telephone call summoned him to meet with

Dumas immediately. He expected a harsh reprimand. Was he going to be judged irresponsible, unworthy of his mission, and end up expelled from the movement, left with no reason for living, erased from the memories of his colleagues? Would his deed, which he had thought heroic because necessary, make him his own victim?

Dumas was waiting for him at the appointed meeting place, near a hotel used by prostitutes. The thick, oppressive, gray twilight clouded the brain. Did it help the occupying forces or those fighting against them? A lookout was posted at each end of the small street. At the first warning, Dumas would disappear into a building across the street, whereas Laurent would be met by a professional beauty.

Dumas lost no time. First, he set Laurent's mind at rest: no one had witnessed the killing. He wouldn't be listed on any Wanted poster. But the Kommandantur felt humiliated; infuriated, it was following the Gestapo's investigation with informers of all types, double agents, and tipsters who, for ideological or opportunistic reasons, mixed in circles close to the Resistance. They were told to move heaven and earth and come back with a name, a photo, a scrap of information, a lead. The Germans said they were prepared to free the hostages if the perpetrator of the Rheims killing gave himself up. In a calm voice, Dumas said, "They're not stupid, the bastards. They know perfectly well that you won't fall into their trap. But they hope to rally the population to their propagandists, who will call us heartless criminals for sacrificing ten human lives in order to spare yours. You'll see what the collaborators will write in their rags."

Laurent listened to him without flinching. Yet an inner voice prodded him: Why don't you sacrifice yourself? It would simplify matters. No more anguish, no more guilt. In any case, if you don't, if your only thought is to save your own skin, what kind of life will you have? How could he silence this voice?

Advice from someone who knew him and loved him—that's what he needed. His parents? Maurice? No. Why add to their suffering? There was Dumas. Why not? But the latter was a step ahead of him.

"I know what you're thinking," said Dumas. "There's no sense in your playing the hero or martyr. If you give yourself up, the Germans will put you through the third degree, and do you think you'll be able to resist their methods? In the end, they'll kill you—you and the hostages. That's what they'll do. And you'll have handed them your future for nothing."

Tense to the point of pain, Laurent knew that Dumas was right. But not entirely. He was right about the torture, but Laurent would avoid it by simply killing himself before talking.

Once again, his superior seemed to guess his thoughts. He went on: "Besides, Laurent, it's not up to you. It's up to the network and the party. You've already made a serious mistake by killing that German; we forbid you to make another one."

Dumas gave him instructions for the days to come. He was to remain where he was. Phone no one. In case of an emergency, his landlord would serve as a contact. He knew whom to call and what procedure to use.

So I haven't been punished, Laurent said to himself. In the eyes of the party, I'm innocent. Tomorrow they might even praise my courage. But who am I in the eyes of the hostages? Who am I for them, their families and friends?

Laurent turned to me and looked me in the eyes with an intensity that made me ill at ease.

"What about you, Doriel? Tell me: Do you see me as a cruel man?"

"I have no right to judge you," I answered. "I didn't live through the occupation as you did. I didn't have to kill."

I was going to continue, ask him if the hostages had been executed, whether they had died together or not, whether his younger brother, Maurice, was still alive, and where his parents were. I would have liked to know if his experiences in the Resistance had played a part in making him decide to go to Israel and take a job in the intelligence services. But I had a sense I had talked too much.

Laurent must have felt the same way. He said nothing more and just smiled. And his smile seemed to me a lesson in optimism.

"Laurent is no longer a stranger to you, is he?" the doctor remarks in her impassive voice. "You said he wasn't a friend; perhaps he is more than a friend. Another aspect of yourself, maybe?"

I could slap her. Anger got the better of me. "You're not going to start again, Doctor? You're the one who needs a psychiatrist, not I. Laurent was Laurent and I am I. You're forgetting the age difference between us."

"All the same, you would have liked to be Laurent."

"I also would have liked to be Moses, Socrates, or Cicero."

"There are times we would like to be someone else and change personalities. It's quite commonplace. Several of my patients would tell you so. For varied and often obscure reasons, they hate themselves. Some even go so far as to kill themselves. Others choose a less radical method, though it's just as serious: they turn their back on reality and live in the imagination. What would be your reasons for acting like that?"

I sit up. "Honestly, you're crazy," I say. "I'll end up agreeing with Karl Kraus, his hatred of Jews and psychoanalysis, 'that disease that thinks of itself as its remedy' . . . I'm wasting my time with you. I think you enjoy making me angry. Plus you get paid. Say, if I was poor, would you still keep me on?"

She is offended and doesn't answer. Immersed in her notes, she doesn't even look at me. Is she ashamed of showing me her face? Have I touched a sensitive chord? And has she understood that she has gone too far? She makes me sick.

Before dismissing me, she assaults me with a final series of questions: "And what about the hostages? Were they executed together? And what about Laurent? What became of him? Did he really find the strength to work, hope, and love? And did he find peace and happiness in the Israeli army?"

I could answer that I already told her he was married and the father of two children. But she irks me, irritates me, infuriates me. I am near the door. Shall I turn back and give her a lesson in respect and courtesy? She still hasn't moved a muscle; her eyes are glued to her notebook. She raises her head, and unexpectedly, as happens each time I'm in front of a woman I don't know, I find her attractive, desirable, mysterious, and I am moved by both her inaccessibility and her femininity.

The following week, I resume the story of Laurent as I remember it.

Six of the ten hostages had been spared, but not Yonel and Yancsi. Dumas told Laurent about their last hours and their behavior in facing their executioners. As Catholics, the two comrades were entitled to the visit of a priest. Just to be provocative, for they were both atheists, Yancsi suggested to Yonel that they demand to see a rabbi. Yonel refused; the Germans were capable of finding one, arresting him, and sending him away in the next transport. In front of the firing squad, under a thick gray sky, they all shouted the same sentence before falling to their death: "Tomorrow it will be your turn, all of you."

Maurice was transferred to the south, but Laurent remained in Paris temporarily. Harsh, necessary, the two brothers separated without tears. They pledged to meet after the liberation. With their parents, of course. They couldn't know then that they wouldn't keep their promise. Laurent was the only one in his family to survive.

Laurent didn't stay in Paris long, and deep down, this was a relief. His great fear was that fate would make him meet the families of the hostages. He tried to reason by telling himself that, aside from Dumas, no one knew the killer's identity. But what if it became known? What could he possibly say to the son or daughter of a hostage, or to Yancsi's fiancée? That wars always make more victims than those who die in them? And yet, several years later, the thing Laurent feared most happened. Dumas and he were dining with their families in a neighborhood restaurant. It was a fragrant spring evening. The conversation was about politics, the theater, education. The two friends had broken with the party at the same time, when the Budapest uprising had been brutally repressed by the Soviets. Why had they waited so long? The question troubled them. But how could they have known about Stalinism's cruel, inhuman face? In spite of everything, they agreed about one thing: they had no regrets about having belonged to a Communist network when they had fought in the Resistance.

Suddenly, a woman sitting at a neighboring table stood up and came to talk to them.

"Excuse me for disturbing you in the middle of your meal. But I couldn't help overhearing a bit of your conversation. You were Communists and in the Resistance. I had a young brother who did the same thing. Perhaps you knew him."

Was it her Hungarian accent? Laurent had the intuition that it was Yancsi's sister who was standing before him. He wished he could leave the table and run away, but he didn't have time. The woman continued. "He was caught by the Germans. They tortured him. But he didn't talk. So they executed him. He died a hero's death."

"Yancsi," Laurent stammered with a lump in his throat.

"You knew him?"

"We knew him," said Dumas. "He was quite a man, believe me. We were proud to be his comrades."

"Proud," Laurent repeated. "But . . ." And he burst into tears.

"When I think about him," Dumas added, "I feel like crying too. But tears are pointless. We could drown our hearts in them."

Dumas lowered his head. Everyone else was stunned; they stared at one another, unsure how to react. Yancsi's sister stammered: "Please forgive me, I'm sorry . . ."

Laurent's daughter, a beautiful little girl whose name was Cécile, was the first to pull herself together and come to her father's rescue. She climbed onto his knees, kissed him many times on his forehead, hair, and cheeks, and whispered: "Don't cry, Papa, we love you."

And then Laurent said to me, "After the war, I had a nervous breakdown and was hospitalized. When I recovered, I lived a more or less normal life, though I had frequent, unpredictable relapses. In Israel, I felt better. I worked with Tamir. Our missions were interesting and often dangerous. In practical terms, they reminded me of the time of the Resistance, only the police I was running away from weren't the Gestapo. Tamir claims that I performed heroic deeds. It's a joke, he's exaggerating. But it's good to hear it."

As I listened to him, I wondered why he was telling me all this, and why Tamir had wanted me to hear it. Was he appealing to my Jewish feelings and my own memories of the Tragedy in the hope that in the end I would accept his proposal of recruitment?

"Do you want to hear something weird?" Laurent added in concluding his story. "For a long time I was unable to cry. Until that meeting with Yancsi's sister. It's those tears that healed me."

———

"And what about me, Doctor? What will heal me?

"In his own way, Doctor, Tamir-Béinish wanted to help me, that's certain. He probably thought there was a remedy for every kind of suffering. But which one would be for me? Throwing myself into the action, contributing to the development of the young state of Israel, might help me. Making myself useful, in short."

"And what did you answer?"

"I asked if I could think about it. I returned to America."

"And then?"

"Then I said no."

"Why? Was it because this new role didn't appeal to you? You couldn't see yourself as an adventurer, or simply a patriot?"

"That's not why, Doctor. I turned it down for an entirely different reason."

"What was that?"

"Tamir didn't trust me enough. In spite of my curiosity, he never really explained why he had left his wife, poor Reisele. I didn't like that.

"I never saw him again. I know he resented me. He thought I would have made an excellent secret agent. He would have trained me and sent me to an Arab country. After I turned him down, he assigned that mission to another spy. I don't know who it was. But I know he was arrested. Tortured. Hanged.

"Instead of me."

# 17

And yet. Yes: and yet. These words have become a kind of contemporary mantra. Remorse? Thérèse Goldschmidt is right: I must continue, I must. Continue to dig into my memory. Giving up would be worse. The incident she is trying to unearth must exist somewhere. A forgotten gesture, a lost word, a wound. Deep under layers of memories, the meaning of what crushes and ruins her patient lies waiting for him since . . . since when? I turn the pages, year by year, reliving one episode and clinging to the next: an event from my childhood, an image from my adolescence. And of course, bravo, Uncle Sigmund, as in the ancient illuminated annals of the early days of psychoanalysis, salvation finally comes. It has been hiding in a word, a simple word: *convulsions*.

Suddenly, my familiar, more or less stable world capsizes once again. I wonder, stunned: What about me, what am I doing in the midst of this? Indeed, I don't know how the upheaval happened. But can it be called an upheaval? *Upheaval* means sudden change, a whim of fate, an unexpected nod from the gods in search of entertainment. No. It is more the consequence, admittedly imperceptible until now, of all the events that have shaped my life, from childhood to maturity: the war followed by exile, the restless years of my education and apprenticeship in America and in the Holy Land, the distractions of love, religious fervor, and the pacifying dazzle of friendship.

Since life is made up not of years but of moments, some gloomy and others cheerful, perhaps these moments should be described, if only to identify some main thread, no matter how tenuous.

It comes. Correction: it explodes unexpectedly, in the middle of a therapy session. Absentminded, I am absentminded. I don't know exactly what I am talking about, but I know—and I knew it for a fact—that my thoughts have wandered miles away. I listen to myself hold forth while wondering what I am doing here, on the couch, staring at a crimson figure on the ceiling and thinking that someone must have forgotten it and left it as is, shapeless and useless, perhaps as a message of love or farewell to a tired mistress.

A faraway voice interrupts my observation: "So, Doriel?"

"So what?" I say, surprised.

"What happened next?"

"After what?"

I have already forgotten what secrets I just shared with the good and unbearable therapist.

"A minute ago you were telling me that when you were young, you used to have migraines. But then you quickly corrected yourself: no, not migraines, convulsions. I asked you to explain the difference. And you replied that human beings have migraines, whereas history undergoes convulsions. That's when you stopped talking."

"I said 'convulsions'? Are you sure?"

"Positive."

I repeat the word, and all of a sudden I see myself as a little boy with my parents in Poland. My heart is pounding, hammering wildly in my chest. And my father, panic-stricken, cries out: "Look, look at the child! Look, he's shaking from head to toe!"

So my mother touches my forehead and, to calm me, kisses it: "It looks like he's having convulsions!" That was the first time I heard the word.

The doctor jots something down in her notebook. I don't know if she looks at me. Maybe she just says: "Interesting, all this. We'll come back to it again the next time."

In the street, I can't shake off the word *convulsion*. All alone, in turn clothed and naked, it lives inside me like a tyrant; it darts off, skips back, runs off again at the speed of wind; it laughs and barks as if to frighten the living and pacify the dead; it slaps me and caresses me, flatters and threatens me. It is as if I have become its plaything or, more ominously, its victim.

As soon as we begin the following session, in a voice that betrays her curiosity, the doctor suggests, "Let's go back to the convulsions, if you don't mind. The word isn't neutral, nor is it innocent. What does it suggest to you? Where does it take you? Let the word guide you."

So the patient sees himself in a hospital, somewhere in California. Hypnotized, he is observing the patient in the bed next to his, a bearded adolescent who is moaning and shaking from head to toe. As though an electric current is going through his body and following a strict, continuous pathway, going from limb to limb, from forehead to neck, from right eye to left eye, from upper lip to lower lip; it is like watching a marionette in the nervous hands of an impassive man, completely engrossed in his experiences. "What's wrong with him?" he asks the examining physician.

"A massive dose of LSD. He's in another world, an unreal, dreamlike world. In his hallucination, he's watching the dramatic battle between life and death, angels and demons. At times, it's one side that's winning, at times, it's the other. Ergo his convulsive movements."

In a refugee camp in Asia. A crowd of children in rags is surrounding an emaciated old man who, head thrown back, is dancing and spinning at a staggering rhythm. "What's wrong with him?" he asks his guide.

"He's a saint. He knows how to make the everyday sacred. His method? His soul goes into a trance; it will soon pick up his body and raise it to lofty heights."

Extreme suffering, inexpressible joy, incandescent love—each is accompanied by convulsions in order to be better fulfilled in the instant preceding birth, death, or the final revelation.

Suddenly, without any transition or apparent connection, I see myself in our house in Poland again, on a beautiful spring Sunday. I am still a child. I am with my parents in the garden. I am basking in the joy of their reunion. It is quiet in the little city. Peace reigns over God's Creation. The spell is broken by Romek's sudden arrival. I already know that I dislike him and should distrust him as someone bringing misfortune and a curse. Yet Romek is all smiles and bearing an armful of gifts. I don't move; I want to listen to the adults. They talk about the war and the clandestine group Romek and my mother belonged to. "Do you remember?" Naturally, she remembers. "And what about . . . ?" Of course, how could he forget? My father barely intervenes. Why do I feel ill at ease? Is it because, like my father, I feel excluded from this exchange and these memories?

Eons later, I wonder why my heart starts beating wildly. Why my breath races until I am filled with a somber, baleful anguish.

It's because of Romek; I can swear to it. The memory of that man who . . . who what? Who managed to come between my father and my mother. As soon as he arrived, a wholesome equilibrium was broken, giving way to a heavy, silent, impalpable tension.

All of a sudden, unexpectedly again—or was it the magical effect of analysis?—I relive an episode that I haven't remembered since the war. Why has it remained hidden? Too painful perhaps. And unpleasant. And certainly annoying, like vague murmurs coming from a neighboring room preventing sleep and impeding one's thoughts.

It is just a furtive image from that same day. The sun is setting. My father leaves the garden for a few minutes. Did he go to get a glass from the kitchen or a book from his bookcase? Romek and my mother remain in the garden. I am standing a short distance from them. That's when I catch Romek's look as he leans toward my mother and speaks to her in a low voice. He is probably asking her a question, for my mother responds right away, shaking her head: "No, it's over." The man insists, and my mother keeps saying: "I told you: it's over. You shouldn't try to break up a family, and certainly not mine." Again, he perseveres. And my mother, in a reproachful tone of voice, replies, "The past is the past; if you keep doing this, you'll only make it ugly."

His head lowered like a culprit, Romek whispers, "Once, just once, that's all I ask." My mother is about to say something, but my father has already returned.

That night I ran a fever. Shivering, my vision blurry, I became delirious. The physician summoned to my bedside explained: "The child must have caught a cold or got a sunburn, causing convulsions." My mother, wringing her hands, said, "Look at him. His whole body is shaking. It looks like he's having a nightmare. Does he sometimes think about Dina and Jacob and not want to tell us about it? Yet he looked happy until now. How could he not be with his parents by his side?"

Actually, I had been happy, but my happiness was shattered with just one look at my mother in the midst of her argument— for that's what it was—with Romek, who talked to her as though he had rights over her. Later on, one question plagued me incessantly, more or less consciously: What would have happened if my father had not turned up again at just that moment?

Could these images and this question have slyly crept into my brain and haunted me, so much so that they affected my behavior with women? Should I admit to this now, though my rational mental faculty has been advancing simpler arguments for ever so long? I was looking, it said, for the right woman, the one and only woman whom fate had picked out for me. But I hadn't found her yet. Or: Isn't it irresponsible of a couple to bring children into the world against their will, a world that isn't waiting for them and that won't love them?

But the real explanation, I discovered with amazement, may be this unavowed, never formulated suspicion that slowly, relentlessly, imprisoned me in the asceticism of celibacy, condemning me to solitude and restless, confused thoughts.

"It's possible," says the doctor, when silence sets in.

I give a start, like someone caught red-handed: Has she read my mind? Have I been thinking out loud?

"What's possible?"

"When we think everything is lost in the abyss, including the sense of orientation and purity, we sometimes cling to its walls. Without even knowing whether it serves a purpose."

The doctor lowers her voice, as though she is talking to herself. "This helps us survive," she says, "but it doesn't help us live."

I don't answer. What's the point? A thought crosses my mind: perhaps we should imagine the gods driven insane by men.

# 18

Martin is reading the newspaper with such concentration that I have to force myself to interrupt him.

"Do you believe in mystical madness?" I ask.

"As much as in political madness," he answers without raising his head.

He irritates me. Why didn't he marry a journalist? For years I've known that I have a rival on Sundays: the press. Both major and minor. The local dailies and the national ones. Weeklies, monthlies, he's interested in everything: current events, news and editorials, the literary pages, sports, cooking. I'm marginal, like a paragraph. "Explain," I said.

"Both are murderous." Since I'm silent, he adds: "The Crusades, the Inquisition, Nazism, Communism . . ."

"But Doriel isn't a murderer. I don't see the slightest hint of violence in him. Anger, yes, but that's it."

A shrug by way of answer—that's Martin when he's reading his newspaper. Usually I keep busy so as not to ruin his pleasure. This morning, I'm too restless. Frustrated.

"I need a book on the dybbuk; I'm sure you have one in your library."

My word, he raises his head. He looks at me. "No doubt," he says. "You can find everything in our library. But why?"

"What do you mean, why?"

"Why are you suddenly interested in the subject?"

Biting my lips, I reply: "Doriel claims a dybbuk inhabits him."

"You believe this?"

"What I believe hardly matters. He seems to believe it. He thinks this explains his behavior, his inadequacies, his illness."

"What does he expect from you? Are you supposed to exorcise him? Only great mystics—and they're rare—could do it. Whereas you, you're . . ."

I don't like his tone of voice. It betrays his annoyance. Clearly this Doriel story and my involvement in it rub him the wrong way. "I'm sorry to have disturbed you, but please, tomorrow, bring me a couple of books on the subject."

The next day I find a bulky file on my desk, assembled by the library's specialist in the occult: a film in Yiddish (with subtitles), a play translated into English, a few essays, and an explanatory note informing me that most of the works on the subject are in Hebrew or Yiddish.

The specialist added a few pages written especially for me. I learn that dybbuks are mentioned neither in the Bible nor in the Talmud. They are featured repeatedly in the literature of the Kabbala and in the popular folklore, especially central European Hasidic folklore. In these sources, the dybbuk is the soul of ungodly persons whose transgressions don't even deserve to be judged, for the greatest punishments would be inadequate. That's why dybbuks wander throughout the world in search of a fragile person whom they can penetrate by force. The Lurianic Kabbalists such as Rabbi Hayyim Vital, Rabbi Israel Ba'al Shem Tov, the Master of the Good Name, and some other masters had the power to heal a victim through exorcism. Actually, the expert explains, there is a kind of handbook that was used to drive a dybbuk out of a body and a life. The ritual is solemn and grave; it must instill fear. The room is lit with black candles.

Everything is black. The cursed soul is summoned by a special rabbinical court and ordered to explain its conduct. Threatened with irreversible, eternal anathema, the dybbuk is compelled to leave its refuge and go into oblivion.

From the psychiatric point of view, this whole story calls to mind symptoms of schizophrenia and neurosis, but I know I'm not sufficiently knowledgeable to tackle the subject.

What should I do?

If this continues, I'll end up believing in dybbuks. Hasn't Doriel become mine?

# 19

A great teacher asks: "Who is the most tragic figure in the Bible?"

A disciple answers: "Abraham, the first believer who was given the order to sacrifice his beloved son to his God."

"No," the teacher replies. "Abraham sensed that in the last minute God would forbid him to carry out the sacrifice."

"Isaac?" another disciple asks. "Bound up by his father and laid on the altar, his life about to be given as the supreme offering?"

"No again," says the teacher. "An inner voice reassured Isaac: his father wouldn't see it through."

"Could it be Moses?" a third disciple suggests. "The most solitary man in the world, forever torn between the commandments of heaven and the needs of the people?"

"No again: he knew his victories would affect the destiny of his people; how could his life be tragic?"

"But then, who is it?" all the disciples cry out in unison.

"It is the Lord, may He be blessed," says their teacher. "From His throne on high, He contemplates what human beings are doing with His Creation. And it makes Him sad."

Recalling this lesson, for some odd reason, as I stroll down the noisy streets of Manhattan after a particularly trying analytic session, I search my mind: Why this hammering racket and the constant need for silence that make my head spin? After all this time spent wandering on the roads of exile, when will I find some rest? And what about God in all this? Could man be the blunder of his Creator, his nightmare, perhaps even his grief, what humans call melancholy? Doomed to despair, whose prisoner or victim is man? Why is he punished and enslaved? How can he save himself? And as always when man comes up against an insurmountable obstacle, I wonder: What about me in all this? Suddenly I realize that I can't answer these questions. I know only that I have followed a path that appears to lead nowhere. Is it too late to turn back? To demand the right to define myself in a world haunted by so many strangers? At my age, it is time he faced the facts. He had been wrong to stay single. Wrong not to get married. Wrong not to start living again when he arrived in New York with his uncle. Wrong not to think about the future, of a life that produces life. Was it too late and irrevocable? Too late to form ties that would promise the possibility of another reality and happiness? Faces flash before my eyes as on a movie screen or as on a stage with changing sets. It's as if, without leaving the footlights, every once in a while, vibrant young girls and women with warm, promising smiles come to join me in my box. The pious young woman from Brooklyn. The singer with flaming red hair on the deck of the boat going from Marseilles to Haifa. The widow who sought to console herself in the arms of strangers. I could have married one of these women. Was it really too late to create an identity as a husband and father, or at least to create a place for myself in the colorful landscape of a community?

In those days, I often felt that everything that happened to me escaped me. Everything glided over my existence: I retained nothing.

As for our sessions, Doctor, I'm confused. I'm your patient and you're my only hope. All my real-life or imaginary stories, all these burdens full of remorse and guilt—it is to you that I show them. Tell me what I should do with them.

———

"I'd like you to explain something to me," says Thérèse. "You're cultured, wealthy, and quite intelligent. How come you never married?"

"I could answer that I'm mad, but not so mad as to take a wife. But joking apart, I've already told you: I always believed that my past and the state it left me in don't allow me to beget life."

"Be frank, Doriel. Is that the only reason?"

It's foolish, but I feel myself blushing.

"What's her name?"

"Ayala."

"Pretty name. And her? Did you love her?"

Her name was, no, excuse me—I called her Ayala. She enriched my life for several days, and it is with her that I hoped—wrongly, of course—for a measure of serenity.

Ours was a chance encounter. I say chance because it might very well have never taken place; everything separated us. She was French, I was American. She came from a rich family, and I had almost no family. She was beautiful, whereas my body had long ago forgotten its vigor. She was twenty-two years old; I was almost three times that age.

We were sitting side by side on a Paris–New York flight. I was going there to spend the High Holy Days with the children and grandchildren of Aunt Gittel and Uncle Avrohom. And, while I was there, I also planned to meet a Yiddish poet, Yitzhok Goldfeld, little known but admired by those who have had the opportunity to read him and approach him. As for Ayala, she was going to join her fiancé, though she didn't know whether she would be marrying him.

She started the conversation.

"This is going to be a long trip," she said. "I have difficulty sleeping in planes. I'll try to read and I'd appreciate it if you wouldn't disturb me. Even when I stop reading. I have to take advantage of these few hours to think." She paused. "Because I have decisions to make. Important ones. There, that's all."

I nodded in agreement. Should I tell her that I also had decisions to make? Reveal to her the real reason for my trip? That my peace of mind was at stake, hence my health, my future? She didn't seem interested. With a brusque gesture she opened her book, and I opened mine. Coincidence? We were reading the same novel. Though badly conceived and poorly written, it was a story set during World War II, the period I'm most interested in reading about, and the book had been on the best-seller list for weeks.

An hour went by. The captain and the crew had ministered to our mood by providing us with information and useful instructions: altitude, speed, approximate hour of arrival, and, in a sober and serious tone of voice, instructions on how to handle the life jacket in case of . . . A buxom blonde offered us paradise: Did we want to drink? Eat? A blanket to help us sleep more soundly? No takers in my row. She had more luck in the next row. All of a sudden, my neighbor began to speak without looking at me.

"If I decide to talk to you, do you promise not to ask my name?"

"I don't know you; I don't have to promise you anything."

"Are you cruel, or stupid?"

"Is that a choice? Can't one be stupidly cruel or cruelly stupid?"

She gave me a withering look and turned away.

"Actually," I said, "I'm rather pleased with your request. Pleased not to know your name. And can I tell you why?

Because, if you'll allow me, I intend to give you the gift of a name, an original name."

"Which one?"

"I don't know yet. Let me think. But in the meantime, talk to me, since you feel like it. Hearing your voice will inspire me. As you surely know, there's a connection between names and voices."

"Fine. But I'll stop when I want to."

"I'm listening."

Her voice. Deep, melodious, caressing: it was her voice that I immediately liked. The voice of someone who is searching while trying to find herself. I was overcome by a feeling of well-being and serenity. I could easily have dozed off, taking her voice with me in my sleep.

"There," she said. "That's all."

I hadn't understood a thing she had just told me. None of her words had stuck in my mind.

"No," I answered, half awake. "Don't stop. That's not everything. It's only the beginning."

"The beginning of what?"

"Of a dream. An affair. A love story. Of a promise made of taboos and sunshine deep in the night. Don't be afraid; I have no intention of courting you. Look at me: I'm old, too old for that, too old for you. Oh, if only I were younger . . ."

"What would you do?"

"I would hold your hand. Yes, your hand. Nothing more."

And the miracle occurred. I felt a hand squeezing mine.

Nothing more, said the voice that seemed to resonate inside me as if to comfort someone in me.

In the darkness that had pervaded the inside of the plane, I started to think about all the human beings I had encountered in my life. Each one had a face, a body, and a name. With each I had had moments of joy that made me want to sing, or grim times that had made me want to weep; and from now on I wouldn't experience either. Yes, with age, the body senses the traps, foresees the dangers, and imposes caution; it has to accept its limits. And yet. What did I have to lose by smiling once more at destiny? In love, everything happens in a flash—with, as a necessary ingredient, surprise, astonishment, and the feeling of a miracle. All I had to do right now was play the game, nudge the story forward, but without moving.

"Don't tell me your name; neither now nor later. My name for you is Ayala."

"May I ask why?"

"Ayala is a doe. She races."

"Please explain what you mean."

"In the Jewish texts, life is sometimes compared to a race, a flight. To a dream too. In the Orient, life is nothing but illusion. A doe carried away by illusion. Or an illusion carried away by a doe."

I expected to see her smile, but she retained her serious expression. "Does this mean I have to get rid of my real name? Throw it to the four winds? Become a virgin again, empty of all memories?"

"Of course not, dear Ayala. For this one night, I take you as you are, with all your baggage."

"And afterward?"

"Let's forget about duration; let's dismiss time."

"And afterward?"

"For madmen, afterward does not exist."

"I'm not mad."

"But perhaps I am."

She withdrew her hand. She didn't like madmen. They frightened her. Something inside me tore apart. A grace—or a curse—of a few minutes had sufficed; all paths had opened and then closed again. It was as though, here in this airplane, we had met, loved each other, married, and divorced. I blamed myself for my recklessness, my lack of maturity and seriousness. I had been foolish and ridiculous. At my age, you don't play games like these anymore. You don't babble rashly and idly. My neighbor surely thought I was an idiot, if not worse.

I don't know for how long we kept silent.

I woke up shortly before landing.

"I like my new name," said Ayala, smiling. "I'll make her discover America. And by way of thanks, here's what I propose: if we ever have another chance encounter, I'll tell you whether I succeeded in separating from my fiancé. And then—"

"And then?"

"And then we'll see."


In the Williamsburg section of Brooklyn, a tall, thin man, whose mouth is deformed by a tic, warns me that it's not easy to see the poet Yitzhok Goldfeld; he is unwell.

"I've come a long way," I said.

"Here geography is an outdated notion. Poetry lies outside and beyond frontiers."

"But my case is urgent."

"Are you sick?"

"Yes . . . no. But he knew my uncle Avrohom."

"He isn't the only person named after our patriarch."

"My uncle Reb Avrohom."

"And the rabbi knows him?"

"They knew each other."

"Are you sure?"

"They knew each other."

Actually, the idea for this meeting had come from my uncle. He had been worried about the waning intensity of my fidelity to God. He had felt that I was distancing myself not from my family or what was left of it but from what he regarded as greater than happiness and peace: the fear of God and the love of God.

We had had many conversations on the subject. He used to present his arguments and I my objections. I didn't question the existence of a supreme judge governing the universe of men, but I questioned his justice. One day, echoing the remarks Gittel had once made, I asserted that, if pushed, I could accept the tragically premature and absurd death of my parents. Perhaps they had sinned before the Eternal and He had punished them. But what about their progeny, their little orphan? What were his sins? Why had he been condemned to grow up and live his life without them? At that my good uncle could only shake his head and repeat: "He knows better than we do what He is doing and why." That's when he advised me to visit his old friend, the mystical poet Yitzhok. "I don't know if he is interested in curing the ailment that is loss of faith, but it's worth a try. If nothing else, you'll discover a great poet." And that's how, several years after Avrohom's death, I decided to follow his advice.

I had been warned that it would be complicated and difficult. This Yiddish poet is practically unapproachable. Everyone wants to spend time with him. Students want to show him what they've written about his worldview. Journalists want to question him on his interpretation of Ecclesiastes and the Psalms. Naïve visitors think he is a wealthy donor. In short, all those who seek hope and help. Like me.

This mystic is my last chance to overcome the ailment undermining me. I've tried everything. The leading medical experts in New York and Paris, Amsterdam and Los Angeles, know my case. I really need a miracle.

This poet must look me in the eyes. May his eyes see what there is to see. May he listen to me. May he talk to me. May he correct the errors of nature in me. Or those of the Lord.

"Listen," I said to the guardian at the door, "don't send me away empty-handed; I'm a grateful person."

"Don't try to bribe me," he answered nastily. "I don't need

your money. I'm a physician. What I need isn't something you could give me."

"What's that?"

"Some *yirat shamayim,* fear of heaven. Do you have any of that to hand me?"

I lowered my head. If he only knew . . . The physician disappeared. He certainly wouldn't rescue me. The minutes passed. He reappeared.

"I have good news for you. You're right, Reb Yitzhok knew your uncle. Return tomorrow morning. If he feels better, he'll receive you. Otherwise, return the day after tomorrow."

"Thank you."

"So, return."

"This word seems to be your favorite word."

"Maybe. For some of us, *teshuva,* 'the return,' also means the desire to repent. What about for you?"

"For me all words are the same."

I kept talking to myself to illustrate what I'd said. Yes and no. Yesterday or tomorrow, joy or mourning. It's all the same. Even a good deed and a bad deed.

The physician scrutinized me at length, evidently wondering if he should get mad or disregard me, and ended up retiring without saying a word.

I could have gone home, but I remained in the neighborhood. I walked into a few small congregations where they were studying the Talmud and singing. I looked at the men and women who had heard one of the teachers comment on the texts and their secrets. Strange, they all understood that each person was given one hour to allow his or her soul to open a door in the celestial palace where everything is accomplished or undone.

One of the faithful recounted that, one day, while the Master of Rovidok, on a visit in Safed, was studying the mysteries of the apocalypse and redemption, a fanatic penitent with a powerful build burst into the home where he was staying and, breathing fire and fury, yelled, in front of the stunned students: "If you don't make the Messiah come right away, I'll kill you." And since the master made no reply, the penitent threw himself on him to strangle him. The only person who wasn't frightened was the old man. He addressed his aggressor in a gentle and melancholic voice: "And if you kill me, do you think the Messiah will come?"

At which point the intruder started to sob. "My last hope has just gone up in smoke."

"No," said the old man. "It will return one day, and, I hope, will lead you before the Redeemer."

Someone asked the storyteller if his tale had a sequel. What happened to the man and his violent streak? One evening he appeared in Jerusalem's Old City, distraught and wild, knocking at doors and windows, yelling loudly: "I'm speaking in the name of the invisible prophet who lives up high, in the celestial spheres. He says to you: Follow me before chasing me, fear me before hating me . . . Man has the choice between the inferno and the dried-out tree . . . I am your first hope! Your only hope!"

And I wondered where that madman had gone—he who was fighting against just one enemy: despair. And what about the ever so serene master, should he be seen as his ally or his opponent?

Another visitor took over from the first. He too had a story up his sleeve. Another madman. I listened to him too. I had time. Then, weighed down with my own stories of faith and disappointment, I asked myself while continuing my stroll: Why not contact my old friends and acquaintances from the yeshiva again, if they're still alive? What if I found Ayala? And tried to convince her to leave her fiancé? A crazy, indecent idea; I was too old for her. And then other preoccupations came to mind. I told myself that I came here, and if I was made to wait, it must be because someone wanted it, programmed it; it was up to me to discover why and with what aim, for I alone could give meaning to that aim.

The next day, the poet received me. In a narrow, badly lit room, sitting at a table covered with books, his eyes both searching and soothing, he let silence set in. My first reaction? I was disconcerted by his age. Like Reb Yohanan before him, he seemed surprisingly energetic. Did he draw his strength from his poetic vision of man in time? His gaze alone was old. My heart began to pound wildly, very wildly; blood rushed to my head. What did he see inside me? What secrets was he unearthing? Why was he remaining silent? Could it be to destabilize me, put me in a state of inferiority, if not guilt? My lips began to quiver unpleasantly.

Finally, he decided to let his voice be heard; it was hoarse, deep, stamped with an indefinable reticence. Speaking was a painful ordeal for him.

"You live alone," he asserted, not letting me avert my gaze from his.

"Yes," I said. "Alone."

"Is that why you've come here?"

"No."

"Is it because you've read some of my poems?"

"No again."

"Is it because you want to discuss Yiddish literature with me and the fact that it is dying?"

"Not really."

"Perhaps you have—how shall I put it?—literary ambitions?"

"Certainly not."

"So why?"

"I don't understand . . ."

"Why are you here? To tell me you're alone? Why are you alone? Have you always been? Yet you had parents, friends? Did you deliberately choose to shut yourself up inside your body and its solitude?"

I felt disoriented, destabilized, shaken, and slightly disappointed. Was I wrong to want to see him? Would I admit to him, "I'm not right in the head"? His questions seemed simplistic and banal to me. Where were his writing gifts and his gift for self-expression? Should I first talk to him about my uncle, and then about my illness?

However, the poet resumed the dialogue, punctuating it with questions, at times specific, at times vague, about my childhood, my religious experience, my inner struggle between the angel of goodness and the angel of evil.

"What do you expect from me?" he finally asked.

"Actually, I don't know. A miracle perhaps."

"What kind?"

"I don't know. All I know is that I suffer from both a deficiency and an excess. From superabundance and complete emptiness."

"Poets experience the same pain."

"But I'm not a poet."

"In that case, what are you?"

"As far as I can read people's gazes, they see me as mad. And I've always felt I was. Mad about my parents first, then about God, study, truth, beauty, and impossible love."

The poet lifted his head and stared at me at length. "For a man like you, writing can become an anchor, a refuge perhaps," he said.

"But writing has an animus toward me. To write, though you have to love words, they also have to love you. Mine scoff at me. As soon as I choose one, ten others spring up and chase it away."

The poet smiled and said, "The opposite happens to me. Ten words turn up before me, because of the richness of my language; but I just want one. And that one often stays hidden."

Since I remained silent, he pursued his questioning. "What about your studies, where do you stand with them?"

"I never really interrupted them. I didn't forget anything, Reb Yitzhok. But my knowledge is of no help to me. Like everything else, I have the impression that it drives me mad. That's the way it is: the madman within me is stronger than I am."

The ailing poet stood up. And I realized that he didn't invite me to sit down. He was tall, a head taller than me. Thin, stoop-shouldered, he bit his lips incessantly. Would he show me to the door? He sat down again in his armchair and motioned to me to take a chair.

"First of all," he said after a sigh, "I want to warn you: I'm not a miracle maker. With God's help, I only know how to make words. God alone can change the laws of nature. And his ways remain secret. I can only help you see more clearly within yourself. Is that enough for you?"

A thought crossed my mind: I'd never met him before, yet he addressed me with the familiar "you." But I didn't reciprocate, and this had nothing to do with age. I respected him, this man whom so many human beings admired.

"At least tell me this: Do you still think that our meeting can help you?"

"I think so," I said in a very low voice. But how? I have no idea. Is the light inside the nightmare any more stable? The meaning of destiny any more apparent? The threat any less close? Would I succeed in better orienting myself within and without, around the traps inside me and the traps encountered along the way?

The physician came in and signaled discreetly to his teacher: he felt the conversation had lasted long enough, but he withdrew immediately.

"Tell me more about your solitude," said the ailing poet. "Why did you accept it? Didn't you know it could lead to despair, sometimes even to madness? God alone is alone. We, His creatures, must build families, a community. You have neither wife nor children. Why? Aren't you afraid of departing from this world without leaving descendants, heirs, traces? Is vanishing forever and ever what you want? Talk. I'm listening. It is in talking to me that you'll better understand yourself."

"It's a long story," I said. "And time—"

"Forget time. You've come from far away. You wanted to see me. You're seeing me. You thought you needed me. I'm here. Right now, I'm here only for you."

Where should I begin? Where would I locate the first cracks? The first falls, the first defeats, the first wrenching torments, the first breakdowns? The invasion of darkness and gloom, their end-of-the-world howling that I carried within myself and that acted as my tutors?

In a halting voice, stumbling over my words, I told him about my exiled childhood, the death of my parents, the feeling of guilt that haunted the orphan I had been and still was. The attraction of the void. Admittedly, more than once, on many occasions, upon meeting a young woman with a voice I liked, I could have started a family. Each time, almost at the last minute, I retreated in fear. I said to myself: I'm not ready, not yet ready to express my trust in man and his humaneness. Not ready to say to the world: I believe in you and in those who mold you; I want to participate in your undertaking and be included in your future. Not ready to give the world my children doomed beforehand.

And then there was my illness. I gave it an inadequate name, but perhaps, with his poetic gifts, he would succeed in describing what was hidden in my innermost being. Since childhood, I'd endured an ineffable feeling of emptiness, of defeat, but how could I make him feel it? I felt guilty about my parents; I was now older than they had been. Did I have the right to judge them, particularly my mother? Did I have the right to suspect her? Should I tell him about the hallucinations that sometimes washed over me like ocean waves and drowned out the last flashes of my lucidity?

I told him about the evening when, weakened, my body

aching from IVs, I woke up in a psychiatric clinic. I had just been rescued from a botched suicide attempt. Voices came to me, some muffled, others deafening. In his delirium the man in the neighboring bed was taking heaven to task. I grasped only one word in three, but they managed to put me to sleep. The next day, I tried to start a conversation with him. Why was he so mad at God? The allusion immediately cut him to the quick. He went through all his criticisms, all his laments, all his accusations: starting with the exodus from Egypt and the Sinai desert to Auschwitz, and including the Babylonian, Persian, and Roman persecutions, the Crusades and the ghettos; there has never been any respite for the descendants of Abraham, Isaac, and Jacob, he said in angry indignation—and why? Why the death of a million and a half children during the great and terrible upheaval? At one point, he stopped and cried out: "We know that for a man born blind, God is blind, but what about a man born mad? Could his God be . . . ? May God forgive me." Strange fellow; he wanted to die because he no longer believed in God—

"Stop. That's enough," said Reb Yitzhak, obviously hurt. "Change the subject. Quickly. Earlier, I thought of using your stories and integrating them into my poems. I give up on this; blasphemers put me off."

"Listen to me for a few more minutes," I implored him. "I have one very recent last story I need to tell you."

I told him about my one and only meeting with Ayala, the young fiancée on the airplane. About the nostalgia that gripped me when I thought of her, a strange feeling, for I couldn't grasp its meaning. I didn't know anything about her, or about how I would react to her; I didn't know if my body would awaken under her gaze and give me long-vanished sensations and joys. And yet she occupied my thoughts; even in this room, she was present, as if she wanted to take part in our conversation.

"Ayala," Reb Yitzhok repeated, his hand on his forehead. "That's a beautiful name for a Jewish woman . . ."

"It's only a name," I said.

"But it is beautiful. I've never met a woman by that name."

"The woman by that name matches her name; she is strange."

"Do you feel guilty about her?"

"No. At least, not yet."

"Because she told you she wanted to break off her engagement?"

"Perhaps."

"But what if she hasn't yet?"

"She has. I'm certain of it."

"Well, then, what do you plan to do? Marry her? Isn't she too young for you?"

I didn't answer. I hadn't come to ask his advice, but . . . actually, why had I come? So he would help me lighten the burden on my shoulders by chasing away the demons determined to possess me and then destroy me? Did I really want him to heal me?

"So," resumed the poet, "do you plan to marry her? If so, is it a challenge to your past or an appeal to what is left of your future?"

"I have no idea," I said. "I haven't thought about it. All of this has nothing to do with—how shall I put it?—my problem. I felt the need to come and see you well before meeting Ayala."

"And what was the original reason for your visit?"

"I don't know what to answer at this point. Can a reason change along the way?"

"I imagine you expected me to rescue you, didn't you?"

"Yes, in a certain sense."

"But rescue you from whom, from what, exactly? From yourself? From fear? From the fear of death perhaps? Or of love?"

"I expected you to lead me to the path that would bring me back to myself," I said to him hesitantly.

He looked at me for a long time without saying a word. Then, lowering his head, in a barely audible whisper, he gave me what I thought was a benediction.

Ayala? I never saw her again. She must have married her fiancé.

Nor did I ever see the Yiddish poet again. But one week later, very early in the morning, while drinking my coffee, the curtain suddenly ripped open. Was it the result of that meeting?

And the young woman with the smile of a frightened child whom I searched for all my life?


Today, when I finish telling my story, I say to myself that the failure was actually my fault, not Thérèse's; she has done her work conscientiously, but I have done everything to put obstacles in her path. She has lived up to her commitment, whereas I haven't. Didn't I agree to let her explore the murkiest corners of my unconscious? Yet I never spoke to her about Samek. She has questioned me several times, without ever being insistent, on how I support myself. But whenever she seemed surprised by my generous gifts ("Goodness, you seem to have unlimited funds. Could you be an Arab prince disguised as an unhappy Jew?") I've dodged the issue with a shrug.


In the end, I don't know if the doctor has helped me very much. My migraines keep coming around, my sleep is still troubled, and my dreams are still haunted. Night is merely an endless wait before the savoring of dawn. My head and soul are at war. I always feel uncomfortable about myself and about my life, dragging around a somber melancholy that has become a kind of second nature.

My therapy has been interrupted. I didn't make the decision; my therapist did. Surprised and offended, I protested: I had come to enjoy our sessions, even when she talked on and on about the

libido and its strange but logical designs, or the unconscious and its mysterious but rational power; even when she shocked me by insinuating that I saw my mother in every woman, and that this explained my consistently ambiguous and fearful relationships with women. I felt at home on her couch, looking up at her ceiling, drawing on images from my earliest childhood. I wanted to continue. Seeing my insistence, contrary to her habit, the doctor agreed to explain her decision.

"I have many reasons," she said. "Professional and not. First of all, there's the undeniable fact that I'm of no help to you anymore. Admittedly, in helping you to remember your convulsions, we made an important breakthrough. But it was the last one. Your preposterous story about a dybbuk left me feeling helpless and depressed. I'm not an exorcist by profession. I don't believe in superstitions; they're for fanatics or simpletons. Not for someone like me, who doubts everything. Whereas you, Doriel . . . For some time now, we haven't been making progress anymore. Earlier, we were moving forward, step by step, with sudden, astonishing glimmers of light. Not anymore. I listen to you, I observe you; you're still living your life badly. An unspeakable suffering is undermining you. You can't understand what you're doing on this earth. And it isn't just a memory problem, whether a failing memory or an overactive one: in either case, it is possible to live a more or less normal life. But in both cases, we could also talk about mental illness. Some have made their choice so as to continue living in society. Only with you, there's something else as well—there's an element that keeps slipping away and scoffing at me. Your illness, in no way pathological, and not necessarily linked to memory, which is inevitably selective, comes from an impenetrable area that you call mystical. Persecuted by the gods, you flee from human beings. But when God is the enemy, I refuse to take part in the fight."

"I thought you were more courageous."

"It's not that I don't have courage," she said, "but faith isn't my field. Appalling situation. It makes me suffer. I don't trust my judgment anymore. We're not getting ahead. Your compartmentalized areas remain obscure; no light, no warmth gets inside them."

The doctor stopped talking, no doubt to reflect before resuming a monologue that could make her admit to shameful things.

"In the beginning, I hoped, though with trepidation, that the Freudian theory would apply in your case. You know, according to the well-known principle of transference, the patient ends up falling in love with his or her therapist. At one point, I came to think that, in order to speed that process up, I should, on the contrary, perhaps adopt an affectionate, indeed amorous, attitude toward you. God is my witness that I tried everything and even risked everything. My husband noticed it before I did, and that led us as a couple to the edge of disaster. Fortunately, we were able to avoid it. But as far as you're concerned I admit defeat. And that's why it's time for us to separate."

There was such sadness in her that I found myself feeling sorry for her, as though she was suffering and not I. How could I help her? Should I have tried to convince her that, lost in my labyrinth, I needed her more than ever—her attentiveness, her knowledge, her way of guiding me and arousing my memories of those I loved, and especially her silence?

Thereupon, she handed me a thick envelope.

"What I'm doing isn't very orthodox," she said. "What I mean is, I'm violating the rules analysts follow. I'm giving you some notes that concern you. Don't ask me why I'm doing this; I don't know myself. Maybe because of the special quality of our relationship. In my office, this is usually not the way things happen. It may be that I also feel guilty about you; I didn't give you the support and help you were entitled to. Now it's your turn. With a bit of luck, you'll cure yourself on your own. Here, take these notebooks and try not to judge me."

At a loss for words that would be convincing and truthful enough, I remained silent. And, contrary to habit, she was nonplussed by my silence.

"Besides," she resumed in a tense voice, "you've overpaid me. I still don't know where your money comes from, and this bothers me. I feel I should give it back to you. Are you a banker? The principal stockholder of a multinational? A Russian spy? An arms dealer?"

I almost burst out laughing but restrained myself. "You have quite an imagination, my dear doctor," I said.

"Perhaps. But I've learned to be wary of people who have too much money to hand out, especially when I don't know how they earn it."

I jumped up and sat down facing her. I asked, "How much time do you have left this afternoon?"

"You're my last patient."

"Very good. Let me tell you a story."

For the first time since I'd known her, she lit a cigarette.


Once again, it's a crazy story. But a beautiful one because it's a tribute to generosity. And it will answer the questions you have about my wealth.

It takes place in Brooklyn, before my trip to Israel, which is still only in the planning stage. I am job hunting. I have to keep busy and pay the cost of my trip. Aunt Gittel has died. My uncle is getting old and is easily tired. I can't count on his help anymore, and I have no profession. In my circle, young men find work easily in business or in the rapidly expanding field of computer science. Computers, neutral in matters of religion, seem to attract them and talk to them—but I'm the exception. I have no understanding whatsoever of computers, and the feeling is mutual. I could become a taxi driver, except I have no sense of direction, and besides, I've never learned to drive. Should I count on a miracle? I've stopped believing in them ages ago.

I was wrong.

I was twenty years old. One fine winter morning, my uncle asked me if I knew someone called Samek Ternover; he had phoned several times and was trying to reach me. No, the name wasn't familiar. His Yiddish was good and he had left his telephone number, my uncle added. Why not call him back? Well, I'd gladly do that favor for the man who almost considered me a son.

My good uncle was right. Samek's Yiddish was melodious and delightful. And he wanted to meet me. As soon as possible. It was rather urgent. Curious, I asked him why. "Not over the phone," he replied.

I felt a vague anxiety come over me. "Why this secrecy?"

"When we see each other, you'll understand."

"Will it take long?"

"Perhaps. That depends," he said, still enigmatic.

Fine, let him come to Brooklyn. No, he preferred to meet me in Manhattan, in his hotel on Sixty-fourth Street between Second and Third Avenues. "When? Right away?"

"Yes, right away."

"Can't it wait until tomorrow?"

"When we see each other, you'll understand."

"There will be no problem? I'll understand in the twinkling of an eye?"

"Perhaps, though a twinkling can be long. In fact," he added, "how can it be measured and with what? Do you know? I don't."

My uncle advised me to go there right away. By subway, it would be quick. He was right. One hour later, I was knocking at Samek's door.

In his sixties, tall and thin, wearing a well-cut suit, he had a hard, burning gaze that shone with a glimmer of gentleness. Ascetic or sick, he gave a strange impression of expectation mixed with resignation. In welcoming me, he held my hand in his for a long time before inviting me to take a seat. He remained standing.

"I've been waiting for this meeting for a long time," he said.

I was going to ask him why, but he beat me to it: "I've been looking for you for years; did you know that?"

I hesitated to reply no, I didn't know he was looking for me, I didn't know anyone was interested enough in me to be looking for me, but something in his behavior made me understand that I had better hold my tongue. His face became clouded.

"And do you know that, aside from me, you're the last living person from a world that has been swallowed up?"

My brain became feverish. Who was he? What did he expect from me? How would I be useful to him? Who was I to him? Why didn't he sit down to talk to me?

"In earlier times," Samek went on, "I had a large family. A brother, four sisters, uncles, aunts, countless cousins of both sexes. I don't have anyone anymore. Nearly all my relatives died in the tempest of fire and ashes. Most of them don't even have a grave."

"I know the story," I said.

"I know you do."

Should I ask him how he knew I knew?

"My brother is the only one who was entitled to a funeral according to Jewish ritual."

"Like my parents."

"That too, I know. You'll be surprised, but I know a lot about you. I know you're alone, like me. But your solitude is different. You have an uncle, first cousins, close friends, whereas I don't have anyone anymore."

He broke off, walked a few paces, stopped to gaze at a photo of an urban landscape hanging on the wall, then turned back and stared at me.

"I don't have anyone from that past anymore, except you."

The familiar "you" startled me. "Me?"

"Yes, you."

He started to pace the room again, from the table to the door, from the door to the bedroom, and finally he came back and sat down opposite me. Then he began telling me about his past. I listened to him, but no matter how hard I tried, I couldn't understand why he had chosen me as his interlocutor. Did he want me to record his testimony? Answer the questions it would raise? I wasn't qualified for that task. But then why? So I just listened.

Suffering, hunger, disease, fear, death; those are the chapter headings. Harassment. Prohibitions. Decrees. Homes abandoned. Families broken apart. The overpopulated ghetto. Fatigue, uncertainty, heartbreak, impotent tears. The first victims, the mass graves. The first nightly convoys to the east through a sleeping countryside. To avoid seeing the disgrace heaped on His Creation, God must have hidden His face.

"My father, the most lucid among us, cited the example of the patriarch Jacob and decided to separate the family in two. My brother joined a clandestine movement of Jewish Resistance fighters. My older sisters and I were supposed to join them several weeks later. But by then it was too late. The Germans invaded the ghetto and chased us to the freight station, where cattle cars were waiting for us."

Should I tell him that I knew? I was too moved to deliver myself of the burden weighing on my chest. How long had I been there? Only since noon? No matter, he resumed his narration. Nightmarish nights, scenes drawn from hell. As if the executioners had been born to kill, and the victims to die from their blows. Oh, what times those were: in those days, under the sign of curses, under the reign of absolute evil, it was human to be inhuman.

One hour had gone by, slowly, filled with the emptiness of dead souls. Samek didn't break off. "My brother spent the war underground while I spent it in different camps. After the liberation of Poland, he went into politics and I went into business. But we remained close. He lost everything, whereas I earned a great deal. So I gave him half my fortune. But the gods are jealous. Just when my brother was about to leave the country, he fell gravely ill. As for me, I wasn't attracted by marriage. I was leading a merry existence with no duties or attachments. I didn't have to report to anyone. What was I seeking? Everyday, immediate happiness. I said to myself: Humanity doesn't deserve that I give it children. I don't trust it. Let everything disappear with me; I don't care. My solitude, I wanted it undivided, unlimited, made of anger and protest against the solitude of the Lord, may He be blessed."

If he hoped his blasphemy would shock me, he must have been sorely disappointed. On the contrary, I felt closer to him; like him, I sometimes had doubts about both the justice and the kindness of heaven. But I still didn't understand why he had been so eager to meet me. While he held forth, I couldn't help wondering: What did I have to do with all this? Nevertheless, I listened intently when he again spoke of his experience in the camps.

"I won't tell you what I suffered and lived through there. Human beings became unrecognizable, stripped of everything, beyond everything. For us, the city narrowed to the size of a street, the street to a building, the building to a room, the room to a cattle car; wealth shrank to a bundle of belongings, the bundle to a mess kit, and happiness to one miserable potato. And man, whose destiny is incommensurable, became nothing but a number, and the number became ash. In a word, I'll tell you what I learned there. I learned that it is possible to live with the dead, and even beyond; it is possible to live in death. Can you understand this at your young age?"

I didn't answer—what can you say to a man who is so tormented? What words can be used to console him, to turn his bare, icy words into a fertile and warm language?

"It's true," I ventured, "it's true that I'm young. But age has nothing to do with it. Even if I were a hundred years old, I wouldn't understand. I would refuse to understand. Yet I'd like to continue listening to you."

He recounted an episode that he described as one of the most excruciating in his life. On leaving the camps, since he didn't know whether his brother was alive, he went home. Along the way, he stopped in Bendin, the small town where he had lived with his parents. Strangers were occupying their home. Irate, they refused to let him in and yelled: "You're still alive, Yid? If you want to remain so, you'd better get away from here, far away." At the police station, he was told that there were no more Jews in the town; most of them had been annihilated. As for the few survivors, they preferred to live in the capital, or in Lodz, Kraków, or Lublin. He was advised to leave too. What was the point of obstinately trying to live in such a hostile place? He should move to Warsaw. Which he did. Shortly afterward, he learned that his brother was still alive. And that he had become an important figure in the new government. Their reunion was very moving. No need to go into it. Samek was dying to go back to see the revolting occupants of their former house.

"I asked my brother to come with me, and we were treated to a different kind of welcome. We had the police chief as our personal protector and guide. When we arrived in front of our house, I wondered how the occupants were going to behave this time. I was due for a surprise. The house was empty. 'Where are the "tenants"?' I cried out. 'Punished, chased away,' replied the police chief. What he forgot to mention was that their punishment was of short duration. The day after we left, they were back, the new owners of my parents' house."

Samek took a deep breath as though he was inhaling cigarette smoke. His hands were trembling. "One must be both daring and humble," he went on, forehead lowered. "One must be able to describe the most horrible things with the simplest words, in a calm voice, devoid of emotion. Some stories deserve more than the immediate emotion they arouse. That feeling only helps us appease our consciences, absolve ourselves, and persuade ourselves that we're not so wicked or blameworthy, proof being that we suffer with the victims."

In Bendin, Samek found the last Jew from his city. How had he escaped the roundups and massacres before being informed on—by whom?—and then deported by the Germans to Auschwitz? No one knew. He alone could have answered. But he was beyond reach, in a hospital, suffering from aphasia.

"Symbolic, don't you think?" remarked Samek. "The only person in the world who could have testified about so many deaths was struck with aphasia. It's simple; the words just wouldn't come out. As if God Himself feared his deposition."

"What do you expect from me?" I asked him. "Why am I here?"

"Patience, young man," he said, slightly irritated. "Do you think I chose you? It's nothing to do with me; life decides, perhaps according to a logic whose meaning we grasp only much later. But first, if you don't mind, let's go back to the last survivor in my town. Do you know why and how he lost the power of speech? When he returned from the camps, he decided to roam the world and tell people about the unspeakable; he hoped to lift the world from its torpor and from an indifference that could lead it to its own annihilation. He spoke, he spoke everywhere, to the point of exhaustion. 'You seek pleasure? Think of its futility. You dream of wealth? *Over there* a piece of bread was more valuable than a thousand pearls. Honors excite you? Where I come from, they were worth less than dust.' At first, people listened to him and wept or kept silent. Then they turned their backs on him. And as he refused to become discouraged, they sought to humiliate him. Nevertheless, he pursued his mission. Then individuals with unsound morals began to accuse him of lying. They interrupted him and yelled: 'You weren't even deported; you're inventing suffering that you never experienced just in order to arouse pity and earn money.' He heard these calumnies even in a school where he had come to talk to a young audience. That's when he fainted. He was brought to the hospital. And since then, he has never uttered another word."

Samek stared at me as if checking to see whether I understood him. Yes, I understood him. I had read enough witnesses' accounts to know that the survivor's tragedy doesn't stop when his ordeal comes to an end. Just as a defiled woman remains one for life, or a tortured man stays one forever. But I still didn't understand why I was there.

Samek stood up, walked around the room again, poured himself a glass of water to clear his throat, and said: "As you can see, I'm ill too."

Then he returned to his story. Unlike his brother, he had been fooled by the Germans and had lived in the ghetto with his parents before being deported with them; he was separated from them in front of the Birkenau ramp. Now I listened to him as I might have listened to a ghost, and I wondered if he wasn't the unfortunate aphasic survivor whose fate he had described to me and who might have eventually recovered.

"My elderly father, my mother, three uncles, and two aunts died that night," he said in a calm, monotonous, impersonal voice. "I was lucky. I passed the selection and was declared fit for the painful, exhausting, inhuman work that isn't sufficiently talked about. Sometimes I said to myself, Thank God my parents can't see the kind of life their son is forced to lead. In fact, it wasn't a life. The cold and the hunger, the fear and the blows, the yelling of the kapos and the barking of the dogs gained the upper hand. Ill at liberation, I was a living dead man. And I still am. It may not be obvious, but I haven't much time left to bring this story to an end. For it remains unfinished. And that's where you come in."

"Me? But I'm not a physician!"

"I know. I told you: I know everything about you—where you come from and what you've done with your life."

Should I ask him for specifics, for details?

"But for the time being I would like to finish telling you about mine. It was very bounteous. Esteem, respect, authority: I could indulge all my wishes, for I could buy anything. Yes, I became wealthy. A multimillionaire. At first thanks to the black market, later because I learned how to invest in the stock market. I had a gift for speculation. I took care of my sick brother. I paid for everything: the best doctors, the most devoted nurses, the most expensive resorts. It's because of him that I remained in Poland for years. Actually, I offered to take him to France, Israel, or Florida, but he always refused. He had his own reasons for wanting to stay near his native city. That's where he's buried. Before dying he told me about his war experience. I knew only what I had read in the official or unofficial newspapers. His feats of arms, his political fights, his return to his origins: yes, as the end drew near, he became interested in Jewish culture and the Jewish tradition. He immersed himself in the sacred texts, and requested that the Kaddish be recited at his grave and during the year of mourning. For that, I hired the services of a Jerusalem yeshiva. But he also told me about his intimate life. Affairs, triumphs of desire followed by romantic disappointments. I was particularly moved by the last one. He was in love with a Jewish fighter his age, a woman who still had some

youthfulness, much grace, maturity, and character, and an innocent quality in her words and behavior. But she was married.
This left him with a feeling of frustration and failure; he resented
destiny. In his final months, he thought only of that woman, imag-
ining her at his bedside, a faithful and fervent wife. After his
funeral, in order to fulfill his last request, though I wasn't sure I
had understood it, I set about trying to find this woman to learn
what she had to say about my brother or to talk to her about
him. It was a difficult and thankless task. I went through government files and national archives; I moved heaven and hell—
in vain."

He fell silent, as if, at that point, it was better not to go on
with revelations to someone who was, after all, a stranger. I took
the opportunity to ask him, without hiding my nervousness, my
own little question: What did he expect from me? Why was I
there?

Suddenly, he became short of breath and blood rushed to his
face. "Excuse me," he said. "I'm familiar with this kind of
malaise. It's a sign I need to pause. Let's leave the rest for our
next meeting. If you don't mind, we'll continue tomorrow. At
the same time."

He disappeared into the bedroom. I went home, my heart
heavy with foreboding.

My uncle, to whom I described the meeting, was just as confused and perplexed as I. He wanted me to describe every last
detail of our conversation. What kind of old or new accent did
Samek have in Yiddish: Galician, Lithuanian, Romanian? I had
no idea. Did he need reading glasses? He hadn't read anything
in my presence. Did he seem to have other problems besides his
health? Indeed, he said he was sick, but what illness did he
have? He had been silent on the subject. My uncle and I talked

far into the night. He wondered whether the strange fellow might be a crook (no), a fighter (no again), an international adventurer (perhaps) trying to find allies or naïve accomplices (no, that was going too far). As for me, even if I dismissed all those possibilities, I had to acknowledge that I had no alternative explanation. All that came to mind was that this Samek Ternover had a more fertile imagination than I.

"But then," my uncle cried out, excited, "since we shouldn't be seeing him as evil, why not see him as good? What if this Samek—or Shmuel—Ternover is the prophet Elijah, protector of orphans, sent by God to help you establish yourself in life and start a family in accordance with the law of Moses and of Israel?"

Noticing my incredulity, he took another tack.

"Perhaps we're dealing with one of the thirty-six hidden righteous men thanks to whom the universe still exists. Perhaps he sought to meet you because he guessed you were a mystical soul who could help him overthrow the order of things? But in that case, may the Lord—blessed be His name—forgive my impudence; it would mean that we've entered the pre-messianic era."

I tried to appease him. I told him not to worry; the following morning I would be seeing Samek again, and we would have all the answers to our questions—except, of course, as concerned the date of the last redemption.

The next morning, Samek was waiting for me in front of the elevator. How did he know I had arrived? Gesturing with his hand, he invited me to follow him. I sat on the same chair as the day before. A beam of sunshine came in through the window, as if to sweep away the shadows. I was grateful for it. Oddly, I felt less threatened. As he had the day before, Samek remained standing. Deathly pale, frail, his features drawn, tired-looking as after a sleepless night, he scrutinized me in a way that was disconcerting, but I held my own against his inquisitive gaze. At last he questioned me in a hoarse voice. "Have you thought about it?"

"About what?"

"About what is happening to you."

"Yes."

"So?"

"My uncle thinks you've come to test me because you're one of the hidden righteous men, working for the coming of the Messiah."

"And what about you? What do you think of me?"

"I don't know what to think. I still have no idea what I'm doing in this hotel room."

"And in life?" he asked.

"I don't understand."

"Do you have any idea what you're doing in your life?"

"Same as you, our wise men would say: helping the Creator make His Creation more hospitable and His creatures more just, more charitable."

He gazed at me for a long time without saying a word, then shook his head in denial. "If you believe in God, you should know that God addresses us in myriad ways, conferring on each of us a specific mission. You and I, the two of us and your uncle, he and every person in the street, each of us lives only for one instant, one event, one meeting. In my case, it's probable I lived, or rather survived, with the sole aim of being face-to-face with you yesterday, today, and for who knows how much longer."

I told him I understood less and less. Why had he chosen me? What for?

He smiled faintly and awkwardly. "I'll tell you the rest of my story," he said. "My brother still plays a major role in it, maybe his final role."

In a low voice, his gaze lost in the distance, he described the love story his brother lived during and after the war. The courage and heroism of two young Jews fighting against oppression, humiliation, and death. Guardians of Jewish honor, they waged a desperate and merciless war against the Germans. For both, this was the most beautiful, vibrant and authentic period in their lives. The liberation separated them.

"My brother's suffering is hard to imagine. Because this woman was special, peerless, unique from every point of view. I alluded to her yesterday. She wasn't free. Her life didn't belong to her. She was married. Yes, married. This didn't prevent my brother from loving her. And like everything he did, he loved her with all his heart—to his last breath. In his final days, he asked me to try to find her. To give her his farewell."

He stopped, as if to catch his breath, his face turning pale and bloodless, then red. And he went on: "I have no idea why this meant so much to him, but that's the way my brother was. Strange, hard to fathom. He often wanted and did things that we couldn't understand. But I gave him my word."

"And did you ever find this special woman?"

"I looked for her for years, but when finally I tracked her down, it was too late. Yet I succeeded in finding her son. He will be very wealthy. Yes, he won't have to worry about money anymore. He'll be able to afford anything he wants. As I said yesterday: like my brother, I'm sick. I have very little time left. The son of that woman whom my brother loved so dearly will be my heir."

"But what about his mother?"

His face clouded over. "She died a few months after last seeing my brother." After a silence, he said, "In France. Leah died in France."

It was as if I'd received a dizzying punch in the stomach. I was stunned, breathless. My memory was suddenly awakened and I was whisked back in time. I should have guessed.

"Leah . . . Leah . . . like my mother," I said.

Samek inhaled deeply and whispered: "It was your mother."

I closed my eyes, and saw myself again as a child, far away. I was in pain; my head was bursting. My heart was beating wildly. Now I understood everything.

"Your brother," I said slowly, trying not to betray my emotion, "I remember him. I saw him."

Samek smiled. "I know. Leah was his great love."

"I think I guessed as much."

Now I understood what I was doing in this room. However, I paused before adding: "But my mother didn't love him, not really."

"That too, I know. She loved only you."

"No. Not just me. She loved my father."

Why was I so upset? Why were my eyes filling with tears? Samek smiled, but his smile had changed: it was buried in his quivering wrinkles. In a gentle, melancholic voice, he started to tell me about Romek, his brother. Describing the last years of his life. His illness, his fear of sinking from one day to the next, unaware, into a physical and mental decline, in short, of becoming an invalid, a "vegetable." His sorrow about not having any descendants. At disappearing without a trace.

"Do you know whom he thought about just before . . . before passing away?" Samek asked.

"How could I know?"

"About you. He spoke your name. He named you as his heir. Theoretically, it was supposed to be me. He told me so. But he added that I wouldn't be his only heir."

As I remained silent, he stared at me with his haunted gaze and mumbled: "You. Yes, you. You're in his will, like me. And since I have no one and my days are numbered, you'll be our only heir."

He let out a small raspy laugh, a mixture of regret, remorse, and humor. "Do you realize what that means? Quite simply, it means your life has changed. You've become wealthy. You can indulge all your fantasies. All your dreams—you're free to fulfill them as you please. Quite a grand moment, isn't it? Admit it's miraculous. It was so I could experience it that I've been looking for you for so long. You won't forget us, will you? Promise you won't forget what you owe us."

"I don't understand a thing," I said, blushing.

A strange feeling of guilt overcame me, and I wondered why. Was it because I recalled my dead parents? Or Romek, who was also dead? Perhaps because of my new wealth, undeservedly acquired?

My head was spinning and spinning. I saw myself at my parents' funeral, surrounded by angry men and motionless women, silent in their grief. They all looked menacing. I was worried, but oddly I didn't know why or since when. What was Samek doing in all this? He has not the one watching out for me; it was his brother. I saw him again with my mother. They were close; that was certain. And he loved her, but this was obvious only now, thanks to this messenger of fate. And my mother, did she love him back? Not continuously, not even a week, but one night, one hour? My head wasn't spinning anymore; it froze and felt like it would burst any minute.

# 20

One morning, I'm walking down a snowy Madison Avenue and I stop in front of the window of my favorite pastry shop. I'm attracted by the distinctive taste of their cakes, and I've been coming here almost every day for the last few weeks. To pass the time, as a kind of entertainment. The warm atmosphere makes me feel good. Observing a silly ritual inherited from my sessions with Thérèse Goldschmidt, as soon as I enter, I allow myself free expression and request whatever crosses my mind: a piece of sky, a cheerful popular song, a white pen and blue paper, a multicolored dove, anything. Today, I'm in the mood for a hot chocolate and a croissant; I order a shirt and necktie. The young waitress doesn't look surprised anymore. She knows what to expect. She gazes at me for a minute, as if checking to see if I had become normal and serious again; then, without any sign of confusion, she agrees to take care of me, in a minute, she says, smiling, in a strictly professional tone of voice. But this morning, something utterly unexpected occurs. Had fate decided to reveal to me her most hidden face, I could not have been more surprised. For, as if she has occult powers, including the power to read my mind, the waitress brings me a hot chocolate and a croissant and says, straight-faced: "I'm sorry, I'm all out of shirts and neckties. But I have black gloves. You'll see, they're lovely, and they'll be perfect for you."

Flabbergasted, I take the tray she is handing me and remain motionless.

"That's five dollars," she says, a hint of amusement in her voice, while looking me directly in the eye. "Over there, on the left, there's an empty table waiting for you."

If her aim was to give me a lesson in humility, wisdom, and good humor, she has succeeded admirably. Should I ask her if she knows my language and my personal logic, the language and logic of my illness? Or ask her if she's mad, I mean mad, not unsettled or out of step, but mad in the head, a bit like me? Can two mad individuals, coming from faraway galaxies or backgrounds, have the same vision, and own the same key, the same code, allowing them to open a vault where they deposit, like treasures, words emptied of their usual meanings and given new ones, known only to them? I should get the waitress to speak more, but she is already far away, busy with new customers. Yet I know it is imperative that we continue our all too brief exchange. It is the beginning of an adventure. I don't know where it will lead us, to which victories and over which enemies, and that's for the best. It's proof that I am living through a period of uncertainty and doubt that has nothing to do with the crises where everything remains clear, rigorous, and inevitable. As in a dream that is not yet mine, I see myself rising from the table, going up to the counter, and saying to the waitress in a voice loud enough for the customers to hear: "I've been waiting for you. You have to come with me."

"But . . ."

"But what?"

"My work . . ."

"I'll give you double what you earn here. Or triple, if you like."

"And what if I'm fired?"

"My offer is good no matter what happens, whatever the circumstance."

"If I follow you, where will we be going? To do what? Are you taking revenge for something? Trying to humiliate someone? Trying to find happiness in another person's misfortune?"

Good questions, I say to myself. Reasonable and pertinent. You'd have to be an idiot to dismiss them, and a poet to reply to them. But aren't madmen sometimes poets in their way, though they don't know it? Where had I read or heard the improvised verses that my lips were about to pronounce? Won't my dumbfounded "public" react, as it should, with an outburst of noisy laughter? Too bad, I'll take the giant risk.

"All I want is to be with you," I say, pleading. "Yes, my young lady, together we'll jettison the weight of memories that don't yet belong to us. Together we'll seek intoxication; the intoxication of gold dawns and of darkness in desolation."

Suddenly she stops playing. Life becomes normal again. The waitress no longer incarnates my dreams of breaking with routine: her feet are on the ground once again. She becomes serious, skeptical, and almost fretful again. And from her lips come these words that can only disappoint me: "But who are you, sir? What weird world do you come from? And who do you take me for?"

She obviously takes me for a liar. I take a wad of bills out of my pocket: "They're yours."

She looks at me, wide-eyed, hands on her hips. I don't look like a Wall Street banker. She's puzzled by me; that's clear. I frighten her. She whispers: "A crook? Are you a big-time crook? An adventurer? A romantic outlaw who is fond of other people's money?"

As I'm convinced she can guess what's going on in my heart and mind, I reply that she must know that I'm not a gangster.

"But then who are you?"

I say it's a long story. I'll tell it to her later. First she must come with me. Seeing her hesitate, I turn to the patrons of this blessed pastry shop; hypnotized, they are watching the scene, chuckling or irritated. I ask them to help me convince my beloved of my good faith. An elderly man, with a felt hat and fur collar, cries out and applauds: "It's a beautiful love story!" And a respectable but exuberant lady approves: "An old man and a young woman! And I thought this only happened in the movies!" One patron urges her on: "Go ahead, miss! Don't pay attention to his age! So he could be your grandfather, so what?" And another patron: "Prince Charming is calling you—don't keep him waiting!"

Then, with a brusque movement, she grabs her coat, comes up to me, takes my arm, and says, "You see: I'll follow you. I'm willing to sacrifice everything. But don't disappoint me, huh; that would be rotten, and stupid to boot!"

"Trust me," I say.

"Oh, I'll watch my step. What you don't know is that I've been through this kind of story before . . ."

"Trust me," I say to her.

Taking her arm, I open the door, and we plunge into a life that doesn't expect us, but whose uncertainties, I know, we're eager to confront.

"Listen to me without interrupting," she says, as though echoing words previously heard in other circumstances. "I'll talk about myself for ten minutes; then you'll talk about yourself. Ten minutes each, is that okay? I can say anything I like, and you too. Lies or truth, it doesn't matter. Then we'll decide if it's worth going on. Is that clear?"

We're sitting in a nearby café, drinking hot chocolate. As agreed, she describes her past. A secular or agnostic Jew, she's not too sure which. Sephardic, born in Jerusalem, American citizen. Age: thirty-six. A degree in the social sciences. As a student, at times mediocre, at times brilliant, depending on her mood. She gave it all up after an unhappy love affair with her philosophy professor. Never married. Various jobs, none worthwhile.

The only daughter of survivors, which should explain everything. Everything? A big word may say nothing, or so little. Weightless, with no depth, like all the others. Perhaps it conceals her impulses, her irrational whims, her curiosity about everything that is out of the ordinary, her rejection of the standards imposed by a hypocritical society, adrift and doomed to perish from its fear of boredom.

"But you didn't say anything about the story." I say.

"What story?"

"The one you'd been through, that's like ours."

"Oh yes, that one."

One day, she went to an elegant hotel to see an American girlfriend who was visiting Paris. She went to the wrong floor and knocked at the wrong door. A stranger opened it. Disconcerted, embarrassed, she mumbled: "I'm sorry, I made a mistake . . ."

He smiled: "No, don't say that. Since you're here, come in." And seeing her hesitate, he added: "I promise nothing bad will happen to you."

"Naïve as I am, loving the unexpected," she tells me, "I accepted. Besides, he didn't look dangerous. He asked me to sit down, which I did. The room had been made up, the bed covered with a bedspread. There was a big pile of books and manuscripts on the table. He explained that he was a novelist. I stayed with him for three months. Three months of trips to the sunshine, of night adventures, of discoveries and learning. Then one morning, while I was asleep, he disappeared without leaving a good-bye note . . ."

"Trust me." Again, this is all I can think of to say.

It is my turn to speak about myself. I just tell her a story told by head rabbi Nahman of Bratzlav:

"One day, the king read in the stars that the coming harvest would be cursed; whoever would eat from it would become mad. He summoned his best friend and said to him, 'Let's both put a mark on our foreheads. That way, when we both take leave of our senses, along with the entire population in the kingdom, we'll know that we're mad.' "

"In other words?" she asks.

I lean toward her.

"I don't understand," she says. "I talked about myself, whereas you're telling me a parable." She was not angry but intrigued.

I then pass on to her the remark of another great master, Rabbi Israel of Ruzhin: a day will come when the parable and its meaning will have nothing in common anymore.

"Plainly stated, what do you mean by all this?" she asks.

"Let's imitate these two great masters, shall we? In this demented, doomed world where the living all seem to be fleeing from a past that is bound, sooner or later, to become their future, we'll be alone together, irremediably alone, but we'll know it."

"We'll know what?"

"That we're mad."

I hope to see her smile, I would give anything for her to smile, but she remains impervious to my sense of humor. Solemn, suspicious, she looks at me as though I'd just dropped down from Mars.

"Really, Mr. Storyteller," she says, "I find you peculiar. I don't know your name and you didn't ask me mine. We're two strangers that a beneficent or evil coincidence brought face-to-face in a pastry shop, where other strangers come for food and indirectly put food on my table. Giving in to one of your whims, I let you tear me away from my customers, my workplace, my milieu, my entourage, my habits. No explanation and maybe no reason. Others have done it before and are still doing it to other young women. But they promise a week of pleasure by the seashore, a costly jewel, lots of exotic memories, meetings with famous people, and even a bit of love and happiness. Whereas you, if I understand correctly, your gift is madness. Right?"

"Let's say I have a one-word answer to that question: yes."

"Well . . . are you making fun of me?"

"No. I'm not making fun of you but of myself."

"And you'd like to use me to better laugh at yourself?"

"There you're mistaken. I'm not using anyone."

Suddenly, she seems frightened. "Mr. Stranger," she says, "let's forget the jokes. Tell me the truth: What are we doing here?"

I lean even closer to her, as though I want my head to touch hers, my life to join hers, or at least to make her smile. And foolishly, at the same time I tell myself that if I don't succeed, my whole life will be ruined.

"You'd like to know what we're doing here. Simply put, I could tell you that we're both trying to change an apparently fortuitous meeting into a story that could perfectly well be placed, with a bit of luck, under the sign of destiny, which has more imagination than we have."

She's a good listener. Silently, she seems to be taking in my words before deciding whether she can fit them into the book of her life. Then she pulls herself together.

"They call me Liatt," she says.

My heart misses a beat; she didn't say, "My name is," but "They call me." I've never known a woman by that name. It's a Hebrew word. It means "You're mine." I repeat: "Li-att."

And finally, no longer resisting, her beautiful oval face, with its harmonious features, lights up with a smile.

"I could tell you my real name, the one I had up until now," I say, "but for you, and you alone, I'd like to invent a new one."

She waits. Her smile seems to deepen. It reconciles sadness and joy, fervor and grace, nostalgia for the past and fulfillment in the present. I scan my mind feverishly for biblical, prophetic, and Talmudic names, a special, unusual, unique name that would reflect the moment I just lived through and the one to come. I look at her intensely, hoping to find it in her. That way, as she gave me the gift of Liatt, I will give her my new name.

"So," she says. "Did you find the name? I'm waiting for it."

I like to have her waiting.

"One word. Hebrew like yours. One syllable: *Od.*

"Which means what?"

"It has two meanings. *Od* with an ayin means 'again.' With an aleph, the word could mean 'thank you, I will give thanks.' "

Is she touched? She takes my hand and says, "Again."

It's been ages since I've been so deeply moved. Or so deeply worried.

This is because a timid but persistent voice within me keeps whispering doubts and warnings: What are you doing? Beware, you old confirmed bachelor. You're about to tread on unknown, dangerous, explosive terrain. This whim could cost you dearly. You're forgetting the negative side of this equation, first of all, your age. This time, it's serious; you're not dealing with a flirtation or a fleeting affair. By what right can you decide to shape or change this young woman's life, to take advantage of her naïveté or simply her curiosity? You, a man with so many complexes, including a guilt complex—think what you're getting yourself into.

However, another voice whispers to me: Remember the women you've known. And who frightened you. Are you sure it isn't the same one every time, who lived several lives before becoming the woman before you now?

"What's wrong?" Liatt asks. "All of a sudden I sense you're troubled."

"I've always been. Sometimes I think that I've let myself be swept away by moments of madness, just to drown out what was troubling me in my life."

But the tiny, insistent voice dares to lecture me: Why don't you tell her the truth, huh? Admit you're too old, with a rather limited future, that you never were able to live like everyone else, in a stable home, with singing children and laughing grandchildren; tell her it's too late for you to start a life as a couple with a beautiful, intelligent young woman who deserves a spouse her own age. Go ahead, tell her . . .

"Listen to me, Liatt."

"I'm listening."

"Liatt, I love that name and I think I'll love you, whose name it is. And the reason I feel like addressing you familiarly, while you don't address me so, is because you're still very young and I'm much older. If we stay together, I know I'll receive a lot from you, whereas you'll receive very little from me."

"Does that frighten you?"

"No, not really. But you're frightened. Or am I wrong?"

"Yes, I am frightened. Frightened of liking my new life too much. In other words, frightened of loving you and then having to leave you."

This day we do nothing but talk. About everything and nothing. About our first memories, our dreams, and our disappointments. Like me, Liatt has already lived a full, turbulent life, with its wounds and joys. But compared with mine, her life is only just beginning. She asks me what I have read and I ask her what she has read. She asks me about my parents and I about hers—professors of biogenetics, they live six months of each year in Israel and six months in California. She asks me about my political opinions, and I ask about her leisure activities. About my Jewishness. I explain my attachment to tradition, memory, community. Our romantic experiences? Scanty on my side, plentiful on hers. She describes several affairs at the university without going into details. At one time, she fell in love with a pseudo Hindu guru. She followed him to his ashram for a week—the worst week in her life. Hell on earth. And the loss of her illusions. But now she is free.

We leave the café at about noon, with the intention of having lunch in a restaurant. She isn't hungry; nor am I. We walk aimlessly through the snowy streets. The coat she is wearing is too flimsy. I offer to buy her a warmer one. She refuses categorically; she will never be a kept woman. Even if I love her? Especially if I love her. Even if I'm far from destitute? Even if I was the wealthiest man on Wall Street. Even if I tell her I have no one else in the world but her? Now she doesn't answer right away. Then it's her turn to ask. Without looking at me, she says, "You never married. Why?"

"I have no idea, Liatt. Let's say that before it was too soon and now it's probably too late."

"Yet you must have met women, and loved some."

"Yes, I think I loved. I was looking for the kindred soul, though I knew I would run away before having found her."

"But . . . why this fear of committing yourself? Why this pattern of running away?"

"My psychotherapist asked me the same questions. With her help, I tried to explore this question in depth. I suspect you don't know analysts; they're a special breed. Their domain is the soul or sexuality, or the two together. According to my therapist, I looked where I should not have, and this caused my psychological problems. Added to that, apparently, is my acute guilt complex for having outlived my parents and siblings. Which is why I refused to imitate them—in other words, I didn't marry, didn't start a family, didn't have children."

"Is that all you discovered?"

"No. There's something else as well. My therapist is convinced that I'm afraid of having sexual relations. What do you expect; she's a Freudian. She clearly implied it: if I had had the courage and not repressed my desire, if I had chosen a woman to whom I was sufficiently attracted and whom I could have loved other than mentally, I would have long ago been rid of what I call my madness."

"And what did you say to that?"

"I told her that, in life, intimate things must remain intimate. But if you require—"

"I require nothing."

Liatt stops in front of a clothing store; we look at the reflection of our two silhouettes and our two faces in the shop-window.

"And now?" she says.

"Now what?"

"Don't you have regrets that you stayed single, I mean, single forever? Without a wife, of course, but also without descendants."

She has been quick to identify my weak spot, the place where I am vulnerable: children. In the past, I was convinced that we shouldn't have children anymore. It was a way of saying to God, echoing my roommate in the clinic: Lord, You witnessed the systematic, implacable annihilation of a million and a half Jewish children. You let the killers get away with it. Well, if that was your desire and aim, if You prefer a world with no Jewish children, who am I to go against Your will? Watch, I'll tiptoe away and say to You: At least my children won't be killed by the enemy. They won't be killed because they won't be born. So staying single was a well-thought-out decision in my case. It was my way of protesting against the cruelty of men and the silence of their Creator. And now, behold, this beautiful, grave woman calls all this into question. Does she want to marry me? Is that the reason for her curiosity concerning my status as an old bachelor? I ask her. She replies with one word: "Possibly."

"What about the age difference, Liatt, what about that? The body has rights and requirements. The irresistible call of life to life is also subservient to nature. And nature requires that a young woman marry a young man. When a young woman marries an older man, it's against nature. For the body couldn't care less about feelings of love."

"I'll answer with a simplistic thought, I admit, which I read in a trashy novel," she says, half amused, half serious. "Love doesn't take age into account."

"But the body does, Liatt, the body does!"

"Well, the body's wrong."

Is it a result of my madness again? I make a quick decision: I am going to marry Liatt. She's mine. Liatt belongs to Od. It must be written in the divine Book where the Creator inscribed the judgments and decrees that were to mark all individuals and all people forever. I'm convinced that on page 1031 at the start of this century, it is recorded that Od and Liatt will unite their lives and destinies.

Suddenly we are in front of my apartment building. Should I invite her to come upstairs with me? She might misunderstand it. Should I send her home? Out of the question.

"Listen, Liatt. I'm going to make a suggestion. You come home with me and we spend some time together. To think over what has just happened to us. Then we'll each decide what we want to do."

Am I afraid of disappointing her? We spend the night not in my bedroom but in the living room. The hours go by. Relaxed, we chat, listen to music, drink coffee. Liatt inspects the kitchen, the closets, looks through the books, and admires the paintings.

Again and again, I feel like going up to her, but a little voice within me, always the same voice, holds me back: Don't, you idiot. You're attracted to her; what of it? Is she attracted to you? Yes, for conversation but nothing more. Don't forget everything that separates you. I let it speak on; I don't answer. It claims to be the voice of reason, but it is really the voice of madness, I say to myself. Isn't it time I freed myself from it? But it keeps talking: The two of you think you have eternity before you, but, poor fellow, what will you do when you're truly attached to her and she's tempted by other men, all more vigorous than you?

Once again, I ignore the little voice and its advice; eventually it will be exhausted, and then it will leave me in peace, free to live my life, or what's left of it, as I please. No one has the right to deprive me of the happiness I anticipate with the woman I've chosen.

However, it is Liatt who makes my will falter. She puts her cup of coffee down on the table and turns toward me.

"I think you ought to hear what I have to say before we make a decision that could bind us to each other," she says.

"I'm listening."

"I'd like you to understand my behavior. Were you surprised by it? I was. I already changed the course of my life once by following a stranger, and I let him involve me in an affair that could have shattered me forever. It was a mistake and I survived it. But I promised myself that it wouldn't happen to me again. Ever."

Frankness, sincerity, honesty, morality: she uses all these words to explain why, even with the best will in the world, there's no chance "it" will turn out well between us. I don't interrupt. She tells me about her fickleness, her volcanic temperament, her mood swings. She is trying to discourage me; that's obvious. But why did she suddenly change her attitude? All those hours of complicity, tenderness, and quasi-amorous affection: Did they vanish into thin air? And those signs of consent and encouragement, her attentiveness and promises: Have they all gone up in smoke? At this point, as usual, I blame myself. Perhaps I said or did something that caused retreat if not an abrupt change of mind on Liatt's part, or at least a hesitation that I didn't foresee a minute ago.

"Then," she continues, "I have to confess something else, something more serious perhaps. I owe you the truth. The reason I agreed to play along with you is that you appeared at the right time in my life. Should I go on?"

"Of course, go ahead, I'm listening."

"It's a banal story. Another one. For, you see, I did it again. I've just been through a painful, demoralizing breakup. A man I loved, who loved me for a while but who no longer does. I know: these things happen, you cry for a while, and then you accept it. He left me because he was tired of me. That's what he told me: 'I'm not blaming you for anything. But I've taken everything from you that you have to give me. That's all. Be happy, but without me. Farewell.' "

I look at her while she's talking. She's ill at ease. It's as though she is forcing herself to speak. Sitting on the couch, she avoids my eyes. Her delivery is slow, fragmented. Does she know she is hurting me? Will I have to take refuge in my dybbuk again, in my familiar and salutary madness where no one can reach me?

"I followed you," she continues in the same tone of voice, "pretending it was forever, not because I thought I could love you, but to punish my lover. So he would hear that a wealthy and kind man chose me. So he would suffer the way I suffer, so he would be unhappy, unhappier than I am." She pauses. "Please accept my apologies. I used you, and I feel bad about it. I shouldn't have, I know. I couldn't help it."

She pauses again; then she asks, "What are we going to do now?"

She gets up, stretches, goes to fetch her coat, and folds it over her arm. Should I help her slip it on? I feel beset by contradictory impulses. Should I put an end to a foredoomed adventure? That would be more prudent and wise. Or should I stop her from leaving, though she's still infatuated with someone else? What would I do if I were younger? Above all, I should remain calm.

"Listen to me, my little Liatt. I'll open the door for you. You'll go home. Think it over carefully. If you return tomorrow, you'll stay with me. And we'll live the few years ahead together. I'll see to it that they're mostly peaceful and never boring. You and I, we know what's what: it won't always be easy for an aging man like me to live with a beautiful, active young woman; or for you to share your days and nights with a man like me. For my part, I'm prepared to try. You'll tell me I'm mad; I'm sure you think it. But so do I. Except I've known it for a long time. I've always struggled with my dybbuk and my demons, without ever really wanting to get rid of them. Which is why I ask: Are you prepared to live with them and not make them yours? You'll tell me tomorrow, if you like. If you don't come back, I won't hold it against you. Whatever happens to us, I'll remember your name."

She is moved. Moved to tears. In front of the door, with a forced smile, she asks me: "Why are you doing all this?"

"Why am I doing what?"

"Why do you want me to be close to you? Why do you want me to join my life with yours, when you've predicted how difficult and risky it will all be? Why this challenge to logic, if not nature?" No longer smiling, she adds: "Why are you so eager to love me?"

To this I know the answer. "It's because of your smile. I've always known that I would love a woman who had the smile of a frightened child."

She thinks for a moment, then leaves without kissing me.

# 21

The next day I go to the cemetery to meditate on my uncle's grave: it is the anniversary of his death. When I have finished reciting the appropriate psalms, I suddenly notice that I am not alone. An old woman with a wrinkled face is standing next to me, wrapped in a black shawl.

"Oh, Avrohom, Avrohom. I knew him. I was close to his wife. Gittel. Also dead. Did you know them?"

"Yes, I did."

"How so?"

"I grew up in their house."

"Oh, so you're the nephew."

"Yes, the nephew. You don't recognize me?"

"I don't like to lie, but . . ."

"I've changed a lot, I know."

She looks at me for a long time. "I'm thinking of something else," she says.

As for me, I am recalling my uncle Avrohom. I miss him. Deep down, he understood, without judging me, what was going on inside me. Convinced that faith was the answer to all predicaments, he suffered from the fact that mine was wounded. But don't hold it against me, Uncle Avrohom. I never betrayed you. Not even in my madness. Sometimes a wounded soul is more open to truth than the others.

"I'm thinking of another day, in another cemetery," says the old lady. Her husky voice has become pensive. "Do you know that this isn't our first encounter? Our first encounter was at your parents' funeral in Marseilles. I remember; you were silent. And also, though it was imperceptible, I saw it and I remember it as though it was yesterday. You were so unhappy that you were smiling. I saw your smile. It broke my heart. It was the smile of a frightened child."

I would like to kiss her, but she shakes her head: no, I shouldn't.


That same evening, Liatt returns.

One year later, she tells me she is pregnant. As for me, I confess to her that during all this time, late at night and often at dawn, while she was asleep, I wrote letters to the two people to whom I owed everything. Indeed, I owed them my life and my survival. They were dead, but they never left me. These are all the things I told my father and mother.

I told them everything.

And now I know that these stories will have another reader: our child.

Then, like the traveler who reaches the top of the mountain, sees the abyss through the clouds, and is seized by a harrowing dizziness, the old man in me suddenly has a mad desire to dance.

## A NOTE ABOUT THE AUTHOR

Elie Wiesel was fifteen years old when he was deported to Auschwitz. He became a journalist and writer in Paris after the war, and since then has written more than fifty books, fiction and nonfiction, including his masterwork, *Night*, a major best seller when it was republished recently in a new translation. He has been awarded the United States Congressional Gold Medal, the Presidential Medal of Freedom, the rank of Grand-Croix in the French Legion of Honor, an honorary knighthood of the British Empire, and, in 1986, the Nobel Peace Prize. Since 1976, he has been the Andrew W. Mellon Professor in the Humanities at Boston University.

A NOTE ON THE TYPE

This book was set in Old Style No. 7. This face is largely based on a series originally cut by the Bruce Foundry in the early 1870s, and that face, in its turn, appears to have followed in all essentials the details of a face designed and cut some years before by the celebrated Edinburgh typefounders Miller & Richard. Old Style No. 7, composed in a page, gives a subdued color and an even texture that make it easily and comfortably readable.

Composed by Creative Graphics,
Allentown, Pennsylvania

Printed and bound by R. R. Donnelley,
Harrisonburg, Virginia

Designed by M. Kristen Bearse